The Serial Killer's Diet Book

A Novel by

Kevin Mark Postupack

Printed in Canada

For information address:
Durban House Publishing Company, Inc.
7502 Greenville Avenue, Suite 500, Dallas, Texas 75231
214.890.4050

Library of Congress Cataloging-in-Publication Data
Kevin Mark Postupack, 1958

The Serial Killer's Diet Book / by Kevin Mark Postupack

Library of Congress Catalog Card Number: 00-2001090319

p. cm.

ISBN 1-930754-06-X

First Edition

10 9 8 7 6 5 4 3 2 1

Visit our Web site at
http://www.durbanhouse.com

Book design by:
B[u]y-the-Book Design—Madeline Höfer

pour Michelle,
toujours mon illumination.

In the spirit of Rabelais…

MANY THANKS are in order. At the top of the list, my parents, Emil and Margaret, who believed in creativity. Ralph Clemens, who instilled in me a sense of standards. Anthony Colantuono, who introduced me to Rabelais and Latin. Michelle Lynch, *semper fidelis*. Doug, for the ol' Mac and countless commiserations. Ted and Kathleen, for trouble-shooting at the eleventh hour. John Lewis, for his steadfast belief. Denyse, ("Any news yet?"). Bob Middlemiss, for the phone call. Madeline, for her brilliant graphics. My lifelong friends, Zid, Steve Crum, Hilary, Trish, Linda, Perry, Greg, Tove, Juan DeRoo, and John Paul. Alexis, Whitney, Harrison, Beth, and the JMU gang. My Southern family, Monty, Pat, LaLani, Eddie, the Grannies, Tessa, and Becky. My basketball buddies, bruisers and bangers all. The Kitty, my editing pal. And last but not least, the "favorite friends".

The longing to transcend ourselves, if only
for a few moments, is and has always been
one of the principal appetites of the soul.

Aldous Huxley

ver perpetuum   always spring

The
Serial Killer's
Diet Book

1

The Devil lived in a modest brownstone on East 54th St. with his cat Cleo. He never played his stereo too loudly, he went to bed at a reasonable hour, and his neighbors never complained. Each morning he went for a walk to the deli on the corner, (where he bought a paper, a bagel, a cup of coffee), and when he returned he put on music. Miles Davis or Bill Evans. The Devil was fond of jazz. There was something about the space between the notes that he particularly liked, as if one was birth, the other death, holding life in its whispered breath between. He was drawn to this because what it held in its beautiful silence was possibility, and this was what he liked most of all. Sometimes when he heard the muted trumpet, or the piano float above the wash of cymbals, he listened to the space and heard a voice—quiet, soft as darkness, speaking words it knew no one would hear. And he smiled to himself because he *did* hear, and then he would go to work. The Devil loved ballads.

The sound of the waves hit his ears like the roar of applause. Sitting back in the sand he watched Sophia emerge from the water. She was Venus born from ocean and sun, and he watched as the water glistened on her shoulders, as the sun caressed her body like eyes, the waves moved over it like lips, and he stared in silence as he remembered her taste and smell. And Sophia saw him watching her, and she smiled. Her dark eyes were dancing spirits opening a door on a room of mirrors, and as he looked he saw every pleasure multiplied a thousandfold, every desire reflected back. In those mirrored eyes he saw himself, and he heard his name on her lips.

"Federico..." she said softly.

"Sophia..."

She stood above him obscuring the sun.

"How was the water?" he asked (in Italian).

"Here, see for yourself." She brought her wet body onto his and they rolled on the beach as they kissed, and when he looked at her again she was coated with sand.

"You look like...a *veal cutlet.*"

She glanced at herself and laughed.

"I think I'll eat you, my succulent baby veal."

And she sprang to her feet and dashed off, pausing once to peel off her sand-coated bikini. And he watched her hair wet against her back as the waves crashed around her, as he tore off his bathing suit and ran towards the sea.

The sounds of the sea became a truck backfiring and the honking of horns, as Fred Orbis stared out the third floor window. It was night. The traffic wasn't so bad at this hour. Cabs wove in and out like leopards on the hunt, and he watched one pounce on its prey—a man at the curb flailing his arms, instantly gobbled up by this sleek yellow predator. And then it glided back to the jungle depths to digest its meal. The ocean seemed far away.

Fred Orbis was frustrated. True, he was a frustrated writer, but so were a million other people in Manhattan. Every waiter had a screenplay dancing in his head where the daily special should have been; every cabbie had a novel in the works; every house cleaner was a poet. And who could blame them? There was this universal quality shared by all human beings, this bent towards alchemy, this insuperable desire to change the lead of their lives into gold. To rise above, to go beyond, to transcend. *Ver perpetuum.* Life was a supermarket, and each of our bodies the shopping cart with the one bad wheel. Our task, to steer this unwieldy vehicle against its will, unerringly towards the dessert aisle. And for Fred Orbis this image loomed uncommonly large. Fred Orbis, you see, was a glutton. Let's be frank. Fred Orbis was fat. Let's be franker still. He was obese. Gigantic. Enormous. He didn't have a back and front, he had hemispheres. Fred Orbis loved to eat, and he parlayed this love into a career. He was editor in chief of *Feast*

Magazine, the monthly journal of eating to excess. Every month the cover featured a sumptuous Bacchanalian banquet, a repast for twelve, and as soon as the final shots were taken and before the photographer put away his camera, Fred had hunkered down to the table and proceeded to devour the food from one end to the other like Sherman marauding across the South. Fred Orbis was fat, and he was frustrated because he wanted to be thin.

He wanted to be someone else. He saw himself on a secluded beach laying in the sun, watching a beautiful woman rush towards him. And in her eyes he was slim and tan, his brown skin pulled taut against muscle and bone as he waited to receive her embrace. He was Federico Orbisini, internationally known novelist, existential philosopher, raconteur, and lover of women. His was a villa on a cliff overlooking the Mediterranean, and an apartment in Paris and New York, and wherever he went women saw in him a depth of passion so great that they would be both overwhelmed and helplessly drawn. In his eyes they would see themselves as they always wanted to be, and for a brief glorious moment their souls would dance.

Fred was hungry. True, he had eaten just an hour ago, but what was time to an appetite? He went to the refrigerator and brought out half a chicken and a bottle of wine, (with poultry Sauvignon blanc). He had tried dieting. He had a bookshelf of diet books, and stacks of exercise videos, and cabinets of vitamin supplements, and refrigerators of protein shakes, weight-watcher frozen lasagna, and non-fat chocolate mousse. He had tried acupuncture, aerobics, homeopathy, and voodoo. He'd fasted like Gandhi and Bobby Sands, and bought smaller plates to make his portions seem bigger. He'd experimented with 12-step programs, hypnotism, and St. Jude's novenas. He'd invoked higher powers from Allah to Zoroaster and done everything short of selling his soul to lose weight, but he hadn't lost an ounce. In fact, the cumulative frustration over the years had resulted in a hundred pound gain, and two or three additional desserts each day as a reward for his suffering. Fred Orbis was trapped inside his body. He was both Ahab and Moby Dick, and his waistline the circumference of the globe on which the whale swam, just out of reach, taunting him, filling him with madness and unspent vengeance. If only he could kill it, destroy it once and for all and peel away its layers of blubber, and watch as its carcass disappeared into the ocean's lifeless depths. Then he could have peace.

He picked at the last pieces of chicken, and as he gnawed at the bones he wondered what kind of pie awaited. Back to the refrigerator—Dutch apple, banana cream, and some kind of blackberry torte. To the table with a pie in each hand, (he'd save the torte for a midnight snack). And this was how he spent his evenings. A dinner (or two or three), and then he sat behind his computer and did battle like a medieval Crusader, as he hacked away at the infidel prolix, at the blaspheming clichéd metaphor and godless hackneyed construction, and brought a kind of sanctified purity to the screen in his search for the holiest of Grails—the Big Book Deal. There is a saying that everyone has a novel inside of them, which is probably true, but to Fred Orbis irrelevant. To him, the question that burned through each of his days was "Is there a *bestseller* inside of everyone?" For years he had been trying to find the elusive formula, to crack the code and find the proper alignment of words that would somehow sing to the hearts of the masses, and make publishers all glassy-eyed. He had four dictionaries placed around his desk, like talismen to the four directions. And they sat like lumps of radium, beaming their energies from north, south, east, and west, and somewhere in their recondite pages, like endless and inscrutable folds in the cerebellum, lay the perfect turns of a phrase, the unexpected twists of plot, the definitive denouement. Somewhere in the *Oxford English* and the *American*

Heritage and the *Webster's Collegiate* and the *Webster's Universal Unabridged* were the right words just now putting on their Sunday bests, gussying themselves up, and strolling on to the town meeting held nightly in his imagination. And like God looking down from on high he accepted his children's offerings, molding them into the sure-fire can't miss 99-weeks-on-the-bestseller-list thriller. Fred Orbis had written two other books, and he knew as sure as visions of blackberry tortes danced in his head that this book, his third, was the one. His only problem was that he had no idea what constituted a bestseller. He was as ignorant of its soul, (assuming a bestseller had such a thing), as Bach in his *Art of Fugue* period would have been to a Top Forty hit single, because in his heart of hearts was James Joyce imprisoned, his soul aching to free itself in the prose on Fred Orbis's computer screen. So that no matter how hard he steered towards bestsellerdom, some plaguing conscience of an inner voice would always speak up at the last moment like a deer dashing across the road, and cause his prose to swerve into a tree.

He looked at the poster of James Joyce that hung on the wall, as he finished the last of the pie. How would Joyce fare in the late twentieth century, he wondered? Joyce's time was altogether different. There was the belle époque, the Great War, the Russian Revolution, the lost generation. There were still places on the globe undiscovered. Japan had barely emerged from its feudal isolationism, Everest had yet to be climbed, the world still held mystery. But now every centimeter of Earth had been mapped out, by satellites which could zero in from outer space onto the mole on your left shoulder blade. Now Japanese in business suits dropped dead from 100 hour work weeks and pollution, rad dude 20-somethings snowboarded down Everest to get corporate sponsors and meet babes, and instead of mystery there was virtual reality. The new Everests raised their peaks in cyberspace, their unscalable summits delineated in spiffy computer graphics. Fred Orbis was convinced that this wasn't his century, and that was another of his problems. The *sixteenth* century, now *there* was a century to be fat! Your coevals: Gargantua, Pantagruel, Falstaff, Henry VIII! What role model did a fat person have here in the twentieth, the *Goodyear blimp*? But that was hardly anything to be celebrated in serious literature. *Ye air-gutted windbag, ye rotund immensity, ye bottled effluvium*...No, he was a castaway, set adrift towards this century's dismal horizon. What would the twenty-first be like? Perhaps eugenics would be perfected and everyone would look like models, and someone like him would be outlawed and sent to Devil's Island. The *Devil's Island Diet*—now there's one he hadn't tried yet. A glance at the treadmill that sat in the corner of the room collecting dust. The first time he stepped onto it the belt jammed, its engine overheated, and it blew up. It was another symbol of his exile in the Elba of his own body.

He sat before the computer screen and typed the word 'FAT'. He watched as the letters ballooned up until they took over the screen, obliterating all other words around them. Then he highlighted this enormous, inflated, gargantuanly obese word until the entire screen was light purple, and he hit the delete key. Just like that it was gone. He looked at the blank screen and typed the word 'thin'.

Darby Montana was heir to the great Polk's Peanut Roll fortune. Her grandfather, Benjamin Franklin Polk, (from the Unadilla Polk's), inherited the family peanut farm, and then took an old recipe handed down through generations from his great great grandfather Thomas Jefferson Polk's plantation, and marketed the family peanut roll, (which was a caramelized nougat surrounded by salty peanuts). Legend has it that the actual recipe came from one of Thomas Jefferson Polk's 1776 slaves. Thomas Jefferson Polk's son, William Henry Harrison Polk, despised his father, and was consequently a fervent abolitionist, and after his father died he granted all the slaves their freedom. However, while making his emancipation proclamation in a torrential downpour, he contracted pneumonia and died, and left the estate to his only son, Millard Fillmore Polk. Millard Fillmore Polk however, was an abject failure. And before the grass was high on his father's grave he had squandered the family fortune, until all that remained of the once magnificent plantation was a small peanut farm, which survived only because Millard Fillmore Polk was crushed to death by a flying cow. Apparently the cow had been sucked up inside a tornado several counties away, and was caught in a wind tunnel until it sailed from a clear blue sky onto M. F. Polk's none-too-businesslike head—as he made his afternoon pilgrimage to his favorite bawdy house, and his favorite bawd, LuLu. But his son,

Benjamin Franklin, or B.F. as he was called, was determined to redeem the Polk name and be a success. And with the inventiveness of his namesake, parlayed the favorite treat of his childhood into a vast financial empire, which would one day surpass even his great great grandfather's plantation, in all of its antebellum opulence. And it was this that he bequeathed to his son, Benjamin Franklin Polk Jr., who also inherited his father's head for business. Today, the Polk family holdings were worldwide, (with even a few satellites orbiting the earth, as part of the communications branch of the Peanut Roll conglomerate). They owned TV stations, newspapers, shopping malls, and a major league baseball team, one of the oldest and most venerable franchises in the American League, which B.F. Polk Jr. moved to Anchorage, Alaska (in order to secure a deal for a major oil field) and renamed the *Akalakmukks*, which was Innuit for *"Whale Blubbers"*—which insured him everlasting fame by being the first person to bring major league baseball north of the 60th parallel, (and in the process, vindicated George Steinbrenner).

B. F. Polk Jr. was one of the richest men in the world, all because of that little two ounce candy bar in the bright yellow wrapper. And in homage to his ancestors he bought back and restored the old family plantation. And although they had only fifty or sixty servants, they employed thousands of people in Third World countries, where they were paid in peanuts for twelve hour days, and from that great plantation in the sky, his great great great grandfather, Thomas Jefferson Polk the patriarch, looked down and smiled.

B.F. Polk Jr. had everything money could buy, including an estranged daughter—christened Dolly Madison Polk, in keeping with the family's long-standing tradition. Dolly was his only child (by his first marriage to the chorus girl and exotic dancer Rita La Flame), and she showed a rebellious streak from early on when she was expelled from Kindergarten, when in response to a classmate's inquiry about her family's peanut roll she replied, "Polk's Peanut Rolls suck." Thereafter she was shuffled around to private schools in Europe and Australia, the further from Georgia the better, to avoid anymore embarrassing scandals. And as Dolly grew to womanhood her father, who had spent the years of his daughter's childhood and adolescence going through two more wives, and amassing seven or eight additional fortunes, called her back to the family plantation for a reconciliation. She was sixteen and he was aging. She was to be his sole heir; his wives all dying under mysterious circumstances. His first wife, Rita La Flame, was consumed by her boa constrictor in an ill-fated attempt at a showbiz comeback. His second wife, Ruby Ruminant, the former Miss Idaho, died of warts. It was the first terminal case of warts in almost 700 years, and to this day still confounds medical science. And his third wife, Rutanya Ruresteva, the Romanian chess champion, who while suffering a sneezing fit during a match inadvertently inhaled her opponent's Bishop and expired there on the board, three moves from checkmate. So the vast Peanut Roll Empire was to be Dolly's alone. However, when B.F. Jr. announced that he had named her sole heir, she instructed him to place his peanut roll in a particular orifice not frequented by the sun, as she left the next day to hitchhike across America. She was sixteen, and like most sixteen year-olds she thought her father was a jerk. A week later she was on a frozen windswept road in Minot, North Dakota, with her frostbitten thumb sticking out, when an 18-wheeler pulled up. The door swung open, she climbed inside, and it was love.

"I'm Bud." said the driver.

She was spellbound. He was everything her father was not. Big, oafish, and uneducated. A flannel-shirted clod of a man, his hair stuck out in forlorn wisps from beneath his Peterbilt ballcap, his eyes holding the vacant stare of a cow. She couldn't decide if he was good-looking or grotesque, (he had one of those faces that seemed to be made of rubber), but she knew that she wanted him. Oh yes. All the way from Minot to Montana she imagined countless scenarios of her losing her virginity to this truckdriving bumpkin named Bud, and when they stopped at a motel for the night in Darby, Montana, she seized the moment. And although her mother Rita La Flame was known for her exotic beauty and knowledge of boa constrictors, Dolly Madison Polk looked more like the snake with her mother inside its stomach. She was not fat, really—more like shapeless, amorphous. Rectangular. And her face, even with an expert makeover, would never make it too far beyond plain. She cut a less than ordinary figure, even as a concupiscent sixteen year-old, but she was willing. And when she whispered to Bud that she was a virgin she became irresistible—at least for the night. The next morning she woke to the sound of an 18-wheeler pulling onto the road, en route to Vancouver and points north. A single sigh, as she watched the plume of smoke disappear, but then she leaned back in bed and smiled. She was a woman now. This was what she wanted. And to celebrate the event she got rid of Dolly Madison Polk, the name she felt was the cause of all her misfortunes, (namely that she was plain with the body of a rectangle), and she searched around for a new moniker. The motel was called the *"Buck Snort"*, not a fitting title for an heiress, but then in a burst of inspiration she rechristened herself *Darby Montana*. The name seemed to embody all that she wanted to be. It was bold, it was fiercely determined, it was exotic. And she got dressed and walked across the street to the Elk Antler Inn, where she applied for a job as a waitress—as she had decided to settle here in her adopted namesake town. On the application she wrote her list of private schools and that she spoke five languages, and the head waitress Hildy thought she was joking and hired her on the spot, since a waitress with a sense of humor was a definite plus, especially where truckdrivers and loggers were concerned, (truckers and loggers comprising the main clientele of the Elk Antler Inn). But after six months of waiting on grimy, unsophisticated backwoods clodhoppers she decided to exchange the greasy spoon for the silver one, and took a bus back to the family plantation where she, like the Prodigal, was accepted with open arms and pocketbook by aging B.F. Polk Jr., who by now was more concerned with the afterlife than the present life. His last six months with Dolly under the roof were happy. The day of the funeral she became one of the richest women on earth, and the day after, she officially changed her name to Darby Montana.

She lived now in New York, an apartment in Greenwich Village, because her new persona was that of a Bohemian intellectual. Each week like Gertrude Stein she presided over her personal *salon*, which she modestly called the Wednesday Afternoon Discussion Group, where the best and brightest would meet. Actually they were people a lot like her—bored scions of huge fortunes, who all shared a kind of misguided aim at solving the world's problems through afternoon philosophizing over cucumber sandwiches. Here, the works of Dante were discussed in relation to wealth versus poverty, and Hobbes and Rousseau in reference to the still plaguing concern of inequality. And as usual, the digressions into old standards like art, music, and how everything could be considered Postmodern, for Darby was nothing if not thoroughly postmodern. The problem was, she would give it all up in a second for the one thing her wealth could never buy. Darby Montana wanted to be beautiful.

Devon DeGroot was a model husband. He loved his wife passionately, he believed in equality, and he shared his wife's feminist leanings. The only problem was that he was a New York City police detective—the commander of the Mid-Manhattan South Vice and Homicide Squad. So consequently each day after breakfast, when he kissed his wife tenderly on the lips and stepped outside, his life was in peril.

But he loved his job as much as he loved his wife. From his earliest days he believed in Good versus Evil, and he knew that it was his destiny to somehow be on the side of Good. He believed that it was possible for a single soul to make a difference, as evinced by the many causes both he and his wife espoused, and in his job Devon DeGroot felt a kind of religious fervor. He was on the front line of battle leading the charge against Evil, and where but in New York City was Evil more apparent. With each drug bust, with each stake-out that bore fruit, with every crooked lawyer or politician brought down, with every murder solved he felt that the light of Good shined a bit brighter. Devon DeGroot loved his work, but lately, as if sensing a shift in the air, he had grown uneasy. His was an uncommon intuition, a sixth sense which guided him, and this was one of the reasons why he was so successful. He read the polluted Manhattan skies and its pot-holed streets as an augury, and he sensed that something was amiss.

"What happened to the *pothole?*" he asked. The police cruiser swerved to the curb and he dashed out. Other cars drove past, and he waved them on as if they were gnats until he stood above where the pothole should have been.

"What is it?" asked Detective Arnold.

"Right *there...*" DeGroot pointed to the newly macadamed road. "They covered up *Big Bertha.*"

Big Bertha was the most notorious pothole in the city. For months she had stood like a gaping maw, ready to devour legions of jaywalkers, schoolbusses full of Kindergartners, and the Macy's parade. She was the Godzilla of potholes, and the police of Mid-Manhattan South always drove down this block with a sense of reverence, bordering on awe. But now she had been filled.

"It's *wrong.*" said DeGroot.

Detective Arnold observed a profound look of consternation on his commander's face—as if he were a Brooklyn Dodger fan after the wrecking ball had been put to Ebbets Field.

Devon DeGroot stared at the black piece of street, and then turned his attention to the sky. Overhead the clouds roiled in ominous waves, as they greedily devoured the sun.

"Something's happening."

Detective Arnold knew of his commander's instincts. They were always right, and now *he* was uneasy. The last time he saw that look was six months ago, the Colombian drug bust when he was shot three times. He decided to double his time at the firing range and get a new bullet-proof vest, and as they sped off, Detective Arnold thought of his wife and two kids, while Devon DeGroot thought of Evil.

6

"No pothole." said the cabbie, in some strange middle Eastern accent.

"What?" the man in the back seat asked.

"Big pothole...gone."

"Hmm..." The Devil's thoughts were elsewhere—a game of chess—as the cabbie drove him to his apartment.

Elizabeth Aphelion was just finishing up. As house-cleaning jobs went this one was a breeze. Mr. Monde always kept the place clean and tidy, and she was usually done in an hour, although she was paid for four. After finishing the bathroom she spent the rest of the time browsing through his library, playing with his cat Cleo, or writing poems. Elizabeth Aphelion was a poet. She had gone to Smith College, like her idol Sylvia Plath, and was working on a book of poetry—a book her professor at Smith promised to show to her publisher once it was complete. It was one of those double-edged swords. Elizabeth wanted nothing more than to be a published poet. She imagined the kind of life she would lead: wondrous winter days in a simple cottage on Monhegan Island, with just the cold gray sea and her pencil and paper. And summers in residence at some New England artist colony, or possibly Santa Fe. She imagined the desert light on her skin, highlighting the radiance she felt would shine from her like a bottled sun. But for now, the sun was held in the hands of her poetry professor, Jacqueline Jimson-Weed. They had been lovers. For Elizabeth it had been an experiment. She had immersed herself in the Romantics, the Libertines, and had always wondered what being with a woman would be like. And then one night during her final semester she accepted an invitation to dinner. Ostensibly to discuss her latest poems, but after two bottles of wine she found herself and her professor naked in bed. She remembered her soft voice.

"You have a gift, Elizabeth, your poetry." her tongue exploring the porcelain intricacies of her ear. "I can help you."

She told her about her publisher, and that when the book was finished she would see that it was published.

Elizabeth tried to hold onto the words, to secret them away like a love letter, but as she looked in her professor's eyes she saw that they were *there*, locked inside.

"We are lovers now." Jacqueline said, closing her eyes, drifting to sleep.

Elizabeth watched her face, smooth and steep as a wall of granite. *"We are lovers now."* What had just happened? The passion she had felt just minutes before had been turned into some kind of Faustian bargain.

They remained lovers. Elizabeth had no choice, because each time she saw Jacqueline Jimson-Weed she saw the bottled sun in her hands. When she moved to Manhattan after graduation she thought she would be free, but Jacqueline appeared every few months for long weekends. By now Elizabeth had met a man and had become *his* lover, but every few months she had to concoct some excuse for a weekend's absence. What had she done? And now her only hope was to complete the book. Once it was published she would no longer need her professor, and then she could break it off.

Elizabeth swept the feather duster across Mr. Monde's bookcase. She was amazed at his collection of books, all appearing to be rare first editions. Her eyes danced over the authors' names: *Dante, Montaigne, Cervantes, Rabelais. Melville, Goethe, Tolstoy. Hemingway, Mann, Joyce.* She brought out *Finnegans Wake*—something she had meant to read since college. Flipping through to the end, she saw that it was 600 pages long. To a poet this was six volumes and a life's work. She put it back and noticed an old book tucked away, its leather cracked and peeling, its cover blank, and when she opened it, loose pages slid out like dried leaves. In a panic she looked at the clock—Mr. Monde would be home soon. Quickly she bent down to retrieve them, and as she did she saw one that appeared to be a title page. In a beautiful cursive hand on thick yellowed parchment was: *The Tragedy of Hamlet, Prince of Denmark.* On another: *Scene I. Elsinore Castle.* She took a breath. They were all handwritten, and every so often a word or a line had been crossed out, and sometimes something new written above it. Just then Cleo trotted to the door. It was Mr. Monde. Hurriedly she put the pages in order, and slid the book back in place.

"Hello Cleo...Hello Elizabeth."

"Hello, Mr. Monde. I was just finishing up."

"Good. I was wondering if you might like to continue your chess lessons today."

A few weeks earlier Elizabeth had mentioned that she wanted to learn chess, and last week Mr. Monde described the pieces and their moves. Today was to be her next lesson.

"Yes, that would be nice." A stolen glance at the book of *Hamlet.* "You have quite a library, Mr. Monde."

"Reading is one of my passions, Elizabeth. One day I hope to find *your* book up there. I'm confident that it will happen. Sometimes, I just get a *feeling* about things."

He walked to the stereo and put on a CD. An acoustic piano—beautifully sad notes rising in the air, tumbling into poignant chords—and then the bass and drums.

"It's Bill Evans." said Mr. Monde. "I think *his* is the best music for chess. Do you like *jazz*, Elizabeth?"

"Well, I haven't heard that much of it."

"He and Miles Davis are both masters of space. Sometimes the notes that *aren't* played are the most important. Like in poetry, the space is as important as the words, do you agree?"

"Yes."

"And in that space there's room for your thoughts...like what move to make." He was seated behind white, studying the board.

"It's sad to me, this song." said Elizabeth. "What's it called?"

"'Re: Person I Knew'."

"Hmm. It's so wistful, like the title."

"Yes, but actually the title is an anagram of the record producer's name."

"Really?"

"But it is a beautiful song. Tell me, Elizabeth, are you fond of anagrams?"

"I...I don't know."

"Well, I must confess, they're one of my hobbies. Take your name for instance...*Elizabeth*..." A pause as he searched her eyes. "*The...Bi...Zeal...*Does that mean anything to you?"

She was silent.

"That's the problem with anagrams, sometimes they're just meaningless." A glance at the chess board. "So, do you remember the pieces, and how they move?...*Elizabeth*?"

"Yes. Yes, I do."

"Good. Then today we'll talk about the opening. This is the most important part of chess. We've already introduced the pieces, now let's get them into play. Imagine the chessboard as a stage.

The pieces all move towards the center, because if you control the center you control the game." He moved his pawn from *King to King Four*. "And now you do the same..."

Elizabeth followed.

"This is most exciting. The pieces, each with their individual strengths and weaknesses, begin to come together." He instructed her to move her Knight, and then he moved his Bishop on a long diagonal.

"What's the matter, Elizabeth? You look dismayed."

"The plot thickens..."

"Yes. Do you remember the moves we've made so far?" He returned the pieces to their original positions.

"Yes."

"Good." And he took the board and switched it around so that she could play white. "Then let's begin."

7

The bookstore window display was always the same as Fred Orbis walked by. It was his barometer of popular culture. The latest mega-bestseller took up the entire window, like baby clones in a nursery awaiting adoption. It wouldn't take long. It was another in the long assembly line of diet books— this particular variation on a theme, *The Priscilla Benson Beach Lookout Diet*. Priscilla Benson was the redoubtable star of the world famous hit television show *"Beach Lookout"*, which featured beautiful bikini-clad women as archaeologists and amateur sleuths, who while searching for clues to a lost civilization buried somewhere beneath Malibu Beach, solved crimes and worked on their collective tan line. Priscilla Benson's first book, *The Autobiography of My Breasts*, was a runaway smash, and told the story of her life, from her silicone implants' point of view.

Fred Orbis was depressed. He thought of his first book *Fortune's Fool*, a massive epic which recalled Joyce, Melville, and Shakespeare. The main character was an aged millionaire who married a 20 year-old beauty. However the woman was not your average 20 year-old beauty. Whether she was angel or witch or goddess was undetermined, but she transported him during their love to different times and places, and he became other people and even animals, and saw life from every conceivable perspective, (and was it a dream or was it real?). The book's scope was all of history, philosophy and religion, the question of God's and man's existence, and a reflection on the soul and immortality. It was Fred Orbis's labor of love, his *magnum opus*. It took over ten years to write, and when it was finally finished he sent it off to publishers, expecting to instantly ascend to literature's pantheon alongside his revered mentors. However, the huge book returned each time like a rain-soaked, chastised mongrel, accompanied by pithy notes of rebuke from the dog-catcher: *"It's too long...No one writes like this anymore... There's no market for it"*. One sympathetic soul even suggested that he familiarize himself with what was on the bestseller lists. And after sulking in a morose cloud of doom for over a year and gaining more weight he decided to take his advice. His second book took only seven years. It was called *Dead Letter*, and was the story of a frustrated writer who one day inadvertently discovers that what he writes in a letter comes true if the letter is opened. So he sends off query letters announcing deaths and gruesome accidents to all of the agents and publishers who had rejected him, and when half the publishing community drops dead he becomes a folk hero to all the unpublished writers. And in the course of the story the book becomes an epic philosophical discourse on literature, morality, and Good and Evil, echoing Dante and Homer.

Needless to say, *this* book, Fred Orbis's "bestseller", received the same response as *Fortune's Fool*. It was then that he began to wonder whether he *had* a bestseller inside him, or was he doomed to be a serious writer that no one would read? He thought of Joyce. The only people who read *him* anymore were college students, and usually through the pacifying filter of *Cliff Notes*. The so-called "Classics" were albatrosses circling the tall ships of publishing houses, hopelessly moored in Manhattan. They were cantankerous grandparents who sat in their creaky rockers, judging everything you did, while you just smiled and waited for them to die.

Fred Orbis's third book as of yet hadn't gotten off the ground. He remembered Melville saying, *"To have a mighty book you need a mighty theme"*, so he tried to go in the opposite direction. The problem was, that it was much easier for him to write a labyrinthine existential epic, than it was to find a bestselling plot. He had become Monsieur Grand in Camus' *The Plague*. Grand spent the entire book working and reworking the first sentence of his novel. He had in fact spent years on that one sentence. Sometimes he removed all the adjectives. Sometimes he removed all the adverbs, and put the adjectives back in. He twisted the sentence like a snake in every possible convolution, until its head became its tail became its head again, and then he looked at it and started from scratch. As all novelists know the first sentence is most important. *"Call me Ishmael."..."It was the best of times, it was the worst of times..."..."a stone, a leaf, an unfound door."* The fate of the five or six hundred pages that followed was in the hands of this felicitous first sentence. And each night after dinners, Fred Orbis sat behind the computer screen and stared at *his* sentence:

Til the soul-departed seas wash your empty shores, and earth becomes a hollowed ball.

It wasn't even a sentence. It was a fragment, really, a statement or imprecation. He wasn't even sure what it meant, but for some reason it had come to him and stuck there on the screen. *"Til the soul-departed seas wash your empty shores..."* He liked the alliteration and the image. *"and earth becomes a hollowed ball."* It foreshadowed something ominous. But *what*? And what did this sentence have to do with a bestselling suspense thriller?

For weeks themes had swum in his head like sharks around a doomed ship. There was the psychotic killer with a split personality, who was also a police detective who ended up arresting himself. There was the head of state who was really a Soviet spy switched at birth, who with the dismantling of his homeland felt a vague sense of anomie, and went to a psychiatrist who was really the antichrist. And there was the story of the minuscule two-dimensional aliens who took the shapes of letters of the alphabet, and infiltrated society by substituting themselves for the letters on the pages of bestselling novels. Actually this was Fred Orbis's hope—to have the alien letters arrange themselves on his computer screen in the shape of some blockbuster thriller that would put him on the literary map. Then he could publish *Fortune's Fool* and *Dead Letter* and be at peace.

He looked back at the bookstore window. Diet books. Diet books by TV stars. Diet books by talk-show hosts. Diet books by the personal chefs of talk-show hosts. Diet books by the friends of a friend of the personal chefs of the talk-show hosts. Everyone and their uncle had a book out these days, but where was *Literature*? It was a lame duck president. It was a fifth wheel. An anachronism, like writing letters. Now you had a famous author's collected *E-Mail*, but where was the *poetry*, not just in the written word but in *life*? Diet books. He thought of the words. *Di*et books was a dactyl, a metrical foot. There was poetry there if you looked at it from the right angle. His perspective changed. Instead of the books, he saw his reflection in the window. The warp and woof of life. Fate pulling the strands into place in this great loom, with each day tightening it further. But wasn't there room for variation? For irregularity? Couldn't one strand be thick and off-color and still fit in? Could this one singular strand change the entire rug?

Fred Orbis stared at his body, like the Hindenburg floating in plate glass, and he heard the words float out from the past. There he was, wedged between his chair and desk in his fourth grade classroom. It was one of those infernal one-size-fits-all desks, with the chair welded to it by immovable steel braces. And it sat like an ancient oak mouth with metal jaws, while each day he sacrificed his body to its unpitying appetite. A glance at the names etched in the old wood like the poetry of a prison cell—a name and a string of days carved into the unyielding cement. How many children had been devoured in that very desk, he wondered, until their brains were sucked dry, their desiccated husks blown from fourth grade through graduate school? He saw his teacher, Mrs. Pressman, before the blackboard now with her list of words. Each week there was a new list which they would learn, and then use in a story which they would compose. Fred Orbis scanned the list and stopped at the fourth word from the top, standing out like an obituary. The word was "obese". He turned to Mrs. Pressman and thought he detected a sinister gleam in her eye, as if for the moment the other children no longer existed, and it was just the two of them locked in an existential battle. She was Death and the word "obese" was her scythe, which would soon swing in an ineluctable arc. A smile of innermost satisfaction appeared on her lips, which was seconds from a sneer, moments from a gloat. Mrs. Pressman had timed the word like the fuse of a bomb. Her dutiful charges read the list from top to bottom. The first word "habit", the second "tablecloth", the third "sobbed", and then the first snicker of comprehension, as one by one the students came to "obese", and one by one turned their heads towards Fred Orbis, wriggling now in his chair-desk, in that last gasp of prey in the mouth of the predator, clinging tenaciously to life, but also realizing that by his own birth this end had been inevitable.

There was silence in the classroom as the students composed their stories. However, Fred Orbis's hearing was acute. Each sound of pencil against paper was a blade against a whetstone. The guillotine was being sharpened and soon he would hear its whistling blade, as each student would march to the front of the class to read their stories aloud. The half hour seemed to pass as an instant and an eternity, and finally Mrs. Pressman stepped forward and asked for a volunteer. Everyone raised their hands except Fred Orbis, and she called on Jimmy Dempster, who stood up and began to read.

"There once was a fat boy who had a habit of eating..." Sensing immediately that he had won over his audience, he continued on with unabashed bravado. "He ate everything including the tablecloth, and when that was gone he sobbed. Fred Orbis was obese, and he had nothing left to eat..." When Jimmy Dempster was finished there was general hilarity. And by the time everyone had read their stories the classroom resounded with good will and hope for the future, like the primitive village that had banded together to burn the Frankenstein castle to the ground. Mrs. Pressman had molded her students into a single battering ram; their stories the flaming torches, the word she'd given them the spark, and they were the tinder. And Fred Orbis, the center of her wrath—the monster.

Fred Orbis stared at the other words on the blackboard: "finished, better, lamb, morning", and then he looked at the story he had written:

> "She had a habit of abuse towards her students. Each morning before school she stared at the kitchen tablecloth, as she finished the last of her coffee and sobbed. She sobbed at the futility of her life. But when she got to class she smiled. The obese boy in the fifth row. Today he would be her sacrificial lamb. Today she would feel better."

"Fred..."

He heard his name like Laertes' sword. It was Mrs. Pressman. "Would you like to read *your* story now?"

She was the incarnation of evil. But then, the slightest smile broke out on his face. Wasn't he a cannon packed with ball and powder? And this bungling overconfident Mrs. Pressman had inadvertently lit the fuse! He started to his feet with the story clutched in his hands, when he got stuck in his desk. And the more he struggled the more he got stuck, and meanwhile the entire class called out like a hideous Greek chorus, *"Obese Orbis!... Obese Orbis!"*, a chant which resounded against the blackboard and into Fred Orbis's ears like the deafening *"Seig Heils!"* at the Nuremberg rally. And there across from him was *der Führer* before her throng of sycophants, wiping the hair on her brow, nodding her head in crazed monomania. The students learned a valuable lesson that day—in alliteration. They took to it like natural born poets, the words dripping from their lips like honeyed wine. *"Obese Orbis! Obese Orbis!"* From that day on Fred Orbis no longer had a first name.

He never read his story. He became so stuck in the desk that the janitor, Mr. Winkbottom, had to come into the classroom and unfasten all the bolts, to extricate him from the accursed desk's rapacious jaws. And from that day on he had a special desk in the back of the class, where he sat like a silent mountain in the distant misty horizon. He didn't read the story but he handed it in, and when he got it back there was a big "F" on it, in bright red marking pen. Mrs. Pressman's victory was decisive and unforgiving.

Fred Orbis stared at himself in the window of the bookstore and then moved on. Whenever he felt like this he got hungry. To the corner deli he went, (as a man with a cat on a leash stepped out, holding a newspaper, a cup of coffee, and a bagel). He walked to the counter and stood behind a small boy, and when the boy turned around he gazed up in wonder, as if witnessing a total eclipse, and Fred moved aside, (as best he could), to let him pass. Fred ordered two submarine sandwiches (the foot-long kind) and a *Village Voice*, and then he walked to his apartment, and sat down with a sandwich in hand as he turned to the classifieds. There was an ad he wanted to see. He found the "Personals section" and scanned through the ads, all of them seemingly reduced to the same simple equation: for women seeking men—"Gorgeous model, long hair, voluptuous seeks wealthy generous older man"; for men seeking women—"Incredibly wealthy and generous older man seeks beautiful female model, 16–21 years old." *Amor vincit omnia.* However, there was a kind of spare, streamlined quality to it which he admired. They had stripped romance of everything but its cynical essence. They had reduced love to a kind of Machiavellian mathematics, and to Fred Orbis this was okay. The airy vicissitudes and sweet nothings of love had always lived in his imagination, but in his reality had remained a mystery. In the Middle Ages of his mind he was Tristan searching for his Isolde; he was a courtly knight with a white rose on his shield, the emblem of his beloved; he was Arthur with Guinevere (with Lancelot off fighting the Crusades). But in the late 20th century, Fred Orbis was a lifeless planet on the far reaches of the galaxy, with not even a dead moon in orbit for company. The "woman question", the *"querelle des femmes"* was a problem that seemed as unsolvable as the quest for the unified field theory, but here in the back pages of the *Village Voice* was the answer. Like Diogenes with his lamp his eyes roamed across the ads until he found it.

"Extremely fat, but also extremely wealthy and generous man seeks beautiful hedonist women for weekly bacchanals."

He gazed at the words as if they were the best thing he had written. It was honest. This, he thought, would hook them in. It was New York, after all—honesty was as rare as green grass and blue sky. They would be moved by his unsparing self-disclosure.

"Extremely fat, *ahh*", they'd think, "'tis a rare man indeed who would say such a thing in a personal ad. This could be the man I've been looking for—a man of resolute courage; of daring. A man not caught up in appearance, like so many of his contemporaries..."

He looked at the next part—*"extremely wealthy and generous..."* Well, that wasn't exactly false. He was quite generous. After all, one doesn't attain the overall girth that he had achieved without a certain generosity at the dinner table. And he had put some money away over the years. True, he was by no means even moderately wealthy, but this "wealthy" could be taken as a wealth of spirit, a richness of character, a largesse of soul, so to speak, and in this regard he felt abundant. He continued on—*"seeks beautiful hedonist women"*, but he was stuck on the word "beautiful". It kind of crossed out the fine picture he had painted of a man not hung up on appearances. But then, appearances had been his entire life up to this very instant! There had not been a moment when he *hadn't* been aware of appearances, namely his own, and how he was so different from everyone else. So with this in mind he could forgive a little lapse on his part. Besides, if he was going to go through the trouble of putting in an ad he might as well ask for what he wanted. And if she truly was beautiful she would see beyond the surface of things to their essence. Fred Orbis was confident that in a beauty contest of spirits his would be as lithe and winsome as an ingénue. He tried to move on, but he was still stuck on beautiful. Perhaps he should have left it out. Perhaps he should have requested someone as fat as himself—after all, what other kindred spirits did he have? But then he remembered the old saying "You can be poor by yourself." All you had to do was substitute the word "fat" for "poor". He could definitely be fat by himself. In fact, he was fat enough for four or five people, and he had no need of adding any more weight to his life, not to mention that the floorboards of this old apartment might right now be on the verge of giving way. A woman who was beautiful might inspire him to lose weight. She might be the Muse he needed to finally get a handle on his bestseller. She could be the person who in one evening could turn his life around. Beautiful was good, he let it stand. His eyes continued on. *"Hedonist...for weekly bacchanals"*, and he was pleased as he read the words. They were literate, clever and lusty, not whey-faced dry as dust, as were most of the other ads. *Hedonist.* The word recalled a thousand pleasures. A thousand pleasures he had never known but had ceaselessly imagined. *Hedonist women.* Images of a seraglio. 17th century Turkey, the smell of cloves and jasmine, sequined silks and incense, and two eunuchs like enormous Doric columns beside the door, as he strode into his bedchamber and beheld the female bodies, spread across the rug like a field of ripe melons. *"For weekly bacchanals"*. He imagined beautiful, uninhibited followers of Dionysus all over Manhattan recognizing his ad as the beacon they had been waiting for to guide them out of their Platonic doldrums. Soon this apartment would be a pleasure dome! But then he noticed the submarine sandwich bursting with cheese and lunchmeat, overflowing with lettuce and onions, dripping with oil. It was a foot long, and after he finished it he would eat another. Reality hung heavy. He looked back at his ad and saw it swallowed up by the other ads, until it became a page of black flies on something dead.

Fred Orbis stared at the page—his ad had become indecipherable hieroglyphics. But it was worth it, he thought, the few moments of release he had felt, the few seconds of joy. There would be no response, that was a given. His opening words were *"Extremely fat"*. He closed the *Village Voice*, and smiled faintly as he picked up his sandwich.

The Wednesday Afternoon Discussion Group was officially supposed to convene at 2 PM. However, since all of its participants wanted to arrive fashionably late this posed a logistical problem, because if one of them arrived late and was the first one there they would be disheartened. So consequently everyone wandered around Manhattan. They visited shops, they grabbed a bite, all the while keeping an eye on their watches for just the right moment to wander back and make their entrance. It became a kind of dilatory dance, a minuet of meandering, a tango of tardiness, and by the time everyone had arrived it was nearly four o'clock—but to Darby Montana this was part of the group's charm. So she was surprised when there was a knock at the door shortly after three.

"Hi Darby."

An elegant man in his late forties stood in the doorway. It was Philep Möthesse, whom Darby had met the other day at an art gallery. She had been impressed by his aristocratic bearing, and his refined sense of idleness, and she invited him to the group.

"I hope I'm not too late."

"No, not at all. Please, come in."

A glance around. He saw that he was the only guest.

"This is Wednesday?"

"You know Manhattan. They usually start filtering in around three-thirty. It will give us a chance to talk before the others arrive. Can I get you a drink?"

One of the things that set Darby's group apart from other discussion groups was that she served her own guests, which she felt lent it an air of Bohemian authenticity.

"Cognac, please."

Philep looked at her apartment, a Parisian salon really, *circa 1920*. The settee and sofa, the lamps and rug all antiques that cost Darby a fortune—not to mention the "Blue period" Picassos on the walls. And there were always roses in art nouveau vases.

"So Philip..." She handed him the drink.

"Phil*e*p." he corrected her. "It has an '*i*' and an '*e*' instead of two '*i's*.'"

"Phil*e*p." she said, trying it out on her lips. "It has an interesting feel." (Although it sounded exactly the same.) "Your name...what is it, it's nationality I mean?"

"I come from a very old family in Luxembourg. The Möthesses go back more than a thousand years."

Darby's family went back only a few hundred. She was impressed. "Tell me more."

"Well..."

"I'll bet you're a count, or a prince or something."

"Well, no. Nothing like that. But two hundred years ago, my great great great grandfather was a king."

Darby looked at his face. He was handsome and fit, his short hair silver and gray, but as she stared at it she suddenly imagined him behind the wheel of a semi, a Peterbilt ballcap on his head...

"Is there something wrong, Darby?"

"No, I'm...I'm sorry, Philep. Please, your great great great grandfather was a king..."

"Yes, the heir to the throne at the time, the son of the king, fell in love with a peasant girl and renounced his title. He married the girl and went off to a life of poverty, and when his father died there was a coup led by my great great great grandfather...and he was made king."

31

"That's kind of a horrible story."

"I know. Most people side with the young heir who marries for love, and they think my grandfather a shameless opportunist. But then, if it wasn't for the shameless opportunists we wouldn't have history."

"And if it wasn't for the young heir who gave up everything for love we wouldn't have romance."

"*Touché.* I'm not proud of what happened then." He grew pensive. "So what about *your* family, Darby?"

She cocked her head and bit her lower lip. Philep would just *love* to hear about her great great great grandfather's 1776 slaves, or the Polk's Peanut Roll fortune.

"I was an orphan." she said. "So what happened to the young *heir*?"

At that the doorbell rang.

"Philep, please excuse me."

"Darby!" A middle-aged woman with a fur coat over a black dress appeared. "Am I *late*?"

It was three thirty-two. Normally this would have been an awkward moment, but since Philep was there her face was safe.

"No, you're right on time. Let me introduce you to a new member of the group...Philep Möthesse...this is Iona Bentley."

"Iona." He took her hand, and kissed it in the manner of an aristocrat.

"Philip."

"It's Phil*e*p...with an '*i*' and an '*e*'." said Darby. "Philep was just telling me the most interesting stories...about kings and *coup d'états.*"

"I believe it's *coups* d'état, dear." Iona turned to Philep. "So, welcome to our little group. I hope we're interesting enough for you."

The doorbell rang again. It was Livingston Good and Anna Coluthon. They had arrived at the same time and neither wanted to be the first to go in, which would then jeopardize their status as fashionably late.

"After you..." said Livingston Good.

"That's so...but *you* go first." said Anna Coluthon.

"Please, come in." said Darby. "Guests have already arrived."

They spotted Iona Bentley on the sofa talking with a handsome stranger, and now they were both eager to meet him.

"Liv Good and Anna Coluthon, I'd like you to meet Philep Möthesse." The former Dolly Madison Polk had a true knack for being the hostess.

"Philip." said Anna.

"It's Phil*e*p, with an '*i*' and an '*e*'." said Iona Bentley.

"Philep." said Liv Good. His tone, confident and manly, as they shook hands. "Möthesse...is that *German?*"

"Luxembourgian." Philep explained, and Liv Good nodded as if he should have guessed.

In a moment two more guests arrived. Barton and Melanie Snide, and then as the clock struck four, Courtney Imbroglio. Courtney was always last. In the world of the fashionably late she was its diva.

"Courtney, good to..."

"Can you *believe* Iona?" she said, calling Darby aside.

"What?"

"She wore that *exact* same dress at the *Met* last week...No paparazzi will ever find *me* in the same thing twice." Rumor held that Courtney wore her clothes only once and then threw them away.

"I believe you meant to say *paparazzo*, dear." said Iona. "What I like about your group, Darby," dismissing Courtney and pouring herself another drink, "is the charming informality...and your *new guest*. Who *is* he?"

A crowd had gathered around Philep, and Darby felt pleased. It was so like Paris, the enchantment with all things new.

"Philip, it's so nice to meet you." said Melanie Snide.

"It's Phil*e*p...with an *'i'* and an *'e'*." said Iona Bentley.

"Iona's niggling stultiloquence continually borders on the umbrageous." said Barton Snide.

Iona looked puzzled, and Melanie stepped in to translate.

"He means that you always know the right thing to say."

"Philep, it's so nice to...so you're from Belgium?" asked Anna Coluthon.

"Luxembourg, actually. So, what do you usually discuss at these meetings?"

"You name it." said Courtney. Her first drink gone, she poured another.

"We talk about...what was it last time?"

"Art." said Darby, turning towards Liv Good. "Liv is an art critic."

"Well, it's just a hobby, I..."

"He writes for *The Times* and *Modern Painting*."

"And that *other* thing, that Postmodern..."

"*Flatulence.*" stated Courtney Imbroglio. Her second drink gone, she lit up a cigarette.

"No Courtney, the name of the magazine is *Afflatus*."

"It means *inspiration*."

"*Thank you* Melanie."

"Like the inspiration of that one artist whom you just *gushed* over." said Courtney. "Tell us again about the artist." And she plopped down next to Philep on the sofa.

"Yes, tell us." said Iona, sitting down on his other side.

Liv was sweating now as he loosened his collar.

"It's about *space*..." he said. "The artist's conception of space is really quite revolutionary."

"He hangs up blank canvasses." said Iona.

"He puts frames around...there's nothing there." said Anna Coluthon.

"They're not *blank*." said Liv. "He's a *painter*. He calls them his *'white paintings'*."

"His *'white paintings'*." Courtney offered an incredulous puff of her cigarette.

"Yes, he uses different shades of white. He varies the sizes of the brushes, and the brushstrokes."

"But they're all *white*." said Courtney. "There's nothing there but *whiteness*."

"Yes, that's his medium."

"His *medium*? I think his medium is lobotomy."

"Now Courtney, you're beginning to sound like a *Philistine*. You have to understand the Postmodern. He's forcing us to look differently at painting. He's trying to show us that all vision is merely perception of reflected light. Look at the world around us. Look outside that window, there's *chaos*. There's crime and pollution and serial killers, and here in his paintings there's this little island of peace."

"But, there's nothing *there*."

"No...*verisimilitude*."

"No...*soul*."

At this Philep Möthesse perked up.

"Let's talk about the soul." he said. "Do you believe in it?"

And everyone was suddenly quiet.

"Do you believe that there's this...airy nothingness inside us that is our purest expression?"

Now Darby was intrigued.

"The body, what is this but a clay urn? But the *soul*...And when we die what becomes of it?"

"Yes," said Darby, "existence versus nonbeing, and the question of the soul. Aren't we more than just bodies? What does it matter what the outside looks like?" (But the words rang painfully hollow in her ears.) "I mean, a Ferrari's nothing without a driver..."

"It's still a damn fine car." said Liv Good.

"We go through life, this whisper of a life, and what matters most is who we are *inside*."

"But the soul can't exist without...it's made by the body." said Anna Coluthon.

"Right, the body makes our soul. It's like...a *chrysalis*."

Darby took a deep breath. To her the body wasn't a chrysalis but a prison cell, with the soul as its inmate. And year after year she sat within its cement walls, because there was no parole from the body or face. It was genetic. It was a life sentence, and her soul, as exalted as she wanted it to be, was doomed to wither away.

"So what if you're dissatisfied with...you don't like your body?"

"Yes, what can you do?"

At this everyone turned to Darby Montana.

"That's a good question." said Philep as he intervened. "If we accept that the body is responsible for the soul, as a teacher would be for his student, then what becomes of a soul in a body the soul sees as unfit?"

"Like in someone who's *obese*."

"I was thinking of...what about *reincarnation*?"

Philep rose from the sofa, and suddenly Iona and Courtney were beside themselves.

"What is reincarnation", he asked, "but another chance for the soul to get it right? And each time the package is different but the soul is the same. And it must work out its new problem, like a puzzle, or a problem in chess. This is the perfectibility of the soul."

"So, do you think it's possible?" asked Darby.

"I think that it's the supreme challenge of a human being."

"Philep's right." said Liv. "Everybody sells their soul on a daily basis...the constant compromise."

"That's Liv's *métier*."

"I'm serious, Courtney. Choices arise every day, and what we choose shapes our souls."

"And we make our Procrustean beds." said Barton Snide. (Barton Snide believed that everyone made their own Procrustean beds, and that they should consequently lie in them.)

"He means that we compromise." said Melanie.

"Right, we compromise our souls." said Iona. "We do things we really don't want to do...like my house cleaner, for instance."

"Your *house cleaner*?...*This* ought to be good!"

"Yes, she's a very nice young woman, and she wants to be a poet...I guess she *is* a poet. But, she cleans houses."

"Maybe she has to *work*." said Darby. "Most people don't inherit fortunes. That's probably why the great artists have all been poor. Their poverty shaped their souls."

"So what's shaping *our* souls?"

"*Boredom?*" offered Courtney, her answer punctuated with a desultory cloud of cigarette smoke.

"So, can our souls be saved, or are they already lost?"

And everyone turned to Philep.

"I believe that everyone is unique, and that you people here have just as much right to unhappiness as anyone else."

"Or happiness." said Darby.

"Or happiness. Every set of circumstances is the best possible one for that individual soul...be it an heiress or a house cleaner... and to both of them there comes a day when they have to make a choice...not the small ones we make every day, but one big choice that determines everything, that determines if we can be happy. I've seen so many people, but so little happiness."

Philep walked towards the door.

"You're not *leaving*?"

"Yes, I...I have to look in on an old friend. But I must tell you all how much I've enjoyed meeting you, and how I look forward to next Wednesday's meeting."

He gave Darby a special good-bye glance, and then walked out the door, into the chaotic world of crime, pollution, and serial killers.

The rest of the meeting was spent talking about Philep Möthesse, and how this had been the best meeting ever of the Wednesday Afternoon Discussion Group. And while the others drank their drinks and exercised their legs on the subject of the soul, Darby Montana thought about what Philep had said. *"There will come a day when you have to make a choice—a choice which determines whether or not you can be happy..."* This, after all, was what it was about—*happiness*. Something stranger and more exotic than the mysteries of the soul could ever be, for even though Darby felt a kind of eternal spirit stirring, in all her life she had never felt happiness. She smiled as she looked out the window and watched Philep Möthesse disappear in a cab, the cab amber and rounded in the late afternoon light like a chrysalis. She saw herself hail it and step inside, and when she emerged she would be happy.

"What's happening?" Devon DeGroot asked, as if expecting news of the Apocalypse.

Detective Kozinski looked up from his newspaper.

"The Knicks lost again."

The past few days Devon DeGroot had the feeling of being inside a storm cloud as it grew darker and more portentous, and he waited for the first rumble, the first flash of lightning.

"Where's Detective Arnold?"

"I think he's at the firing range." Detective Kozinski scanned the box score to see how many points the Knicks' new hotshot guard had last night.

DeGroot went to his desk, and found that somebody had spilled coffee on it.

"Who *sat* here?"

"What? I don't know, boss. Donalbain or Macduff. Why?"

"Well get their asses in here! They spilled coffee all over my desk!" He grabbed some paper towels to soak up the spill, but when he was through his eyes were drawn to one of the towels, the shape the coffee made in the paper as it was absorbed. Laying it flat on his desk, he studied the shape—like a large sack with several openings.

"Kozinski, what does this look like to you?"

Detective Kozinski stared at the coffee stain on the paper towel.

"A *coffee stain*, boss?"

"No, the *shape* of it...think *laterally*." Devon DeGroot was a tireless exponent of lateral thinking.

"You mean, like if it was a *Rorschach*?"

"Yes."

"It looks like..." He studied the coffee stain as an art appraiser would a Caravaggio. "Michigan, boss." And he stood back from the paper towel, pleased with his discovery.

"*Michigan?*"

"Yeah, the upper peninsula."

Detective Donalbain arrived.

"What's goin' on?"

"Did you sit at my desk this morning?" asked DeGroot.

"It must have been Macduff."

"Well, tell me what you see in this..."

Donalbain stared at the coffee stain on the paper towel, and then turned back to his commander.

"Is this a trick question, boss?"

"Think *laterally*." urged Detective Kozinski.

At that moment Detective Macduff walked by and glanced at the coffee stain.

"That looks like a stomach." he said. "Hey, sorry boss. I guess I spilled some coffee this morning."

"What did you say?"

"I said I was sorry about the coffee."

"No, about the stomach."

"Yeah, my kid had to watch this science program the other night, on human organs, and *that* looks just like a stomach." He glanced at the others and then went back to his desk.

"Get me *Gray's Anatomy*."

"What, boss?"

"*Gray's Anatomy*, we must have a copy somewhere. And Donalbain, get me a dictionary."

"Here you go, chief..." said Kozinski. "I've been using it as a doorstop."

DeGroot turned to the section on the stomach as Donalbain searched for a dictionary.

"*There*..." He placed the diagram of the stomach alongside the coffee-stained paper towel.

"We got a match!" said Macduff.

"I still think it looks like Michigan." said Kozinski.

"What kind of dictionary do you want?" asked Donalbain. "We got the *Oxford English*, the *American Heritage*, the *Webster's Universal Unabridged*..."

"Bring them all." Devon grabbed one and turned to the word stomach. "Here...*Definition 1: a large sacklike digestive organ of the alimentary canal*..."

"Hey, isn't that in Jersey?" asked Macduff.

"What?" asked Donalbain.

"The Alimentary Canal."

"Yeah, but you don't want to swim in it!" said Kozinski.

There was general jocularity as DeGroot pushed on to definition 2. "*Informal. The abdomen or belly*...", and then, "*Definition 3: An appetite for food*...", and then, "*Definition 4: A desire or inclination.*"

Devon DeGroot stared at the last two definitions for several minutes as the others went about their work. It was a slow day in Mid-Manhattan South, but for Devon DeGroot, in the case that had yet to be a case, he had found the first clue.

10

"It's your move." said Mr. Monde.

Elizabeth was distracted. She couldn't take her eyes from a painting on the wall.

"What is it, Elizabeth?"

"That painting, of George Washington...Have you always had it there?"

Mr. Monde turned in his chair.

"Oh yes, always."

"I guess I never really *looked* at it."

"Well, you know what *Picasso* said, the only way for a painting to be noticed was to hang it slightly crooked. That way your eye was drawn first to its *crookedness*, *then* to the painting. Otherwise it disappears."

Elizabeth looked back at the painting, (slightly crooked).

"Like with books. They all blend together on the shelf, but then one day a single book sticks out as if it *spoke* to you. Has that ever happened to you?"

There was a pause.

"Yes."

"Our intuition is a most underrated sense, Elizabeth. I think the answers to our questions are right under our noses. We just have to open ourselves to the possibilities. That to me is my favorite word."

"What, *possibility*?"

"Yes, it has poetry, don't you think?"

Elizabeth thought of the word, and then saw Jacqueline Jimson-Weed. A cold slab of a table, a book laid out before her. On the book her name, *Elizabeth Aphelion*, the title: *Possibility*. Her professor was dressed as a surgeon, and she watched as she took a scalpel and sliced away the first two syllables.

"Pos-si...a *pyrrhus*...both unstressed." And then she cut again and held up what remained before the class. "*Bil*-i-ty...a *dactyl*...a stressed followed by two unstressed."

On the book now was a new title: *We Are Lovers Now*.

"It's what makes life interesting." said Mr. Monde.

"What?"

"Possibility."

She needed to change the subject.

"I've seen that before. Isn't it *famous*?"

"You mean dear old *George*? Yes, the most famous of American portraits. I'm not usually one for trends, but...well, that has... sentimental value."

"But I've *seen* it, in a museum."

"The Boston Museum of Fine Arts."

"Yes, when I went to Smith, we went there. So this is a reproduction?" But then she recalled the old book of *Hamlet*, written in longhand.

"What if I told you it was a *gift*, Elizabeth, presented by General Washington himself?"

She smiled.

"Would you like to hear a story? We can...we can finish our game later."

"Sure. What *kind* of story?"

"A story about George Washington...A story that's never been told before."

"Yes, I'd like that."

"Good, then sit."

From the wine rack he brought a dusty bottle. Mr. Monde insisted that Elizabeth never dust the wine rack. He preferred the bottles with a layer of dust.

"A toast," he said, "to *possibility*...Are you familiar with the Faust legend, Elizabeth?"

"Yes, but..."

"It was December, 1776...what many believed the coldest winter in memory. The war was going badly, and Washington desperately needed a victory. His army was a shambles, frozen and half-starved. Many had no coats or shoes. And to make matters worse, on December 31st their enlistments would be up. Out of an army of 10,000 men, only *2000* would remain, and without an army the war would effectively be over.

"You see, America at this point was still an *idea*. The *army* was the country, and Washington understood this from the beginning. He knew that the only hope was that it could stay together, because if it stayed together long enough, the British would leave. But then he asked himself, why would *anyone* re-enlist? The soldiers all needed food and clothes. Many hadn't been paid in six months or more. He had written Congress again and again asking for money, but there wasn't any. And to top it off, the people had lost faith in him."

"In *Washington*?"

"Yes."

"So what did he do?"

"He devised a plan. It was bold. Audacious. The last thing anyone would expect from a half-starved, half-frozen army on the verge of collapse. He decided to attack. The last few days had been milder, and the ice on the Delaware River had broken up enough to cross...although only Washington saw this as a possibility. His plan was to cross the Delaware on Christmas night, and attack at dawn. Imagine the *daring*..." Mr. Monde paused to take a sip of wine.

"But as in all great men, Washington had great doubts. The army had suffered a string of demoralizing defeats, and the more he thought of his plan, the more foolhardy it seemed. On Christmas Eve he sat in his tent and brooded. Outside the wind howled, it had gotten colder again. In a few days the Delaware would be frozen solid, and the British would march across and attack Philadelphia, so there was just this one window of opportunity...Think of it, to see the fate of your country come down to a single day."

"So what happened?"

"There was a knock outside. One of Washington's young Captains, Alexander Hamilton. Hamilton was only 20 years-old, but he was a brilliant thinker and a daring soldier, and Washington trusted him. They talked of the plan and drank more brandy, and in the course of the evening Washington believed that his plan would not fail, and more importantly, that America would survive and become a great nation."

"You don't mean..."

"Alexander Hamilton was the *Devil*," he said with a smile, "and on that winter night George Washington made a bargain with him that ensured America's freedom...Remember the key word, Elizabeth...*possibility*. If we knew the real story behind most things we'd be constantly amazed."

"Okay, so how did it happen?"

"Well, as you can imagine, George Washington was incredulous. After all, here was this 20 year-old Captain informing him that he was...But, the brandy, the cold, who knows? We see Washington now with wooden teeth and a wig, but I assure you that he was a very modern man, a man not bound by conventional thinking. Did you know he played *chess*?"

"No, I didn't."

"Yes, he was quite good in fact. But, back to the story...The following night they crossed the river in a snowstorm. They could barely steer the boats through the ice. Frost-bitten, almost blinded by the snow, many without gloves, many with blankets instead of coats. Washington's plan was to attack at dawn, but the army didn't get across the river until after three. And it wasn't until well after four when they were all assembled and ready to march. It was at this point when he considered turning back. They had lost the cover of darkness. By the time they reached Trenton it would be light, and for Washington, this was his moment of truth. He decided to push on.

"They marched for nine miles in a snowstorm, many leaving bloody tracks behind, all the while keeping strict silence. But then, fortune smiled. Because of the weather the Hessians had withdrawn their pickets, and Washington's army was able to advance right on the town. The Hessians were still asleep, hungover from too much Christmas cheer, and when they finally woke up it was too late. By nine that morning Washington had put them to rout, and taken almost a thousand prisoners. The Americans had no dead and only a few wounded. Imagine General Washington, looking out across the field as an officer told him that the enemy had struck their colors. He was in disbelief, but then he looked and saw the Hessians with their hands in the air. An officer said he noticed tears in his eyes."

"But, he had made the bargain." said Elizabeth.

"The bargain was so America would one day be free. Crossing the Delaware was all Washington. His *will* made it succeed. And then, an amazing thing happened. Almost overnight, people around the world hailed the *Battle of Trenton* as it was called, as one of history's great victories, and placed Washington alongside Alexander the Great. And like a house of cards, the British fell and withdrew from New Jersey, and the colonists suddenly believed that they were invincible. That battle was a huge stone tossed in the water, and when the last ripple went out, the colonies were a free nation called America."

Elizabeth drew a breath as she looked across the chessboard. "That's some story, Mr. Monde."

"Yes, and one you won't find in any history books. Do you believe it?"

"Well..." she smiled.

"What is history after all but an *opinion*? It all depends upon who holds the pen...What are the histories that *you* believe, Elizabeth?" He reached over and refilled her glass. "Do you believe in the Faust legend? Do you believe that someone can sell their soul, like in the story? And I don't mean in a metaphorical sense, the *'quiet lives of desperation'*, as Thoreau put it. I mean the real thing."

Elizabeth was silent. She thought of what they were talking about—certainly the oddest afternoon of house-cleaning she had ever spent.

"I don't know, I...I think I would be afraid to consider it."

"What did Hamlet say? *There are more things on heaven and earth, Elizabeth, than are dreamt of in your philosophies...*"

"So what happened to George Washington?"

"Do you really want to know?"

"Yes."

"Well, the story I told you is just the beginning. People have the wrong idea about the Devil. He's really an okay guy. He's witty, well-read. He's the life of any party. He involves himself in matters of philosophy. One could safely call him an *existentialist*. I mean, who else is more concerned with man's plight? So, imagine him coming upon someone like Washington. The Devil admired him. He respected him. The deal he gave him was different. Instead of the usual *quid pro quo*, he was given the chance to redeem himself."

"Washington?"

"Yes. He would live to see his country a great nation, and after he died his soul would be reincarnated four times over the next two hundred years or so, and in each incarnation it would be

47

presented with a *test*, if you will... perfecting certain aspects of his character. And if he passed all four tests, at the end of this time his soul would be cheerfully returned, with no further obligation."

"So, he didn't really *sell* his soul then."

"Well, he kind of deposited it in a bank account for two hundred years, and the Devil lived on the interest. And if he passed all four tests his soul would be returned intact, and he could finally rest in peace."

"So, how has he done?"

"So far he's passed the first three with flying colors."

"And the fourth?"

"The fourth test has just gotten underway, and *this* is the most difficult of all."

"I want to hear more. What's the fourth test?"

"Elizabeth, you don't strike me as the kind of woman who rushes straight to the denouement."

"Sorry, I...I just got caught up in the story. Can you tell me about the *first* test then?"

"Yes. It would be my pleasure...but *next* time. My voice is tired, and we have a chess game to finish."

"But, can I ask you a question, about the story?"

"Certainly."

Mr. Monde walked to the stereo and put on Miles Davis's *Seven Steps to Heaven*.

"It's about Alexander Hamilton. Wasn't he killed in a duel with Aaron Burr?"

"Aaron Burr, yes. A despicable man."

"But if he was..."

"If he was the *Devil* then how could he be *killed?*...The Devil takes on many guises, Elizabeth. It's one of the fringe benefits of the job. Besides, his business with Washington was finished, it was time for other things. The duel, that was his own idea, going out in a flourish. The Devil's a ham, what can I say? He's really not a bad guy. You'd like him...Next week we'll continue the story, but for now," he surveyed the battlefield that was the chessboard, "it seems that your *Knight* is in danger."

Elizabeth scanned the board, and then moved her pawn to counterattack.

"You learn fast. To me this is one of the most exciting parts of the game, before the first piece is taken. The calm before all Hell breaks loose." Mr. Monde captured her Bishop, and then smiled as he placed it on the side of the board. "It's your move, Elizabeth."

11

Fred Orbis was fat inside the womb. He consumed so much of his mother's vital forces that by the fifth month of her pregnancy she could barely move around freely, her energy sapped by the feeding of her voracious unborn. By the seventh month she could no longer stand upright without toppling over like an upside-down bowling pin. By the ninth month she had become a sprawling estate, and she labored for an additional month before finally freeing herself from the fetus. The doctor's first words were *"Gott in Himmel!"*, and then *"Arghh!"*, as he threw his back out trying to lift the baby, (in order to hold it before its mother in the age-old fashion of pediatricians and midwives). Several nurses and an orderly were called in to assist, and they gasped at the sight of this child, the size of your average Kindergartner. Mrs. Orbis's first words were "I beg of you, *please*, tie my tubes!" And as the doctor was wheeled out on a stretcher with a blown sacroiliac, and the nurses and orderlies and Mrs. Orbis all gazed in awe at her baby, Fred Orbis uttered *his* first words, *"I eat! I eat!"* The nurses and orderlies gasped again as he searched the room for some food, and when his eyes came upon his mother's breasts she let out a shriek of horror before fainting away. When she awoke she was informed that the doctor who delivered her child was suing her for malpractice, for causing him to throw out his back. It was the first time in the history of medicine that a doctor sued a patient for malpractice. Thus was Fred Orbis's first day in the world.

Milk trucks stopped several times a day at the Orbis residence, as the thought of breast-feeding her young filled Mrs. Orbis with a catatonic dread. For weeks she was speechless. She wandered around in a delirium, her days spent mentally flagellating herself for her sins like St. Jerome. And whenever she looked at Fred in his makeshift crib, (which was a double bed with pieces of plywood nailed around its sides), she became nauseated—one of the rare cases of post-natal morning sickness. In the bedroom it was even worse. Mrs. Orbis lay rigidly in bed a barely animated cadaver, her limbs plastered to her side, her eyes staring vacantly into the void. And at the slightest touch from Mr. Orbis, at the slightest tremor radiating across the bed as he turned disgruntly over, her body gave itself up to an interminable shuddering, the likes of which had only been seen in shipwrecked castaways on ice floes in Antarctica. A month later Mrs. Orbis, who had already mastered her vow of silence, got on a bus, left town, and entered a convent—*Our Lady of Perpetual Nervous Tics*, (a more modern ecclesiastical order)— where she spent her days doing God's will, ministering to the poor and sick, (providing that the poor and sick weren't obese).

Meanwhile Fred Orbis Senior took to spending more and more time at the local tavern.

"How's the kid?" his friends would ask.

"You mean the *blob*?"

"How's Junior?"

"You mean the *furnace*?"

To Mr. Orbis, his son was a kind of engine that had to be continuously fed. He went through baby food like cordwood, and an entire room of the house was given over to its storage.

"I shoulda' named him *Jupiter*," he said, "after the planet." And then he bought drinks for the house, because in a way he felt a kind of pride—that through his seed he had done this.

Fred Orbis Senior beamed like any proud father the day little Fred, then six months old and 125 pounds, was on the cover of the *National Inquisitor,* one of those tabloid magazines. A photo of Fred Jr., in all of his layers of baby fat, with the headline: *Enormous Baby to Play for Green Bay Packers!*

"He looks like the Michelin tire mascot!" said Mike McAlchy the bartender.

"No, more like King Kong." said P.J. Pumice, an out of work longshoreman.

"No, he's like *Mrs.* Kong, when she was pregnant with Son of Kong!" said Roger Centgrabber, the local used car salesman.

"No, no, he's like...What was that big plane that Howard Hughes built? The one that never got off the ground?" asked Monty Briefsoiler, the local shyster lawyer.

"Yeah, I know it..." said Mike McAlchy. "It was enormous. What was it called?"

"The pine pigeon?" suggested P.J. Pumice.

"No, that's not it. But you're on the right track. It has a tree and a bird in it." said Monty Briefsoiler.

"The Mahogany Merganser?"

"The Walnut Warbler?"

"The Oak Ostrich?"

"The Maple Mosquito?" offered Maury Bund, who had just joined the conversation, and was three or four sheets to the wind.

"No, you moron!" they all called out. "The mosquito's not a bird."

"I got it!" announced Roger Centgrabber. "The Cedar Waxwing!"

"That's a bird, but it's not a tree."

"What, cedar's not a tree?"

"The Hemlock Hummingbird?"

Suddenly it seemed as if hours had passed.

"The Koa Cormorant?"

"The Hickory Hawk?"

"The Teak Termagant?"

"Termagant's not a bird..."

"Well, what is it then?"

"It's your wife!"

"I got it..." said Mike McAlchy as he stared at the others in triumph. "The Zamian Zander."

"What the hell's *that*?" asked Roger Centgrabber.

"It's a rare tree and a rare bird." said the bartender.

"Rara arbor, rara avis." Maury Bund muttered to himself, as he stirred his drink with a swizzle stick the shape of a shillelagh.

"First of all," said Fred Orbis's father, "the zamia isn't a tree, it's a plant, with a short tuberous stem, and a crown of palmlike pinnate leaves."

"And isn't the zander a fish and not a bird?" chimed in P.J. Pumice.

"Exactly."

"Hey, what do I know, I'm only the bartender, right?" Mike McAlchy wiped the bar rag across the counter in a defiant sweep.

"What about a zygodactyl?" asked Maury Bund, his eyes like two pearl onions.

"But that's *of a bird*," said Fred Orbis's father, "it's not a bird itself."

"The zygodactyl zeppelin." said Monty Briefsoiler.

"That's neither a bird or a tree."

"The zaftig zeppelin...*zaftig*, doesn't that mean *fat*?"

"How do you spell that, with an '*a*' or with an '*o*?"

"Both, I think."

"I got a '*Z*' word for you..." said Maury Bund, gazing into his empty glass. *"Zymurgy!"*

"Now *there's* a word I like!" said the bartender. He tapped a keg and poured everyone a round of Stegmaier. "To Fred Orbis Senior, and to his son...If only I can stay in business until he's of age."

They raised their glasses to the family Orbis, and the mystery of Howard Hughes' wooden plane was never solved.

Edo ergo sum. I eat therefore I am. This was Fred Orbis's philosophy of life. By the time he was six his father sent him off to military school. The tuition was expensive but it included room and board, and this, the board, was what stuck out for Fred Orbis Senior. It seemed like a bargain. It was here as a six year-old when Fred Orbis Junior was given his first official nickname, "Tank" Orbis, in keeping with military tradition. But after only a year the school administrator explained to Fred Orbis Senior that his son could no longer attend the school, because they could no longer afford to feed him. So he was given up to the tender mercies of a public education, and the name "Tank", which Fred Jr. had grown to like, was rudely eclipsed by his fourth grade sobriquet—*"Obese Orbis"*.

Fred Jr. was the only child to carry two or three lunch boxes to school, each crammed with a Thermos of soup, and as many sandwiches as it would hold. There was so much food in fact, that the time in the cafeteria wasn't enough, and he had to continue eating on the playground while the other children played. And when he was finally finished, as the other boys played football or baseball or dodgeball, he hovered on the periphery like the Goodyear blimp.

One time though, he *did* ask to join in a game of football, and one of the captains, envisioning Fred Orbis as the entire offensive line, picked him for his team. But when Fred bent over to hike the ball he collapsed under his own weight, and when he clambered to his feet the ball lay squashed on the ground. From that day on Fred Orbis was an outcast, and he silently watched the others from the edge of the grass, as he ate the box of donuts he had brought for dessert.

The only thing Fred Orbis had going for him was that he was uncommonly intelligent. In fact, he would rightly have been considered a genius if it wasn't for Mrs. Pressman, his Medea-like fourth grade teacher, (whose own mother was so fat that she constantly filled the young Mrs. Pressman with a sickened revulsion, which Mrs. Pressman as an adult took out on anyone who was obese). Fred Orbis would have scored in the highest percentile in the battery of standardized tests given that year, however after class, Mrs. Pressman erased Fred's name and switched it with Jimmy Dempster's, putting Fred's name on *his* test. Consequently six weeks later, Jimmy Dempster, who had previously been considered a bully and a dunce, was hailed as a genius, and even awarded a blue ribbon by the mayor for his achievement—whereas Fred Orbis scored in the lowest percentile, and spent his days staring at Jimmy Dempster in bewilderment. Jimmy Dempster, an avowed dullard, dimwit, pea-brain and nincompoop, yet hailed now as a genius; while Fred Orbis, who had taught himself Latin, and had already written a cycle of sonnets in iambic pentameter, was shunned as an ignoramus.

Fred Orbis watched as the years passed, and Jimmy Dempster, buoyed by his unexpected test results became the most popular boy in school, the president of his class, the captain of the football team, the king of the Senior Prom. He was given a full scholarship to Yale and was now a state senator. Meanwhile, Fred Orbis languished in obese obscurity, (or obscure obesity). And even though he got a perfect score on the SAT's, the only number anyone in college admissions noticed was his weight, and for that reason they became less than inspired. He ended up at the City College of New York where he was valedictorian, although during the commencement exercises all honor and praise were given to the salutatorian, with

Fred's name mentioned only in passing. "And the valedictorian, Fred Orble..." Somehow the last two letters had been misspelled. The only reason he got a job after graduation was because he started his own magazine, and in the twenty odd years since, *Feast Magazine* had become moderately successful, and Fred Orbis had found his niche. He worked each day at a job he liked, and he couldn't help but notice the similarities between the word editor, which he was, and the Latin *edo*, or eat, which he did. And then each evening was spent writing his novels, as the years, and the decades blurred quietly by. But now something had happened— something that made this day different from all the rest. He had received a response to his personal ad.

Fred had gone to the Post Office as he did each day, in the hope against hope that somehow there might be a letter waiting. He had rented a Post Office box just for this purpose. Actually, he had one of the temp workers in the office rent it for him, under the name *"Gustavus Silenus"*. *Gustavus,* for the first King of Sweden who led the revolt against Danish domination, and who was a renowned gourmand; and *Silenus,* after the Greek *Sileni*. In the days of Socrates, Sileni were little boxes decorated with harpies and satyrs; mythic figures after Silenus, the master of Bacchus. The outside of the box was frivolous, and belied what was inside, some rare and precious drug such as ambergris, or precious stones. It was said that Socrates was like a Silenus, because his outward appearance was coarse and ugly. His manners were that of a rustic, he had the face of a fool, he was unlucky in regards to the *querelle des femmes*, and he spent his days laughing, eating, drinking, and generally making light of himself. But inside he had a far-reaching compassion, a marvelous insight, a divine wisdom. And this was how Fred Orbis saw himself—as a large...an *extremely* large Silenus. So he ordered a temp worker named Juan DeRoo to run down to the Post Office, and get him a box in the name of Gustavus Silenus. And then the next day Juan DeRoo's job was finished, and he decided to go to Europe in time for the plum harvest in northern Spain—the result being that there was no trail leading to Fred Orbis. This, he felt, was something that had to be kept completely *sub rosa*. No word must leak out that he had put in a personal ad, because then his co-workers would needle him relentlessly. True, he was the boss and they were his underlings, but Fred Orbis held little faith in the generosity of the human spirit. He hadn't heard the word "obese" since the last day of high school, and then he moved to New York City, where he felt he could better blend in and escape its ceaseless echo, which had resounded since that fateful day in fourth grade. And now as an adult he had no desire to ever hear it again.

Fred Orbis took the day off. He tried to remember the last time he had done this, and he vaguely remembered a day off, ten or twelve years ago—pneumonia or something. But today was different—the day of his big date, and he was too nervous to go to work. The letter had arrived on Monday, and he waited until Tuesday to call, which took a Herculean effort of will power—he didn't want to appear too anxious or desperate—and now it was Wednesday. His mind drifted back to the phone call.

"Hello, is this Belle Horizonte?" He had liked her name from the first moment he saw it. *Belle Horizonte...Beautiful Horizons.*

"Yes, this is Belle."

Her voice like nectar poured from the phone, and he drank it down like Tantalus.

"Hi, this is Gus...*Gus Silenus*...You answered my ad in the *Voice.*"

"Let's see, which one were you again?" In the background was a TV, and what sounded like a baby crying.

"Extremely fat..."

"Oh yeah...and extremely wealthy and generous." She liked his voice, so deep and resonant...like a *banker*. Perhaps he was brimming with insider information.

"It's so good to speak with you, Belle." (The perfect gentleman. He had reread *The Art of Courtly Love* in preparation for this phone call.)

"So, you wanna *meet?*" she asked.

Fred was favorably impressed. She was direct, strong, like Eleanor of Aquitaine. Here was a woman he could respect.

"Yes, but don't you want to know anything more about me?"

"You're everything you said in the ad, right?"

Her tone was bold and challenging, and brought to mind Mary Queen of Scots; Joan of Ark.

"Yes. I'm extremely fat."

"And extremely wealthy and generous..."

There was a slight pause.

"Yes."

"Well then, good. Let's meet. How 'bout tonight?"

"*Tonight?*" He could barely contain himself. What just a week before had seemed a chimera was now a reality. "Yes, tonight would be fine. Where shall we..."

"Pick me up at the corner of Madison and Fifth...You understand I can't give you my address yet. There are a lot of creeps in New York."

"Yes, I understand perfectly. The corner of Madison and Fifth would be fine. How will I recognize you?"

"I'll be the beautiful blonde stepping into your stretch limo."

He was silent for a moment, as he realized she wasn't joking.

"About seven then?"

"Yes. Seven."

"What was your name again?"

"Gus...Gus Silenus."

He's Greek, she thought. Some Greek tycoon.

"That's a nice name."

"Thanks." *She obviously appreciates the finer things. Perhaps we can discuss Socrates...*

"Good. See you tonight at seven."

He started to say good-bye, but she had already hung up.

"That's a nice name." Belle had said. Fred Orbis heard her voice as he sat before the computer screen. He was so nervous he thought he could take his mind off the impending date by doing a little writing, and he stared at his sentence.

Til the soul-departed seas wash your empty shores, and earth becomes a hollowed ball.

He gazed at it like a jeweler searching for a flaw in a gem, and then his fingers danced over the keyboard. "Til the seas wash your shores and earth becomes a ball." He had removed all the adjectives. It was pithier now, more Hemingwayesque...but then he noticed the metaphor. Hemingway *hated* metaphors, and Hemingway had been a bestselling author. More typing. "Til the seas wash your shores on earth." That was better. No high-blown metaphors cluttering up things. A look back at the sentence, but still something wasn't right. The first word, the poetic *til* for *until* suddenly seemed pretentious. Keep in mind your audience, he told himself. "Until the seas wash your shores on earth." Maybe it should be "on *the* earth." He typed it in. *Now* he was getting somewhere. But then again, it was too prolix. He lopped off the *the*, and left earth by itself. He could almost see the second sentence materializing. But no, one mustn't rush things, he thought. "Until the seas wash your shores on earth." Still, it wasn't a complete sentence. It seemed that the very first sentence of a bestselling thriller should at least be complete. Staring at it, he raced through the dictionaries, thesauruses, and encyclopedias of his brain, and came upon a new tack. "The earth was washed by the seas." He had eliminated *until* and *shores.* It was obvious now that they had completely obfuscated the sentence's meaning, and as it stood now it made sense. "The earth was washed by the seas." What could be truer than that? It was a strong, forceful beginning, it said something that made sense, and what's more, he had pared down the original sentence, which floated in an ambiguous ocean of fourteen words and twenty syllables, to a sleek, streamlined seven words and seven syllables. It had been a pokey ocean liner, but now it was a hydro-foil built for speed. The words flew by, they could barely be contained on the page, and this of course was the hallmark of a bestseller. "The earth was washed by the seas." But then he looked again at the sentence. Even though it was brimming with celerity it was missing something. Maybe it was still too poetic. After all, he didn't want to offend the sensibilities of his readers—they wanted a suspense thriller, not Shakespeare. Simplify, he thought. "The seas wet the earth." *There,* that was *it!* More to the point. It had a kind of classic quality to it. "See Spot run."..."The seas wet the earth." There was the same kind of timeless lyricism. But then he thought of the original sentence and the sense of foreboding he had felt from it. His fingers rushed back to the keyboard. "The seas *will* wet the earth." Now there's *suspense.* The seas haven't wet the earth *yet,* but they *will*...but then, "The seas *might* wet the earth." This increased the suspense even further. Now you're left wondering whether or not the seas will actually wet the earth. Rereading the new sentence he was pleased. But then, what about that business with the soul? "The soul-departed seas." What did that mean? He was glad he had rid the sentence of the word "soul"...too many New Age connotations. But then, he thought of the image of the earth as an empty ball. It was a good image. How could he get that in there somehow, without ruining the integrity of "The seas might wet the earth."? "The seas might wet the *empty* earth." It had alliteration; but it had an adjective, and he had eliminated all adjectives and any semblance of metaphor. But as he mouthed the words he liked their sound. He looked again at the word *might*. True, it provided suspense, but wasn't it sort of wishy-washy and noncommittal? After all, shouldn't the opening sentence be unequivocally bold, with no pussyfooting whatsoever, but at the same time imply mystery? That's where the word *Til* came in. It provided the element of the unknown. He put it back. "Til the seas wet the empty earth." Now the word *wet* stuck out, suddenly so banal. It snapped in the air like a smelly locker-room towel—not the image to have in an opening sentence. "Til the seas *washed* the empty earth." Better. But still it was too general. You don't want general, you want striking. "Til the seas washed *the shores* of the empty earth." But now he needed to make it more personal; give it a human element, imply a character and a character's struggle. "Til the seas washed *your* shores..." It was about someone now, but all of a sudden the last part, "of the empty earth" seemed to run on a bit. Maybe if he broke up the sentence differently. "Til the seas washed your shores *and*...something, something..." His mind was a blank. He thought back to the first part. Maybe he should change "washed" to "wash" to give it more suspense. It implies that it may or may not happen. He typed it in, and then he looked at the word *your*. This had personalized the sentence, but maybe he didn't go far enough. Maybe he should disclose something enigmatic about this as of yet unnamed person. Shine a light on the character's inner life, give a hint of his struggle and pain, perhaps imply an element of destiny. "Til the soul-departed seas..." Yes. It came off the tongue like ambrosia. "Til the soul-departed seas wash your shores." No. "Wash your shores" sounded too much like "wash your clothes", and that would only work if the enigmatic person he was hinting at was a charwoman. He thought of Cinderella and shook his head. Back to the sentence. It needed a word, a modifier between "wash your" and "shores". Glancing at the end of the sentence, he snatched the word empty from the clutches of the earth, and planted it like Columbus's flag in the welcoming soil of the word "shores". Yes, he thought. "Til the soul-departed seas wash your empty shores..." And now to the matter of the troublesome last part. With *empty* gone all that was left was earth. What *about* the earth, he asked? He needed to describe it, give it some substance... or maybe, his eyes lit up, a *lack* of substance! Yes, that would continue with the sentence's enigmatic nature, and might possibly even add to its mystery. The earth was empty, barren. These were good enigmatic words. They conjured up nice existential images. The earth was empty...but then he saw that he had already introduced *empty* to *shores*, and as he looked back the two seemed perfectly cozy, he couldn't bear to part them. *Hollow.* It just came to him. The earth was hollow. And this word implied that other word *"hallowed"*, which added the element of the sacred. It introduced the dichotomy of Good and Evil, and in addition, the image of a "hallowed" earth made "hollow" was poignant, and provided all sorts of metaphysical overtones. The earth was hollow. No, it *becomes* hollow...more suspense. It becomes a hollowed *ball*. A ball, an ordinary thing made extraordinary by this juxtaposition. "Earth becomes a hollowed ball." His fingers flashed over the keys. "Til the soul-departed seas wash your empty shores, and earth becomes a hollowed ball." There! That was it! It said everything he wanted to say. He gazed at the computer screen. It was the best of all possible first sentences, and as Fred Orbis sat back he let out a deeply contented sigh. In this day off he had accomplished a lot. He saved the sentence and turned off the computer, and then he reached for the letter, the letter which he had held in his fingers and recited these past two days as if it were the Rosary.

"Dear Advertiser," it began.

True, it was a photocopied form-letter. But this was the end of the millennium; a *New Age* was dawning, and with this a new way of thinking. Once again he looked upon this woman as uncompromisingly direct. She saw through the dense thicket of duplicity that crowded everyone's lives. To the heart she slashed, with her naked sword of truth. Her letter showed uncommon prudence and circumspection. "Dear Advertiser..." Wasn't that what we all were, going about our days, advertising things about who we think we are, hoping someone will be interested enough to buy? What was the first rule of salesmanship? *Sell yourself!* It was the mythical "getting your foot in the door", which paved the way to all things good. She recognized this, and in this impersonal photocopied form-letter there was recondite wisdom. A bond existed between them; a kind of Socratic meeting of the minds. Fred Orbis saw her for who she truly was, and he savored the rest of her words.

"I enjoyed your ad in the..." Here there was a blank space where she had written in: "The Voice". His eyes danced with the words that over the past two days had become so familiar. "How exciting it must be to be extremely wealthy, and how personally rewarding to be generous." She was quoting from Scriptures. *"It is better to give than to receive."* "I admire both of these qualities and am very giving myself." It's obvious, he thought. "As for me I am extremely beautiful, with long blonde hair that flows to my waist. I have been told that I am as gorgeous as a model, and I am also quite voluptuous. I am 22 years-old, and my experience of the world is still rather limited. Perhaps we can explore it together and go down to some exotic places. I look forward to meeting you..." And then her name, Belle Horizonte, and her phone number. *Belle Horizonte*, the name like a Brazilian greeting. A wish for happiness. *"May you enjoy beautiful horizons...Belle Horizonte."* A blissful

63

glance at the clock. It was barely lunchtime; he had almost seven hours to wait and he couldn't sit still, so he decided to take a walk.

Fred Orbis went to his favorite bookstore and saw that the window display had changed. The latest bestseller was now the confessions of a convicted serial killer known as the *"Alphabet Killer"*, for his penchant for picking victims with alliterated names. He began with *"A"* and then ran through the alphabet, murdering them all with a method corresponding to their letter.

Alma Abramowitz was asphyxiated.

Betty Blumenthal was beheaded.

Carlissa Clarendon was cleavered.

Dolores Diplodocus was dehydrated.

Ethel Edleweis was electrocuted.

Fiona Florentino was fricasseed.

Gwynneth Gottlieb was gashed on the gourd with a glockenspiel.

Hildegard Hilderssön was halved by a harrower.

Inez Iguanodon was immolated.

Jezebel Jardin was jambalayaed.

Kevina Kneff was knifed, knotted, and knoosed.

Lolita Lambada was lulled into a false sense of security, and then rent limb from limb by a locomotive.

Millicent Maplethorpe was mangled, mauled and mutilated by a mastiff.

Nora Nebuchadnezzar was nailed with the nose of a narwhal.

Oriana Oglivie was obliged to listen to ocarina music until she opted for being offed.

Prunilla Paganini was pecked to death by a pugnacious penguin.

Queeny Quincunx had some bad quince.

Ramona Redfern was ravaged by a rabid Rhodesian Ridgeback.

Sari Satyagraha was soaked in saffron and sauted.

Tallulah Tengallon-Hatte was given a tracheotomy with a trombone.

Üma Ümlaut was taken unawares by ursus horriblus.

Vera Valpolicello was the victim of voodoo.

Wanda Waitabit was wacked with a wurst.

Xanthippe Xenomorph was Xeroxed.

Yolanda Yevtushenko was yanked, yoked and finally yodeled, (as she was forced to listen to 72 continuous hours of Slim Whitman, before leaping from the 27th floor into the wild blue yonder). But before Zelda Zylinski could be boiled in a vat of molten zinc, the police finally caught up with the killer. And he consequently became a celebrated author, in the Mailerian tradition; his face smiling out now on his adoring public, from the windows of the best book-shops in Manhattan.

Fred Orbis was depressed again. And as he turned around he heard a middle-aged woman in a fur coat, talking condescendingly to another as they passed by. "No, I think the word you're looking for is *éclaircissement*, dear." He watched them walk into the bookstore and then he continued down the block—like an ocean liner cutting through a sea of bodies—until he was confronted by a huge poster on the sidewalk. A perfume advertisement, a beautiful willowy model, with beckoning eyes, and lips that held the whispered words he always longed to hear. He searched her face for the slightest recognition, her lips for the slightest sound. And...what was *that*? She moved her head, did you see it? She looked in his eyes. She took a breath and was about to speak. And wasn't that the beginnings of a smile on her beautiful face? Fred Orbis took a bold step forward, but then, from out of another poster (this one for men's cologne) stepped a man in black. Young and lean with tight jeans and boots, and an angular face with the perfect three-day growth of beard, he stood before Fred Orbis like a giant erect penis. And after giving him the once-over his face became a sneer, and he swaggered into the perfume poster, the young model leaping into his arms. And Fred watched as they cavorted with all the license of Youth and Beauty, as he felt suddenly naked to the world. And in a window he saw himself, an enormous blob of flesh oozing lard-like down the sidewalk. In a panic he hurried to the nearest restaurant, his face dripping with sweat, because whenever he felt like this he got hungry—the only remedy, to *eat*.

The afternoon ticked slowly by as Fred Orbis sampled the lunch buffet, the brunch menu, and then the early dinner special, until it was time to pick up the limo—although he faced the evening now with decidedly less enthusiasm. He had rented a stretch limo for the night, as per Belle's request, but he insisted on driving it himself, (he didn't want some busy-body chauffeur sniggering in the front seat), so consequently he had to pay through the nose.

The drive to Madison and Fifth was timed so that he would arrive exactly at seven. A crowd of people stood at the corner, but as the light changed and the people filtered across, a single woman remained—tall and beautiful, with blonde hair that flowed and kept flowing. Like a goddess she was, and as he stared in awe she looked at the limo and smiled, and in that smile Fred Orbis was reborn. Never had he seen such a smile, and now this smile was for him—(well, actually it was for the *limo*, but what the hell!). As she approached the car he watched her lean over, her breasts aching to be released from her dress which confined them like Rapunzel's tower. The window opened and she smiled again, thinking him the chauffeur.

"Are you *Belle*?" he asked.

"Yes, are you Gus's driver?"

"Actually, I'm Gus."

For an instant her smile was obscured by clouds.

"Please, come in."

"What, does your driver have the night off?" She sat down and closed the door, and then looked over her shoulder at the rest of the limo, which seemed to stretch on to the threshold of paradise as she sat in the front seat.

"I prefer to drive." Fred explained. "It's such a lovely evening for a drive, don't you think?"

"I guess so." She fidgeted in her seat, and played with the long strands of her hair. "You *are* Gus Silenus?"

"Yes...Gustavus actually, after *Gustavus I*, the king of Sweden in the 16th century. Do you like the 16th century?"

"What? What did you say?"

"I was talking about the 16th century. It's my favorite century."

"Whatever...You *are* extremely wealthy and generous?"

"Oh yes. And you, I might add, are extremely beautiful and voluptuous."

"Thanks."

He noticed the peculiar look on her face.

"What is it, Belle? Is something wrong?"

"Well..."

"What? Please, tell me."

"Well, it's just that..." Her eyes were like one of Columbus's ships as she looked at his body, sailing the infinite expanses of the ocean. "It's just that...you're *really fat*." And now that she had said it she felt better.

Fred Orbis felt hot flashes, cold sweats, heart palpitations, and irritable bowels. He tried to compose himself.

"Well, the ad *did* say 'Extremely fat'."

"I know, but maybe..."

"What, what is it?"

"It's...*nothing*. Can we please not talk for awhile?"

Fred was more nervous than ever, and whenever he got even slightly nervous he got hungry. He spotted a sidewalk burger joint in brightly-lit neon, and he pulled to the curb.

"What is it? Why are you stopping?" She was suddenly afraid that he was going to kick her out before she even got anything.

"It's nothing. I'll be right back." And a few minutes later he returned with a foot-long meatball sandwich.

"I thought we were going to *dinner*?" She had hoped to salvage at least a free meal from this evening, which was turning out to be a bad date.

"We are..." He took a huge bite of the sandwich. "It's just that when I get nervous I get hungry. I thought I'd eat this on the way."

"You're eating on the *way* to dinner?"

"Like I said, when I get nervous I eat." Fred Orbis sensed that things were going terribly wrong. The conversation wasn't at all as he had hoped.

"Well, you must get nervous a *lot*." A glance at his enormous stomach, at his huge paw-like hand as it clutched the sandwich. "Maybe you should try *Xanax*..."

"What, what do you mean?" Sweat dripped from his forehead and fell onto the sauce-covered meatballs.

"I *mean*, maybe you should have described yourself better in the ad."

"What? What are you *saying*, Belle?" There was coldness in her voice, and he felt the familiar panic; the waves of heat. The rest of the world no longer existed, and he had become the Hindenburg hovering over Lakehurst, New Jersey.

"I'm saying you should have used a different word to describe yourself. Something a little more accurate."

He was mute.

"Like *Blimp-like!...Humongous!*" She tossed her beautiful hair to the side as she searched for the definitive word. "Like...*Obese!*"

There was a blinding flash of light as a Hiroshima went off in Fred Orbis's head. The limo careened into the nearest alley and pulled to a stop, slamming into several garbage cans and waking a sleeping bum.

"What did you *say*?" Fred asked. He was Mt. Vesuvius and she was Pompeii, oblivious to the wrath that was about to be visited upon her.

68

"I said you're *OBESE!*" And then she folded her beautiful arms in defiance over her forbidden breasts.

There was a rustling of paper, and as she turned towards it she saw a foot-long meatball sandwich, (minus an inch or two), making its way like a runaway train hell-bent for a tunnel. Before she could react, the sandwich had been crammed down her throat, until only a small bit of crust and a piece of green pepper jutted from her mouth.

And he watched as the light of life winked from her beautiful eyes. In a moment it was over. Belle Horizonte had crossed into the beautiful horizon, and as she did Fred Orbis felt a remarkable sensation, something he had never before experienced. For the first time in his life, (including the time in the womb), he wasn't hungry. It was unprecedented. Monumental. He searched his central nervous system for a leftover of hunger, a midnight snack of appetite, a crumb of craving, but he came up empty. He tested himself, imagining steak and lobster, fried chicken, bags of cheeseburgers, chocolate eclairs dripping luscious cream...*Nothing*. In fact, the images even repulsed him. For the first time in his life Fred Orbis was repulsed by food, and as he looked over at the beautiful, dead Belle Horizonte, he smiled. Slipping her body out the door he stepped on the gas, and as the limo stretched itself from the darkness of the alley into the brilliant, shocking light of the Manhattan night, he was welcomed into an utterly beautiful and glorious world.

The doorbell rang shortly before two. Darby was usually getting out of the shower about now, but each day for the past week she had risen unusually early—today before eight—because since last Wednesday's meeting she had been too excited to sleep. She remembered that day in Kindergarten when she announced to the class that *"Polk's Peanut Rolls suck."* How they gasped at the forbidden word, and how her red-faced teacher blustered over in a huff. What power could exist in a single word, she thought, and it was because for that instant it took on her spirit; it was the Mongols at the gate, ready to lay waste to the unfortified minds of her classmates, as her teacher rushed upon her like the wrath of the Crusaders. In that singular instance she felt filled with possibility.

Then came the private schools, the shuffling from country to country. Ironically, that one word created ripples that brought her further away from her finest moment. A rebellious spirit by itself wasn't enough. It needed an outlet.

She tried her hand at writing, and with her contacts in publishing she had a book published. But whenever she thought of it now the word *"suck"* reappeared. Next came music; then painting. *Suck*, and *suck*. Although she was uncommonly intelligent she lacked creativity, which to Darby Montana was a combination fatal to happiness. For awhile she was an activist. She travelled the world, saving the whales, the walrus, the bandicoot, the bee; she painted her face like a skeleton and marched before nuclear reactors; she tossed red paint onto women wearing fur coats; she became an ovo-lacto vegetarian macrobiotic. But it was someone *else* doing these things, and she watched from that Kindergarten classroom as her life flashed by, and when she looked back, all she saw were empty desks—square and lifeless. The soul is a product of the body. This Darby believed. That's why she never considered cosmetic surgery. A weed was always a weed, just as a flower was always a flower. But now for the first time she saw herself as a weed about to evolve. Her spirit was alive, and it was dancing.

The doorbell rang again.

"Darby," said a breathless Iona Bentley, "I hope I'm not too early. Is he *here?*"

"Iona, *I'm* barely here. It's not even two o'clock."

"My watch says 2:05."

"It's fast."

The bell rang again. Anna Coluthon and Liv Good, followed by Barton and Melanie Snide.

"Is he here?" they all asked. When they saw that he wasn't they milled restlessly around the bar, like hounds impatient for dinner.

The doorbell rang again, and all eyes turned towards the door.

"Hi Darby." It was Courtney Imbroglio. Even though she was two hours early she was still fashionably late. "Is he *here?*" And then she saw the disappointed looks, and went over to fix herself a drink. For some reason Philep Möthesse had captivated the entire Wednesday Afternoon Discussion Group.

"Darby, I just want to tell you how much I enjoyed last week's meeting." said Liv Good.

"Yes." the others agreed.

"That business with the soul...real interesting stuff."

"Where *did* you find him, Darby?"

"At a gallery...the Sutton West. There's a Postmodern exhibit there now. The entire gallery's empty."

"What?"

"It's Dolus." said Liv. "He's a genius."

"What do you *mean*, it's empty?" It was Courtney Imbroglio, alerted to the scent of prey.

"There's nothing there." said Darby.

"The artist is making a statement on the emptiness of our lives." said Liv Good. "He's commenting on our need to fill our own emptiness with someone else's vision...the gallery being empty comments on the futility of this...that we ultimately can't fill ourselves with things external to ourselves."

"So there's nothing on the walls..."

"Nothing."

"It sounds like he's commenting on the lack of his own imagination."

"Courtney, why do you find the Postmodern so difficult to grasp? It's the logical result of 500 years of art history."

"It's a scam."

"A simulacrum." said Barton Snide. (Barton Snide believed that everything was a simulacrum.)

"There's no...where's the *beauty*?" asked Anna Coluthon.

"Exactly. Thomas Wolfe said *'The object of the artist is the creation of the beautiful'*."

"It was *James Joyce*, dear." said Iona.

"And you only said half the quote," said Liv, "*'As to what the beautiful is is another question.'*"

"So what is Beauty?"

At this Darby's stomach tightened, as it always did whenever the topic of beauty came up. The doorbell rang, and everyone dropped into a dead silence.

"Darby, I hope I'm not too early."

"Actually, you're fashionably late."

"Philep!...Philep!..." They cleared a path for him to the couch.

"We were having a most wonderful discussion on *Beauty*." said Iona Bentley.

"Beauty and the *lack* of beauty." said Courtney Imbroglio. "I mean, there aren't any standards anymore, am I right Philep? That's why art is in such sorry shape. There's no longer any difference between a Raphael and dog shit."

"Courtney, you're so...erudite."

"But there *is* a difference. Raphael couldn't get a showing in a gallery these days."

"*Philep*..." Courtney turned to him as if he held the answers they all sought. "Darby tells us that you met at a gallery, and that the gallery was empty."

"Yes, Dolus's exhibit."

"Well, what did you think of it?"

A pause as Philep looked at everyone's face.

"What if art can no longer be seen in reference to the past?" he asked.

"What do you mean?"

"In the Middle Ages people were easily defined. Their roles in society. The church. God. But then there was Martin Luther, and a *new* kind of man, the *individual*. And now, 500 years later, this is the result, *ecce homo*. Think of God. He once existed inside us, but he's been replaced. Now instead of the icons of saints, we have billboards. And what's become of *Beauty*? Everywhere we look we see how we're supposed to be."

"And we think it's about freedom." said Darby. "We think we have choices."

"Unlimited choices. Isn't that what it's all about? The quality of the choice is beside the point. What we have now are arbitrary opinions which change each day. So in a primordial soup such as this how can you deny the Postmodern?"

"We're a global village...and our choices become everyone's choices."

"Like that *TV* show," said Iona Bentley, "*Beach Lookout*...Do you know that it's the most popular show on earth!"

"I didn't think you *watched* TV?"

"It's our number one export."

"But people can *discriminate*!" said Liv Good. "They can choose this over that."

"But what if all the choices are *bad*?" asked Courtney.

"And if there's nothing but arbitrary opinions," said Iona, "then where's *Truth*? Where's *Beauty*?"

"But this is our world..." said Darby. "A world we can't change."

"Then what's the point?"

"I...I don't know. That we can change *ourselves*?"

"So Darby, what does our world say about the soul?" asked Philep.

"That it's dying?"

"What do you mean?"

"Well, nothing is infinite, right? Except God. Everything must reach a conclusion. So what we're witnessing is the conclusion of the human soul. Its denouement."

"Now you're sounding melodramatic, dear."

"No, I'm serious. Do you remember what we talked about last week? About the individual soul improving itself with each incarnation? What if the collective human soul has to do the same thing? It has to go through...I don't know, untold millennia to perfect itself, and *this* is its last chance."

"Now you sound like Nostradamus, dear."

"And what if *this*," Darby motioned to the world outside, "is the human soul's final expression?"

"Then I'd say we're in deep shit."

"Courtney, you truly have a way with words."

"If the soul contains the truth, then what is this truth?"

"And what is *Beauty*?"

"Fructu non foliis arborem aestima."

Philep Möthesse gave Darby a soft smile.

"Judge a tree by its fruit, not by its leaves...Do you believe in Fate, Darby? Good and Evil? God and the Devil?...Do you believe that we're here for a reason, or is this really Hell, and we're all Sisyphus?"

"You're talking about hope."

"Hope and the *absence* of hope."

"What do you mean?"

"Think of Sisyphus, doomed to spend eternity pushing a rock up a hill, only to have it always come tumbling down. What could be more pointless?"

Darby was silent.

"What is it that causes our pain but *hope*? Hope for the future...for things to get better...Here's Sisyphus, each day he pushes that rock, and maybe this time..."

"But it always comes down."

"And what does *hope* do? Imagine Sisyphus without it, like Camus. He saw Sisyphus as happy because he'd given it up."

"But then, what's the difference between that and the worker on the assembly line?"

"Consciousness is what makes for tragedy. Remember *Oedipus*? We can do almost anything without a thought as long as we remain unconscious. But for Sisyphus it's different. He knows about eternity. He *knows* that the rock will never stay put. But he smiles anyway because he's superior to his fate."

"I'm not sure I understand."

"'There is no fate that cannot be surmounted by scorn'."

"I *know* that." said Liv Good.

"It's Albert Camus."

"So what about *God*?"

"How do *you* picture God, Darby?"

"I don't know, I guess as this absentee owner."

"What?"

"Yes, the world is this beautiful country estate, right, but he's been gone so long it's all overgrown and falling apart. I don't really *see* him...But, I can't blame him. I mean, if *I* were God..."

"If *you* were God, Darby?"

"Well, I can't see him as this caretaker, you know, fixing the ceiling and mowing the lawn. Or as this omnipresent *ear* listening to everyone's perpetual whining. I mean, he'd create the universe, he'd move on. He'd do something else...I don't *blame* him for being nowhere to be found. I'd do the same."

"So you're saying that even *God* would feel the need to transcend?"

"Yes, I mean, it's like some basic law of creation. Maybe he's completely different since he created the universe. Maybe he's changed so much that we wouldn't even recognize him."

"Darby, 500 years ago you would have been branded as a heretic."

"Or *today*, in the South." said Courtney Imbroglio.

"So, how do you see the *Devil* in this ever-transcending cosmos of yours?"

"I don't know, I guess the same way I see God. Someone with limitless possibilities...For all I know the Devil could be *Iona*."

"Your time with me will be pleasant, Darby. Because you're such a good hostess you will attend to my many guests."

"You've hit on another good word." said Philep. *"Possibility."*

"So do you believe in...what about *Destiny*?" asked Anna Coluthon.

"Good question. Do you think our lives are determined before we're even born?"

"This gets back to what we talked about last week, about reincarnation."

"But this implies that if we knew where to look we could find out all about our lives."

"Like through some sort of divination?" asked Iona.

"What, like a *palm reader*?" asked Liv.

"*Chiromancy.*" said Barton Snide.

"Or tea leaves..."

"*Botanomancy.*"

"Or dreams..."

"*Oneiromancy.*"

"What about *'Personal ads'*?" asked Iona. "Courtney's been thinking of putting one in...*Fashion conscious dominatrix seeks...*"

They turned to Barton Snide, to see what kind of *"mancy"* casting your fate to a personal ad in a newspaper was.

"Destiny..." said Philep. "It depends upon whether you want to look at your life as a chess match played by someone else, or whether you want to see yourself as a free agent who can make his or her own fate. The question is, what if it's *both*?"

Everyone was exhausted now, and the conversation drifted to Courtney's current boyfriend as Darby surveyed the expanding universe of her mind. She looked at Philep's face, smiling at the others, and she saw Sisyphus, his shoulder to the stone, humming a single beautiful word—*Possibility*.

13

"There was a murder." said Detective Donalbain.

Normally this wouldn't merit a raised eyebrow. It was New York City after all, and they were police detectives working homicide. *Now if it had been that the coffee machine was broken...*However today upon hearing the news, Devon DeGroot's face became a stone, and he stopped under its weight by Donalbain's desk.

"What *kind* of murder?"

"An *unusual murder*, boss." Donalbain reached for the photos. "A young girl found in an alley."

"The cause of death?"

Another glance at the photos.

"Well, it looks like a meatball sandwich, boss. She was found like that, with a foot-long hoagie crammed down her throat."

At this Detective Macduff walked over.

"Actually, it was more like ten inches."

"What?"

"The Coroner said that about two inches of the sandwich had already been eaten."

"By the girl?"

"No."

Devon DeGroot stared at the pictures as Detectives Kozinski and Arnold walked in.

"Looks like your hunch came true, boss." said Kozinski. "That stomach on the paper towel...Too bad for the girl it wasn't Michigan."

Detective Arnold watched silently as his commander sorted through the photographs. The ominous feeling that had hung over him since the day of the pothole was beginning to materialize.

"Who's the girl?" asked DeGroot.

"Her name's Belle Horizonte. She lived on the west side...22... single...no visible means of support."

"Hooker?"

Kozinski shrugged his shoulders.

"She has a two year-old daughter. She's with relatives now."

"What about friends...*boyfriends?*"

"Well, we talked with a friend from the building where she lived. She said that the deceased didn't have any boyfriends that she knew of, but that she had talked once about dating an older guy. A guy with money."

"So she's a gold-digger," said Macduff, "some rich guy's mistress. The wife got sore and..."

"And in a fit of jealous rage she killed her with a meatball sandwich?" said Arnold.

Macduff went back to his paper work.

"Pretty strange murder weapon, huh boss?"

"Where was this alley where the body was found?"

"West 71st."

Devon DeGroot turned in his footsteps.

"Let's go."

"They found the body over there." said Donalbain.

As Devon DeGroot walked through the alley his head became a radar dish, searching for the slightest tear in the cosmic fabric. At that moment a truck on the street blared its horn like

Roland calling to Charlemagne, and as the truck passed the alley it sent a huge Satanic breath into the air.

Donalbain nudged Macduff as their boss gazed into the black cloud.

"Pyromancy." said Donalbain.

"No," said Macduff, "*capnomancy*...Pyromancy is divination by fire...*Capnomancy* is divination by smoke."

Devon DeGroot's eyes covered every brick of the buildings like pollution, every inch of the ground like asphalt until they came to a puddle.

"Hydromancy." said Donalbain.

"No, he's looking *into* the puddle." said Macduff. *"Lecanomancy."*

"You're *right*," said Kozinski, "divination through a reflected image in water."

"The *Voice*..." said Devon DeGroot.

"He said *'the voice'.*" whispered Donalbain.

"Sonomancy." said Macduff.

"The *Voice*..." DeGroot said again. And then he called the others over. "Look, in the puddle..."

The other detectives gathered round and saw a copy of the *Village Voice*, submerged on the murky bottom.

"Get it out." ordered DeGroot.

"Looks like a recent issue, boss."

"Let me see it."

"Careful, boss. It's pretty water-logged."

DeGroot looked at the *Voice*, and then turned back to the detectives.

"Were there any witnesses?"

"One, boss...but he's not much of a witness."

"A bum," said Macduff, "sleeping over there by the garbage cans. He said there was a bright flash of light, and then he started quoting from Scriptures."

"Revelations 5:6." said Detective Arnold. *Dread. Creeping dread. With each minute it got closer.*

"And then the bum said that this black cloud appeared, and out of it fell the girl."

"Belle Horizonte."

"The deceased."

"A black cloud." said DeGroot. And then he remembered the truck, the plume of smoke from its exhaust. "Maybe it was a truck, or a car."

"A car?"

"Yeah, limos are big and black."

"A stretch limo."

"And that would fit the profile of our gold-digger and her sugar daddy. Get me a list of all the stretch limos in Manhattan."

"Stretch limos in Manhattan," said Kozinski, "that should only take...a *week*."

"Talk about a needle in a stack of needles!"

"And check out all the fast-food places, burger joints, sub shops, and greasy spoons in a twenty block radius."

"There can't be too many of *those*."

"So what do you think, boss?"

He was silent.

"You want us to show the picture of the girl at the greasy spoons?" asked Donalbain.

"Yeah, but I have a feeling she stayed in the car. The sandwich was barely eaten. They got it to go."

"But it doesn't make sense. I mean, a stretch limo and a take-out meatball sandwich. It doesn't add up."

"I know." DeGroot looked at the *Village Voice*. "Well, you better follow up on those leads."

"What are you gonna do, boss?"

"*Me?*...I'm gonna go home and read the paper."

81

The house was empty when Devon DeGroot got home. It was Thursday—his wife's day to volunteer at the local soup kitchen. As he closed the door their big dog Lafayette rounded the corner and leapt up onto his chest.

"Hi, boy. I've got another job for you." He led the dog downstairs to the basement, and then spread the damp *Village Voice* over the cement floor. "Let me know when you're through."

He walked back upstairs to the kitchen, and halfway through a boiled ham sandwich he heard Lafayette bark, which meant that the deed was done.

"Good boy!"

Downstairs, the dog had left his inimitable mark on page 97, and Devon DeGroot rushed to the phone.

"Yeah, Kozinski, look to see if you have a copy of last week's *Village Voice.*"

"Hey Donalbain, do we got a copy of last week's *Voice* hangin' round somewhere?"

A shuffling of papers.

"Yeah, here it is."

"Yeah, we got it, boss."

"Good. Turn to page 97."

More rustling of paper.

"The *Personal Ads*?"

"I want you and Donalbain to scour that page with a fine-toothed comb."

"What are we lookin' for, boss?"

"Anything to do with *stomachs*, or *food*."

"You got it."

"How are the other leads coming?"

"Okay. We already got five pages of stretch limos. And Macduff and Arnold are checking the greasy spoons."

"Good, I'll be back soon...Remember, with a fine-toothed comb."

"You got it, boss."

Devon DeGroot hung up the phone. He started to take another bite of the sandwich, but then saw Lafayette standing before him at attention.

"You're right," he said. He tossed the rest to his dog and then grabbed his coat. "I gotta go to work."

14

"Mr. Monde, you said you would tell me about George Washington's first test today."

"Yes, Elizabeth..."

As they sat on the sofa Cleo hopped up between them.

"She doesn't like to be left out of the conversation." said Mr. Monde. The cat lay on her back as he stroked her stomach, and for a moment the man and the cat exchanged a glance that Elizabeth found disconcertingly intimate. "Are you familiar with the *chanson de geste*, Elizabeth?"

"*Chanson de geste*...I haven't heard that since college. It was a medieval poem or something."

"Yes, one of the early French epic poems. The story of the tragic hero. A knight finds his destiny by falling hopelessly in love with the wife of his king. He struggles desperately with his passion, but since it's part of his destiny he can never escape it, and it can never be fulfilled without him violating his honor. And this is what separates him from other men."

"And it usually ends tragically."

"Always. Think of Tristan and Isolde...Tristan, the faithful knight, escorts the beautiful Isolde to her marriage with the King. On the way they both accidentally drink from a magic potion, and they fall so deeply in love that it brings about both their deaths. Love always has its price, doesn't it? Which brings us to George Washington."

"George Washington, the tragic hero?"

"Not how history usually paints him, is it?" He turned to the portrait on the wall. "But to understand his passion is to understand his greatness. Washington was a young man when he fell deeply in love with Sally Fairfax, the wife of his patron and close friend. He wrote her long letters, of *'a Destiny which has control of our actions...Misconstrue not my meaning; doubt it not, nor expose it. The world has no business to know the object of my Love, declared to you when I want to conceal it. But adieu to this till happier times, if I ever shall see them.'*

"It's beautiful, and...*sad.*"

"What he wanted most was denied him because of his sense of honor. He tried to forget, but it was with him all his days."

"And Martha?"

"A love of respect, not of passion. And from passions suppressed comes rage. Washington's temper was notorious...but, that's *another* story." he smiled. "To control his passions Washington adopted a stoic reserve, and this is how we see him today."

"So what happened, with..."

"Sally Fairfax?"

"Yes."

"He loved her until the day he died."

"But then, when he made the bargain with..."

"To George Washington, love wasn't as important as honor... What is the one thing that fills our lives like the sun? That shines a light on all our dark places?"

"Love?"

"Yes, if we have it it guides our life. If we don't, then our destiny becomes the quest for it." Mr. Monde reached into his pocket and took out a dollar bill. "Here's our old friend. Do you see the eye above the pyramid? And these words beneath it... *Novus ordo seclorum...*"

"That's Latin, isn't it?"

"A new age now begins. Remember that Christmas morning? We look at Washington's destiny, to win his country's freedom, but if we look at it another way. If we turn the bill around we see Washington the stoic, and something altogether different. What if it was Washington's destiny to have this great love, which he *denied*?...What if, in the inscrutable scheme of things, this was the grand design set forth for him, and in the course of his denial he made history? What if Washington is remembered, but for the wrong thing? This was Washington's most profound regret...which brings us to the first test...

"There was a young prince, the heir to the throne. A tiny country near Luxembourg, no longer there, I'm afraid, where the young prince had come of age. His name was Marius, and from the time he was born he had been groomed to be king. He was his father's only son, and all his life he had been dutiful and obedient. Then one day he was out hunting when a shot rang out. His horse collapsed from beneath him, and he sailed through the air and was knocked unconscious. Highwaymen. They took his money and his rifle, and the signet ring given to him by his father, and they left him for dead.

"A short time later a young peasant girl, a milkmaid, was on her way to town with a cart-load of milk, when she came upon the young prince, although she had no idea who he was. The ring with the royal seal had been stolen. So she brought him home with her, and attended to his injuries. And when he awoke he was in a bed next to a fire, and on a stool beside him was a lovely young girl.

"How do you feel?" she asked.

"My head hurts. What happened?"

"Your horse was killed. Robbers."

"Where am I?"

"You're with me, at my house. I'm Nell."

"I'm Marius." He looked at her face and saw that she was beautiful. "You saved my life. I must *thank* you...you and your husband."

"My husband is dead." she said, and they were quiet.

Nell tended him until he was well, and after that he came back every day to see her, and soon they fell in love. But always, he kept the secret of who he really was."

"How come?"

"Because a marriage had already been arranged. A girl from Luxembourg whom he had never met. And this weighed heavy on his heart, because you see, he loved Nell desperately, but he couldn't summon up the courage to tell his father. He had never disobeyed him. And of course, it wasn't just a marriage that had been arranged. It was a consolidation of fortunes, a political alliance."

"It was good for his country."

"Yes...Young Marius began to despair, but finally he knew what he had to do. He went to see his father and he told him everything. But his father was not pleased. In fact, he became so enraged that he banished his only son, and told him never to return.

"So Marius went to Nell and confessed, and it was then that she knew the depth of his love. They were married, and the young prince, the heir to the throne, spent his days milking cows and bringing milk to market. He had lost everything, his wealth, his position, his father, his country, but somehow he looked upon those days with Nell as the happiest of his life.

"It's funny," said Mr. Monde, "the image of a stone tossed in a still pond, the ripples it creates continue outwards in all directions. While Marius and Nell were enjoying their happiness, a certain faction within the government decided to exploit the fact that the young heir had been banished. One of the King's ministers, in collusion with an unscrupulous Duke from Luxembourg, devised a plan. A messenger was sent to their simple cottage, and Marius was informed of a plot on his father's life. He was advised to come back to court immediately, but when he returned he found his father already dead, a dagger in his heart. And as Marius knelt down and wept he didn't hear the Duke from Luxembourg, or his father's loyal minister. Within hours, a story had circulated of how the young prince, embittered over his banishment, had come back to confront his father, and in the ensuing argument they had killed each other. The Duke's army had been waiting in the forest, and now they rode in to maintain order as the Duke assumed the throne. He promised the minister who had betrayed the King a vast estate, however, the next day the minister was found with his throat cut. Five years later France invaded, the Duke fled, and the country disappeared. It became part of France, and the young prince and his tragic story were forgotten."

"That...that was *terrible*." said Elizabeth.

"Yes. And it's a story that no longer exists, except in a few memories. The world is a vast tapestry, and history is its many intertwining threads, threads which wind deep beneath the surface."

"It...it was so tragic. At first like a fairy tale, but then..."

"But Washington passed the test. He embraced his great love, regardless of the cost."

"But he lost *everything*."

"A great love is complete, Elizabeth, in every moment it exists. Have you ever had a great love?"

She turned away.

"You will. Sometimes I *see* things."

Elizabeth saw Jacqueline Jimson-Weed, and she dashed the thought.

"Was the Duke, the evil Duke from Luxembourg, the Devil?"

Mr. Monde laughed.

"History is a play, and we are all but poor players..."

"So the duplicitous minister could have been Benedict Arnold?"

"Well, that would be in keeping with the story."

"But if life is a play, and we're all merely players assembled to further some plot..."

"Then who's the *dramatist*?"

"Yes."

"Do you believe in fate, or free will?"

"I, I don't know. Sometimes I feel as if I have, you know, what we talked about before, possibilities. But other times it's like I'm swept away."

"It's something for you to think about." Mr. Monde rose from the sofa. "I have to go. I have an appointment to keep, and you have other houses to clean."

"Don't remind me."

"Sam Adams said, '*Nil desperandum*', Elizabeth...never despair. It was his motto...Think of free will. If it's true, then you're doing the best you can to make your life the way you want it to be. And if it's up to Fate, well, perhaps even now things are conspiring behind the scenes for your benefit. Remember, never underestimate the mysterious inner workings of the universe... Next week we'll hear of Washington's *second* test."

Mr. Monde put on his coat as Elizabeth grabbed her bucket of cleaning supplies. They rode down the elevator in silence, and when they got outside they went in opposite directions.

"I'll see you next week, Mr. Monde."

"Good-bye Elizabeth."

She walked the few blocks to her next house, and thought of *nil desperandum*, never despair...And then she remembered the phone call she'd received the night before. Jacqueline Jimson-Weed was coming to Manhattan at the end of the week, to spend the weekend.

89

Fred Orbis stared at the computer screen and saw the world before him as a blank slate. He remembered the blinding flash of light, the searing heat, the meatball sandwich. He had killed someone. He had taken a life—something he had never imagined doing—but now that he had done it he felt oddly composed; as if he had come to a crossroads, and it was the next step which would determine his future.

All his life Fred Orbis had been on the inside looking out, stuck in this padded cell of a body, while outside Life was being lived. It was definitely not a one-size-fits-all world, it was of slim and slimmer. His attempts at weight loss were legion. Years before, he had signed up for an aerobics class. He even went to the health club in his XXXXXL sweatshirt and sweatpants, but when he looked inside at the slim men and women, moving like a flock of graceful birds to the music, he knew it was hopeless, and he went home and ate two or three dinners, and five or six desserts. So what was the price of a life, he wondered? The life he had taken, or the life he had been given but hadn't lived? And suddenly he saw Caesar crossing the Rubicon, saying, *"Jacta est alea"*, the die is cast. His fingers raced to the keyboard, and in minutes the phrase appeared in the middle of a beautiful sheet of paper. On the wall behind his computer was an old, yellowed page—a phrase from Phaedrus—*Fructu non foliis arborem aestima*. It had been his motto. All these years it had looked down upon him, reassuring him that it was the fruit that mattered, not the leaves, but now he had discovered the truth. To the world he was *fat* and nothing else, and was it wrong that he felt rage for his wasted life? He yanked the old motto from the wall and it instantly succumbed, consumed by his enormous hand, and then he turned to his new motto— *The die is cast.* With these words he had recreated himself, and he stuck it to the wall where it would shine out and be his guide.

So then, was he a *monster*? True, he had killed someone, but the irony was that all of his life he had been moral and good and the world had seen him as one. At least now it would be justified.

He grabbed the newspaper and read the article:

Young Woman Found Dead in Alley. Dateline: New York City. A 22 year-old Manhattan woman named Belle Horizonte was found dead in an alley near West 71st St. Cause of death undetermined.

Fred Orbis read it again. It was the first thing he had gotten published, the first serious work of his to appear in print. True, it was only on page 17 of the News. And it was a bit too pithy and cryptic...this *"cause of death undetermined"*. But there was a sort of Hemingwayesque quality to the reportage which reminded him of *The Sun Also Rises.* He turned back to the computer.

"So, I'm to be a *villain*, then." He thought of Richard III. True, he wasn't *fat*, but as villains went he was a pretty good role model. "So be it."

And his fingers began to type.

Young Woman Found Murdered in Alley by Meatball Sandwich. Dateline: New York City...

And then a pause as the inspiration took hold.

What is this Life, which in scope is God-like,
but in aspiration demeaned? Whose mirror'd gaze sees a
factitious face, and society's sinister refraction...

Yes, he said to himself, his fingers racing across the keyboard.

Skewed, we look out from blackened cellar windows;
Possessed, we sell our dearest possession—until this human form
of infinite variety and measure conforms itself to the
needle's slender eye. And the rest, out of
compass left. Outcast and aberration; and
God's glorious gift—an advertisement on page 97...

A pause for a breath and to survey his work. Not bad, but he sort of lost the train of thought. This was an announcement of a death...but, *yes*! That's exactly what he had written. The death of a soul!

And what of Life, this demimonde,
euphonious of name but erroneous of mind?
And what of me? To the world a fiend,
but on reflection an illuminating flame! A torch to the
pyre of *Avarice, Illusion*—the familiar face,
like Sisyphus pushing his rock, comparing itself
to what is ever unattainable...

A tear came to his eye.

How many spirits lie unmourned in this smouldering field;
their bodies carrion in this army's brutal wake?
The question of identity, the answer without,
And Death, (the beautiful horizon), retains a
certain poetic *flavor*. As one sun sets another rises
on a fortunate soul resigned to Fate,
and the blazing light and awe of this new day...

There...True, it kind of rambled a bit, but in a spirited, Shakespearean sort of way. Fred Orbis looked at his words. Had he just offered up his soul? But it was too late. And besides, for the first time he felt truly, completely, wonderfully alive, and it was a feeling he wanted to savor.

He reached for one of the letters on the desk. Three more responses had come to his ad, and he shook his head in amazement. How could he have been so concerned with the human condition all these years, his finger on the existential pulse of mankind as it were, and yet remain blind as to what had become of love? Currency. A commodity. Bodies traded as stocks with the same aloof objectivity. Promises of love made as business deals. Now the only "courtly" love had to do with endless litigation; and divorce as tango or lambada, with everyone slithering up to an endless succession of partners in heat. But it wasn't *hedonism*, or even *libertinism*. It was a blind rage to consume. This was what had become of Man, *homo consumptus*. *Homo consummatus*. The complete human, finished, perfect. This was as good as it got, and the experiment was a failure.

He looked at one of the responses:

"Dear Extremly Fat, but also extremly wealthy and generous..."

She had misspelled "extremly". Oh well, at least it wasn't a photocopied form letter. It was handwritten, its letters like well-fed geese waddling in formation, and at the end of each sentence flying off into a kind of Pollyannic blue sky. Above each *"i"* was a circle instead of a dot, which floated like the proverbial cloud with the silver lining. But as Fred Orbis read her words he lanced them with his sword until their vital fluids seeped out, and the letter became a sanguine battlefield.

"I enjoyed your letter in the Voice. I am a 21 year-old model and I appeared in several magazines, although nothing big yet. But my agent says I'm going to be a Supermodel. I enclosed a photo so you can see for yourself..."

A glance at the photo. Her body obviously naked, but positioned in such a way that her most intimate regions were fig-leafed by folded arms, and opportunistic shadows. Her hair long, her face the kind he saw every day, gazing from ubiquitous billboards and magazines.

"My name is Sylvia Scarlatina and I would very much like to meet you. Call me soon..."

If only the Alphabet Killer could have met Sylvia, Fred Orbis thought. He shook his head again and dialed her number.

"Hello?" It was a woman's voice sounding tired beyond her years.

"Hello, is this Sylvia Scarlatina?"

"Yes, who's this?"

"This is Calvin Igula...you answered my ad in the *Voice*."

He was Richard III, Caligula, Pontius Pilate crucifying Christ.

"Extremely fat, but also extremely wealthy and generous..."

"Yes, I'm glad you called. What was your name again?"

"Calvin Igula. It's Armenian. But you can call me Cal."

He was Hitler gazing out from Berchtesgaden, at the world like a ripe piece of fruit.

"Cal..." Her voice dusky now, breathy like a perfume ad. "I like your voice, Cal."

"I like yours too...and the photo you sent. I hope you don't mind me saying so, but you are extremely beautiful."

"Oh, thank you, I..."

"In fact, I have several important contacts in the fashion industry, and if you don't mind, I'd like to show them your photo. Do you have any others?"

"Oh yes!" Her voice rose in a triumphant trumpet-blast. "I have lots, including some nudes...although the quality of those is not...well, not that they're...but anyway I...well, maybe I won't bring those."

"No, please, bring them all. Are you familiar with *Dante Alighieri*, the famous fashion designer? I'm sure he would love to have you model for him."

Listening to her voice, he felt a curious mixture of compassion and the desire to corrupt completely—like the Devil, who had once been an angel.

"This is so exciting, you have no idea!"

She was a child. She saw the world at its most cynical, and this she saw as beauty.

"I don't know what to, I don't know what to *say*, Mr. Igula..."

"Please, Cal..."

"Cal."

"You have something, Sylvia. Something the world desperately wants."

Mundus vult decipi...the world wishes to be deceived.

"When can I see you? I must tell you, I'm leaving for Europe at the end of the week, and I'd like to take the photos with me when I see Dante in Rome."

"Well, oh, I don't, how 'bout, *tonight?*"

"Tonight, let's see..." A pause as he shuffled through the newspaper and Belle Horizonte's death notice. "Yes, I can make some time tonight...Seven o'clock?"

"Yes. That will, that'll be *wonderful.* I live at..."

He jotted down the address.

"Fine. Be waiting in front of your building at seven *sharp.* My limousine will pick you up."

"Cal, I...I don't know what to say. This is more than, than I ever *imagined*...My friends, you know, they told me I shouldn't answer an ad, with all the weirdos in New York and everything, but I...I don't know, I'm just so...*appreciative*, you know...I can't wait to show you how much."

Shameless, utterly shameless.

"Yes."

"And I'll bring the nudes...I mean, they're not bad...I mean, do you *want* me to?"

"Yes, bring them all. I'll see you tonight."

Before she could say good-bye Fred Orbis hung up. Her letter tossed in the trash, he looked at his new motto on the wall. *"The die is cast."* He had the entire afternoon to kill before his date so he walked to the refrigerator and looked inside, but with a disgusted look he shut the door. He'd had a bowl of shredded wheat for breakfast. And a banana. He wasn't hungry.

16

"Literati..."

"Illiterati..."

"Intelligentsia..."

"Umm...*stupidentsia?*" Courtney coined a new word as Iona's eyes rolled in counterpoint to her yawn. They were playing *"Opposites"*.

"Here's one...*anomie...*"

"Where's Philep?"

"Yes, do you think he's not coming?"

"I've decided to quit smoking."

"Are we playing *'Non Sequiters'* now?"

Like an archaeologist Courtney dug in her purse, until she unearthed a small two ounce candy bar in a bright yellow wrapper.

"What's *that?*"

Darby blanched at the sight.

By now Courtney had unwrapped it, and had half of it in her mouth.

"Izza Polth Peeuh oh..."

"What?"

"She's speaking in tongues."

"No, she's speaking *without* a tongue..."

"It's a Polk's Peanut Roll." she said again.

"I think *I'll* have a cigarette." said Darby.

"But you don't smoke."

"They're helping me to quit smoking." said Courtney. "Eight or nine of these a day, no more cigarettes."

Darby hovered over Courtney Imbroglio's shoulder like a vulture, her eyes peeled on the Peanut Roll.

"Where's Philep?"

"Yes, what time is it?"

"Almost four."

"Goodness, we've been here for *hours*."

"Where's Philep?"

"Iona, three weeks ago nobody *arrived* until four."

"I know, but..."

"What were we talking about last week?"

"Sisyphus..."

"And..."

"Hope."

There was a knock at the door.

"Darby, sorry I'm late."

"That's all right." In an instant the Polk's Peanut Roll wrapper was snatched from the coffee table and banished from sight. "I've been thinking about what we talked about last week, Philep..."

"Yes."

"And about *Pandora's box*."

"The coming of *Evil* into the world." he smiled. "What about it, Darby?"

"Well, Prometheus steals fire from the gods, right, and gives it to Man. And for this, Zeus chains him to a rock...Would you like a drink, Philep?"

"Yes, thank you."

"And each day this eagle comes down to eat his liver. But Zeus still wants his revenge on Man, so he gives him a gift."

"Pandora's box."

"Right. He creates this woman, Pandora, and he gives her this chest which is supposed to contain great treasure, but she's told never to open it. But of course she *does*! And all the evils are loosed into the world...famine, disease, war..."

"Postmodern art..." said Courtney Imbroglio.

Liv shook his head.

"And Pandora is paralyzed by fear, but she finally manages to shut the box, and the only thing left is..."

"Hope." said Philep.

"Right. And this was what enabled mankind to bear all the other evils."

"That's a good myth, Darby. But, what if hope wasn't meant to be *good*?"

"What? I don't understand."

"Because now all the horrors can be endured, but never eliminated. Think of religion, right, the opiate of the masses. Or television. Anything to put a buffer between ourselves and life. Remember what we talked about last week? You can do practically *any*thing if you remain unconscious, but if you question hope, if you hold it up and examine it, then the true existential dilemma comes into view."

"Which is..."

"Camus said it was whether or not to commit suicide, and his answer was *life*."

"But a life without *hope*."

"But what's life without hope, Philep?"

"And if there's no hope, then where's *God*? I mean, isn't he the sum of our hopes?"

"That's a good question. If we give up hope do we still need God?"

"But the thought of...with nothing but ourselves is..."

"Frightening."

"Yes."

"Fear and hope go hand in hand. But if we can let go of *both*..." Philep paused. "There's a word...*Cathexis*."

"The investment of emotional significance in an object, activity or idea." said Barton Snide.

"Yes. We have an idea about a relationship or a person, and in this idea we invest our emotions. And what is this but an investment in *hope*? We meet someone, we fall in love, and before we know it we've emptied our emotions into them, and then we hope that they'll give us something back."

"But Philep, you make love sound like opening a bank account."

"Well, in a way it is."

"But, what's the alternative, to be *unemotional*?"

"No, but to not be ruled by our emotions. Freud saw this as the cause of our problems. It wasn't the relationship *per se*, it was the emotions we invest in the relationship, and how we invest them. Emotions are what make us human but they're also hard to control, and sometimes they control us."

"So we should get rid of fear and hope." said Iona Bentley, as if she had thought of it herself.

"And God."

"Quite a day..." said Liv Good. "We've eliminated fear, emotions, hope, and God."

"But what about the *Devil*?" asked Darby Montana.

"The *Devil*?"

"What about him?"

"Darby, if there's no God then how can there be the Devil?"

"I don't know, why *can't* there be?"

"Because the Devil is causally linked to God. Because he..."

"But what if God exists because we *allow* him to exist?" Darby's face aglow with the suddenness of her idea.

"*What?*"

"Well, let's say there existed this entity, this being called *God*, and it..."

"He..."

"She..." said Darby. "She decided to create time...and then she created the universe, and people..."

"Go on, Darby."

"And so she creates the human race and instills in them this belief in her, right, like children believing in their parents. But what if over time the people she created, the human race, no longer believed in their mother?"

"Like rebellious teenagers!"

"And what if through this belief God had come to derive her existence?"

"Through *cathexis.*" said Philep, smiling as Darby's idea became clear.

"Yes. God invested more and more emotional energy into mankind until it was all gone, until human beings possessed it. And then..."

"They stopped *believing*...Darby, that's brilliant. How come you didn't write about things like this in that book of yours? The one you..."

"I just thought of it." She glared at Iona, for reminding everyone of her sucky book.

"Yes!" said Liv Good. "It *is* brilliant, Darby. And so the human race just stopped believing..."

"And then God realized what He'd done."

"She, dear."

"But it was too late. She'd given up her emotions, and she couldn't get them back."

"God as co-dependent."

"Something *you* know all about, Courtney."

"So God just...she *vanished.*"

"So what's left, the *Devil?*"

"Why not? I mean, it's easy to see evil, it's all around."

"But look at *42nd Street*, dear. How they cleaned it up. Surely *that's* good."

"It's a simulacrum." said Barton Snide.

"Barton, I think *you're* a simulacrum."

"So, what do we do with a world where evil exists, and there's no God?"

"But maybe it's like what Darby said last week. Maybe God *transcended*, and now he's the Devil and the Devil's God, and..."

"So we should embrace the *Devil*?" said Liv Good. "Or maybe we should *all* just sell our souls!"

At this Philep stepped forward.

"What if I were to say to you that *I* was the Devil, and I'm here to buy a soul..."

"Well, I'd say take *Iona's*, but I don't think it's in demand."

"How painfully tedious."

"I'd ask you what you had to offer," said Darby, "and what were your terms."

Philep gazed into her eyes.

"For you Darby I will grant you your innermost wish. The secret you've kept hidden from everyone else on earth."

"Darby, you're blushing."

Philep's eyes remained fixed.

"You will no longer fear, and your emotions will be yours to command. There was a moment for you, Darby, when you were young, and this was the highlight of your life. This was *you*, who you truly *are*...but, what happened? Somehow, you changed. The years went by, and you look in the mirror and you're someone else, someone you never thought you'd be...But you're still there, aren't you? Trapped inside."

"Darby, do you know what he's talking about?"

"And what would I have to give you in return?"

"Why, your *soul*." Philep smiled. "The standard agreement. In exchange your soul would be mine."

"And when I died…"

"You mean, *Hell*?"

"I need a drink." said Iona Bentley.

"Me too." said Liv Good.

"Me too." said Barton and Melanie Snide.

"Have you ever *acted*, Philep? Because you sure had *me* going."

"Yes, it was amazing. How are you at charades?"

Philep looked at them and smiled.

"Maybe we should play sometime."

"Yes, these talks have gotten quite…"

"Intense." said Liv.

"Yes." said Iona.

"I need a cigarette." said Courtney.

"Darby, are you al…"

At the window now she looked out on the street. Puddles reflected the sky, and trucks went past with buildings in their windshields. Steam rose from a manhole cover, and taxis rumbled by. She tried to imagine Hell, but all she thought of was New York City.

"Darby, are you all right?"

"Yes." She walked over and poured herself a drink.

"I need a cigarette."

"You already said that, dear…moments ago."

"Or have another of those…*peanut rolls*."

"Yes," said Darby, "I hear they're pretty good."

Her eyes were drawn to Philep but he was turned away. She wanted him to face her, but her will weakened, and she stared at herself from the still reflection in her glass.

17

"These are all the *same...*" said Macduff.

"Tell me about it." said Donalbain.

"I mean...*Extremely wealthy and generous older man seeks voluptuous model...Extremely wealthy and generous distinguished man seeks gorgeous model 17-21...Extravagantly rich CEO seeks model 19-22 to accompany on world cruise.* What gives?"

"We've spent a week on that." said Donalbain. "It'll make you wanna become a monk."

Macduff scanned the page.

"Here's a variation on a theme...Extremely wealthy and well-endowed older man seeks *plain* but *intelligent, older* woman..."

"What?" Donalbain and Kozinski reacted with shock.

"Just kidding. Actually he wants a *gorgeous model, 20-23.*"

"And what, aren't regular garden-variety models good enough anymore?"

"Yeah, now they have to be *gorgeous* models."

"Isn't that redundant?"

"These extremely wealthy and generous CEO types leave nothing to chance." said Macduff. "That's why they're movers and shakers."

"Lookin' for gorgeous models to *move 'em and shake 'em.* I mean, if these *CEOs* have to advertise for dates, what chance do schmoes like *Donalbain* have?"

"How *droll.*" said Donalbain. "That's a *word*, isn't it? *Droll?*"

"Any luck?" It was Devon DeGroot. He had walked in holding a steamy cup of coffee.

"Well, there were *117* ads on page 97, boss."

"We put them into categories. Show 'em the pie chart."

Donalbain grabbed the pie chart, as well as several graphs from the desk.

"*See,*" he pointed with a cinnamon cruller, "the red area is what we call the *'Rich Geezer Meets Teen Model'* zone."

"Extremely wealthy..."

"And generous..." The cruller caught Macduff's eye.

"Older man seeks gorgeous model 17-21 *blah, blah, blah.*"

"*Ad nauseam.*"

"Hey, you got another *cruller*?" asked Macduff.

"The red area accounts for 78% of the ads on page 97. Then there's this black section, boss..."

"Leather, whips and chains, so forth and so on."

"17%."

"Yellow...4%...urolagnia and coprophilia..."

"*What?*"

"You know, golden showers, steamy brown massage, that kind of..."

"That's a big ad nauseam!"

"Only *4%*?" asked DeGroot.

"Well, they have other categories towards the back that are more...*specific.*"

"Right. These ads are primarily *'boy meets girl'.*"

"Charming."

"Rich old coot meets 14 year-old with big tits."

"Ah, romance..."

"So what's this *white wedge*?...1%..."

"That's what we call *'Alien Love Secrets'.*"

"Men seeking space aliens."

"*Female* space aliens..."

"*Gorgeous model* female space aliens..."

"So out of 117 ads, 53 mentioned food or eating or some reference thereof. 36 mention dinner, usually in some exotic place like Paris, or...what's that other place?"

"Côtes d'Azur...It's in the south of France. The French Rivi..."

"I know where it is." said DeGroot.

"What's that little thing above the '*o*' again, in *Côtes*?"

"It's a circumflex."

"From the Latin *circumflectere*..." said Macduff. "To bend around."

"Hey, how do you know Latin?" asked Kozinski.

"It was on *Jeopardy* last night."

"As I was saying, 53 mention food directly. And then there's a couple o' fringe ones." Donalbain looked back at the paper. "Here...Extremely wealthy, *blah, blah, blah*..."

"*Ad nauseam.*" the others said like a Greek chorus.

"Seeks beautiful young girl with large mammary glands to smear with honey."

"Did he really say '*mammary glands*'?"

"Hey, it's a *family* newspaper."

"And there's this...Extremely fat, but also extremely wealthy and generous..."

"That's a nice twist."

"Seeks ad nauseam for weekly bacchanals. Doesn't a bacchanal have to do with food?"

"It's a drunken or riotous celebration in honor of Bacchus." said Devon DeGroot.

"*Jeopardy*, boss?"

"Education. But it could involve feasting." A solemn look at his detectives. "So...?"

"Nothing yet, boss." said Kozinski. "We've spoken to about half the guys who put in ads relating to food. You'll never guess who some of them were. That one about the honey-smeared mammary glands...the *Archbishop*."

"Hmm. Well, check the rest. What about the limo?"

"Well, we got 18 pages of stretch limos, boss. And that's just in Manhattan."

"18 *pages?*...What, does everyone in Manhattan drive a stretch limo?"

"Yeah, you'd think they'd be embarrassed."

"Freud would say it was an extension of their..."

"Sometimes a limo's just a limo." said Macduff.

"So far, of the ones we checked no one's ever *seen* the girl... chauffeurs, mostly."

"What do you mean, *mostly*?"

"Well, sometimes people rent them *without* a chauffeur. You know, rich college kids going up for the big game. High school proms, that kinda stuff."

"Check 'em all out. How 'bout the greasy spoon? Any idea where that meatball sandwich came from?"

"Well, on the night in question," said Detective Arnold, "429 places were opened within a twenty block radius that could have sold our sub. We need more man-power, boss. We checked out about 200 so far, but..."

"I know...*budget cuts*!" the words spit out like bile. "They won't give us any more men until we have more to go on than..." He was going to say than his dog doing his business on a wet newspaper.

"But boss, you broke that Colombian drug ring by looking at that guy's guts."

"Yeah, the guy they left disemboweled by the pier."

Detective Arnold shuddered, because that was the bust when he got shot three times.

"*Anthropomancy...*" said Macduff. "Divination by inspection of the entrails."

DeGroot tossed his head to the side in an exasperated twitch.

"Well, they're not into lateral thinking upstairs."

The phone rang and Donalbain picked it up.

"Yeah...yeah when?" He jotted down an address. "Alright, we'll be right there. There's been another murder...the Village... young girl with a ham sandwich rammed down her throat."

At this Detective Arnold sank into despair. The bad feeling was getting worse.

"She looks like the other one, boss. Young, beautiful..."

"A propensity for not chewing her food."

"Found in an alley, choked by a ham sandwich. What a way to..."

"It looks like *baked Virginia ham.*" said Kozinski. "Just like the other one, no sign of a struggle."

"So our man is strong." said DeGroot. "He just rams it down their throat before they can react."

"Ah, boss?" said Detective Donalbain. "Looks like we got ourselves a witness. This officer was first on the scene. He found that bum over there behind the dumpster."

"Another *bum...*" DeGroot sighed. "All right."

"He was sleeping when we found the body," the police officer said, "but he says that...Well, you better talk to him." He motioned to the vagrant, standing by the dumpster with the other officers.

"Good morning, sir. I'm Detective DeGroot of Mid-Manhattan South, Vice and Homicide."

"Dr. Jared." said the bum.

The officer leaned over towards DeGroot.

"He keeps saying that he's a *doctor.*"

Devon looked at the bum. His coat was torn and soiled and smelled of garbage. His hair was matted to his head, with a piece of celery or cabbage stuck by his ear, and his face was covered with a dirty mask of gray whiskers.

"Dr. Jared, you saw what happened?"

"Yes, last night, I was having dinner..."

"He means over behind the dumpster." the officer explained.

"When I heard this noise..."

"What kind of noise?"

"A voice, a man's voice."

"Wait'll you hear *this*..." The officer nudged Macduff in the ribs.

"And what did this man's voice say?"

"Gosem pher, gezumpher, greeze a jarry grim felon! Good bloke him!"

There was a moment of profound silence.

"Gosem pher, gezumpher, greeze a jarry grim felon! Good bloke him!" he said again.

"Okay." DeGroot turned to Kozinski. "Bring him in and get his statement."

"But boss..."

"Bring him in anyway." He searched the alley for a clue, but all he saw were overturned garbage cans, and indecipherable graffiti on sooty brick walls. The filth of Manhattan had gathered here like a malignant tumor in a remote extremity, as a block away on the street, the body Manhattan continued on, oblivious to its cells' degradation.

Back at the station Kozinski and Arnold questioned the bum, while Macduff and Donalbain dug up more info on the girl.

"She was a model."

"Surprise, surprise. So, our man is somewhere in that red pie chart."

"What else did you find on the girl?"

"Well, her name's Sylvia Scarlatina...She's 21, a model... nothing to write home about...*This* is her..." Donalbain handed him a cheesy magazine, with a naked girl on the cover doing her best to expose her breasts, while at the same time covering them with her hands.

"Hotties?" said DeGroot. "The name of the magazine is *Hotties?*"

"Yeah. There's more of her inside. Apparently she has some agent, name of Vince or Vinnie something."

"Vinnie DeCastro." said Macduff. "So far I haven't been able to reach him. It appears he doesn't have a phone. And his office is where a parking garage is."

"Some agent. Find him...Where did the girl live?"

"10th St."

"And the body was found in an alley on 8th...And the first one was on West 71st." DeGroot's face lit up. "So, he puts in an ad, and women from all over Manhattan respond. That first one, Belle Horizonte...she lived on Fifth uptown, and was found 20 blocks away. But this one was just a few blocks from her apartment. What does that tell you?"

"That the second one was *deliberate*, boss?"

"He picks up the first girl, and they're on their way to dinner. But they get into an argument, and for some reason he has a meatball sandwich with him..." Stifled laughter around the room. "And he shoves it down her throat, and then he dumps her in the alley. But then later, he thinks about what he did and he *likes* it...so *this* time..."

"He doesn't mess around."

"Right. He picks her up and...Any luck at her apartment? Any friends? *Anybody* see who picked her up?"

"No. Apparently everybody in that building just keeps to themselves, boss. I showed her picture around, and her next door neighbors didn't even recognize her."

"Ah, New York. That's why we love it, right gentlemen... Anything in her apartment?"

"No, apparently she wasn't much of a house-keeper. It was pretty messy. So, if this guy put an ad in the paper..."

"Then the women are coming to *him*." Devon DeGroot took a sip of coffee and immediately spit it out. "It's cold."

"Where you goin', boss?"

"To check on our witness, the good Doctor...and to get some coffee that's *hot*."

Outside the interrogation room DeGroot listened as the bum spoke to Detective Arnold.

"Poolbeg. Cookingha'pence, he bawls Donnez-moi scampitle, wick an wipin'fampiny..."

"He's been going on like that." said Kozinski. They watched from behind the two-way glass.

"Fingal Mac Oscar Onesine Bargearse Boniface...Thok's min gammelhole Norveegickers moniker..."

"What language is he speaking?"

"I'm not sure."

"Klikkaklakaklaskaklop..."

DeGroot and Kozinski stared at each blankly.

"Patzklatschabattacreppycrotty..."

"Whad'ya think, boss?"

"Let him go." He walked back to the office and glowered at Donalbain and Macduff. "*Any*thing?"

"No. What about the 'Doc'?"

"Goddamn it! I can't get a cup of coffee in this whole goddamn police station! All right, who didn't make coffee?"

"It was Donalbain." said Macduff.

"I made it last time." said Donalbain.

"Uncle Flabbius..." said Kozinski, as he and Arnold walked in.

"*What* did you say?"

"Uncle Flabbius...*Uncle Flabbius Muximus to something Flappia Minnimiss*. It's what that guy, the *'Doctor'* said. It just kind of stuck with me."

"Uncle Flabbius Muximus..." said Macduff. "It's from *Finnegans Wake*. James Joyce. It was on *Jeopardy* last night. *20th Century English Literature*."

Devon DeGroot's face brightened.

"Maybe we should have you watch *Jeopardy* full-time." He turned to Donalbain. "Do we have a copy of *Finnegans Wake* laying around?"

"Finnegans *what*?"

"*Wake*...It's a novel by James Joyce."

Donalbain rummaged through the books that crowded the wall behind his desk.

"Well, we got *Ulysses*...and *Dubliners*...but I don't see any *Finnegans Wake*, boss."

"Run down to that bookstore on the next block and get a copy, alright." He turned to Arnold. "Where's the bum?"

"You let him go boss."

"Well, get him back."

Ten minutes later a copy of *Finnegans Wake* was on the desk before Devon DeGroot, along with a cup of fresh coffee and a box of cinnamon crullers.

"Where's the bum?"

"He, um...well, he...he left and...well he, he *disappeared*, boss."

"Go back to the alley." DeGroot flipped through the pages of *Finnegans Wake* and read aloud. "*The great fall of the offwall entailed at such short notice the pftjschute of Finnegan, erse solid man, that the humptyhillhead of humself prumptly sends an unquiring one well to the west in quest of his tumptytumtoes...*"

"What the..."

"Sounds like the 'Doc'." Macduff read over his shoulder. "*Corpo di barragio! you spoof of visibility in a freakfog, of mixed sex cases among goats, hill cat and plain mousey, Bigamy Bob and his old Shanvocht!*"

"I thought you said it was *'English'* literature." said Kozinski.

"It *is*. It was the *'Daily Double'...20th Century English Literature for 500.'*"

"But what does it...I mean, is it *poetry*? What did they say on *Jeopardy*?"

"That's all I remember, *Uncle Flabbius*, because then my wife started calling me Uncle Flabbius..."

"That's *great!*" said Kozinski.

"I told you you should work out more." said Donalbain.

"I know, but who has the..."

"Gentlemen..." said Devon DeGroot. "What was the first thing that bum said? The man's voice he heard in the alley..."

"I have it right here, boss. *Gosem pher, gezumpher, greeze a jarry grim felon! Good bloke him!*...And then he said he saw the girl's body. No car or anything. Her body just appeared."

"Like out of a black cloud...Find me this bum. I want him back here ASAP!"

"Do you want us to look through this book, boss?"

Kozinski had picked it up and was reading at random.

"If the proverbial bishop of our holy and undivided with this me ken or no me ken Zot is the Quiztune havvermashed..."

"No. Call around. Find if there's some expert on James Joyce, specifically *Finnegans Wake*." He took a bite of the cruller and washed it down with the coffee. "So our man's educated...some kind of scholar or eccentric...anybody who quotes *Finnegans Wake* while he's shoving a ham sandwich down someone's throat...Get me a list of all the people in Mensa in Manhattan."

"What's that, some men's group, boss?" asked Donalbain.

"Ha!" laughed Macduff. "A group that *you* obviously aren't in."

"Shut up, Uncle Flabbius."

"It's a society for high I.Q.'s...geniuses."

"So this guy's some extremely wealthy and generous hard-up genius, with a penchant for delicatessens." said Macduff.

"Penchant...that's a good word." said Donalbain.

"Penchant...predisposition, inclination."

"Propensity, proclivity, predilection." added Kozinski.

"What, do *you* watch *Jeopardy* too?"

"Crossword puzzles."

"I just spoke to Columbia." said Detective Arnold. "They said they used to have this professor there, the world's foremost authority on *Finnegans Wake*."

"And..."

"He got canned five years ago, boss...budget cuts. They cut a third of the English department."

"What was his name?"

"Doctor Randall Jared, Ph.D....*Doctor Jared*."

"Budget cuts!" Devon DeGroot grit his teeth and smashed his cruller on the desk, and for a second the air was filled with a cloud of cinnamon sugar.

Detective Arnold continued.

"They said he disappeared right after he got sacked."

"Find him!" DeGroot looked at the mangled cruller on his desk, and started reciting the Vice-presidents in order to restore his calm. *"John Adams, Thomas Jefferson, Aaron Burr..."*

"Hey, boss..." Kozinski called out. "I just spoke to his ex-wife... you know, of our dumpster-diving Doc..."

"And..."

"She said she hasn't seen him in almost five years...since the divorce. She said he couldn't handle being fired and he took to drink. She said he owes her back alimony for the last four and a half years, so if we should find him to..."

Macduff brushed the mangled cruller from the desk into the wastebasket, and then he crinkled up the napkin and tossed it in, and they all watched as Devon DeGroot stared fixedly at the napkin.

"What is it, boss?"

"I'm going over to the girl's apartment. What was her name?"

"Sylvia Scarlatina."

"Why boss?"

"There's something in the trash."

"But the whole *place* is trash." said Donalbain.

"You have her number. Call me if you get anything...and if you find the world's foremost expert on James Joyce."

"So what about *this*?" Kozinski held up page 97 of the *Village Voice*.

"Keep digging. I want every ad checked...especially the ones that have to do with food. He's there *some*where, I can feel it."

"What about the latest murder weapon?"

"The baked Virginia ham sandwich..."

"Concentrate on the personals, that's where it is. And whatever you do, Uncle Flabbius," he said to Macduff, "keep a lid on this sandwich thing. All we need is for the media to get a hold o' this." Devon DeGroot rushed from the office, coffee spilling in his hand, and repeated *Gosem pher, gezumpher* as he hurried to his car.

"He called you Uncle Flabbius!" said Donalbain.

Macduff administered a withering glower.

"Find the Doc, genius."

And they turned back to page 97, and the poetic paeans of the lovelorn CEOs, seeking their 17 year-old gorgeous model soulmates.

18

Her eyes followed the icy walls from the rim into the hollow of the cirque, and came to rest on the lake. There was a face, floating faintly in this oval mirror, and beneath the water's surface, a cave. This was where it all went, everything unwanted. She reached around for her bucket—the brush, the cleanser. *Bon Ami*—good friend—and she watched as it snowed down these porcelain walls, hidden in this remote region of the house. She was one of the few who explored this place, but she wouldn't call herself intrepid. The brush moved the water in a swirling cloud, an overcast sky, winter's dim petrifying gloom. Never had she known a toilet this well. The winds from the streets of Manhattan blew into this valley, the waste of each day sounded its depths and she saw herself, a part of its poetry. Pressing the handle she wiped it clean, and in a moment the walls glistened, the water was clear.

Elizabeth shifted on the floor, until she loomed above the bathtub. The ring of grime ran round the walls like a layer of history, a cross-section of time, but instead of dinosaurs and early Man, it told her that a week had passed. In a way she was like God in this silent bathroom, in this silent house, and every seven days she created a brand new world, which by Friday afternoon, sparkled and gleamed. This place was the repudiation of shit.

Elizabeth went to the sink. Cleanser and sponge, some hot water, then quiet. How she loved the quiet. In it she felt the house's presence, more than she did the people who lived there. They were a check under a flower pot, a piano never played, an antiseptic kitchen. The house something feminine and unrealized, like a womb.

Before the mirror she stood and saw Jacqueline Jimson-Weed, her hands like serpents on her shoulders, and she sprayed the *Windex* until the mirror was covered. An ancient memory—of going with her father to the car wash. The deep breath she took as the car buckled and latched onto the track, and then glided effortlessly into the cavern. Jets of water blasted from the sides and whirlpooled across the windows, and she felt comforted. Outside the windshield was a swirling pool of suds, and for a moment they were shut off from the world. A snowstorm. A remote ice station above the Arctic circle. A scientist in the midst of the most terrible of blizzards. But then the snow washed away, the last of the spray trickled down. Spring thaw and sunlight. Daybreak, as they drove into the light.

She wiped the mirror with the rag until it was clean, and then she was through. A final glance to make sure she hadn't forgotten anything, and then she walked to the living room. There was a book on the coffee table—one of those sprawling photo books of wildlife and wilderness—this one of Yellowstone Park. Beneath the book was a single penny. Elizabeth had placed it there four months ago, and each week she checked and it was always there. Wild rivers and geysers, elk and grizzly, stuck in this Manhattan townhouse, never venturing beyond those closed covers. She put the book on the penny and grabbed her bucket, but hesitated as she moved towards the door. In another hour Jacqueline Jimson-Weed would be here.

Walking home she thought of the poem. All through the quiet a poem had lived inside her head. This was how she could do this, day after day, because while her body was that of a charwoman's, her mind was free. As she walked along the sidewalk her footsteps beat in time with the words.

I've been weaned of love—
sucked ev'ry drop from the
desiccated breast
until I had no taste for it.

I've been weaned of love. But the poem wasn't finished. She grabbed her mail and caught the elevator. Quiet again. So much quiet in the city, if you knew how to find it. Her apartment was a mess. After cleaning other people's houses all day it was the last thing on her mind, but Jacqueline was sure to notice. She was the type of person she cleaned houses for. Elizabeth glanced through her mail. A card from Northampton—Smith College. A reproduction of a Gustav Klimt painting. Two naked women standing side by side, and inside a poem called *"Reunion"*...

I remembered your eyes
Black, like obsidian
And when I saw you
with your hair pulled back
I imagined the taste
of your neck
on my lips.

"I wrote this after the phone call." Jacqueline said in her note. "I can't wait to see you. I have good news about the book."

The book, her Procrustean bed. And how she would contort her body in every possible way to fit its mattress. She closed her eyes.

"Did you like the poem?" Jacqueline would ask.

"Yes, very much."

Hands on her body—she could barely breathe.

117

She looked at the clock as its blade sliced away time, dismembered the hour. The buzzer rang. Harsh, like an electrocution.

"Elizabeth..." Her voice, dewy and damp. She pressed her body close. Lips and tongue, the taste of cigarettes. "It's good to see you."

"It's good to see *you*."

Jacqueline walked in and put her bag on a chair, her eyes falling upon the clothes strewn about, the unwashed dishes in the sink, the cleaning bucket not put away.

She took off her coat and Elizabeth noticed her breasts. That first night, weren't they beautiful then? Supple beneath her hands, lovely and milky white. Hadn't she traced them with her tongue, kissed them with her lips?

Jacqueline stood by the unmade bed. She took off her sweater and bra, and the rest of her clothes.

"Come to me. I want to feel you inside."

And Elizabeth knelt down as before a wrathful God. Hands stroked her hair, and pulled her close. Musk and ammonia. Rigid hairs; the moist softness of an overripe peach. She imagined peach blossoms and bitter almond, *(was that from a poem?)*. And ammonia and porcelain walls, *(good friend)*, as she moved the brush and scraped it clean. This was where the waste gathered, all things unwanted. A shudder as her face pressed in deeper. Soon it would disappear. Another shudder, and she was left staring into the gaping wounded earth.

Jacqueline bent down until their faces were together, until she tasted herself on her lips.

"Take off your clothes."

Elizabeth moved as in a dream. No sound, a disheartening sky. Her clothes fell as dead leaves, leaving her naked before winter.

An hour later they were in a restaurant—the glimmer of candles and silverware; the hush of linen napkins and muffled footsteps. As they ate their meal she was safe. They would have a drink, and another; and maybe they would go home and fall asleep and this first night would be over. She had told Michael that she was going to Martha's Vineyard, to meet her publisher.

Jacqueline Jimson-Weed poured the wine. Pouilly-Fuissé. Wasn't this what Elizabeth Aphelion imagined her life as a published poet would be like? Dinners with important literary figures?

"I spoke with James the other day. He says he loves your work. He wants five more poems."

A month ago he had wanted five more and she gave them to him, and now he wanted five more.

"And then will it go to print?" She could barely taste the wine or the food.

"And then it will go to print. Just think, Elizabeth, your first book published! Do you have a title for it yet?"

"Tantalus."

Jacqueline laughed.

"Don't worry, it will happen. This is publishing, one delay after another..." She reached across and touched her fingers.

"When Days Are Overcast."

"Yes, from your poem."

Being alone is having
questions without answers.
A mother's daughter
an only child
fatherless,
seeks him in every face.
Is he already there?

A hill overgrown with tangled limbs,
a barely discernible path leads
to a hoary sky
a windsong I begin to recognize
most clearly
when days are overcast.

"It's a beautiful poem, Elizabeth."

But she was thinking of a different poem—one she called
"Existential Poem No. 1"...

Sometimes there are days
when you just
shit and piss
and eat and breathe.

"So it *will* happen? It's been so long."

"I know. I remember waiting for my first book to come out. The longer I had to wait the more I was convinced that it never would. And I thought that if it didn't happen soon I'd dry up inside, and whatever poetry I had would wither away."

For a moment Elizabeth felt compassion, forgiveness—but then she remembered how Jacqueline had used this against her. How it made her close her own eyes. It was a means to an end but she never saw the end. She thought of another Klimt painting, *"The Gorgons"*—three naked women, with wanton hair and acid eyes. This was her portrait—she and Jacqueline Jimson-Weed, and a third woman watching *them*. Her spirit. Her essence. She felt a moist palm on her wrist, and Jacqueline's gaze. *We are lovers now.*

They finished the wine and went to a Lesbian dance club. Eyes no different than the eyes of men covered her body—leering and moist like some mortal sin, or priests with little boys. Weren't women supposed to be *better* than this? Didn't they hold something inside like a prayer, that had to do with creation and birth? Hope and salvation?

The music was machinery and grinding gears, the sweat of metal, the hiss of steam. Oiled bodies as replaceable parts, of friction and the heat of glistening steel. What was the music and what were the people? Where did one leave off, the other begin? She felt a hand along her ass. Faces like masks; cold echoes of metallic hallways, dimly lit and subterranean. Voices becoming tongues, fingers, moans. The noise was frantic, the smell overwhelming, and she felt sick because they were inside her, this place. She had created it.

"I have to get *outta* here."

For a second Jacqueline disappeared, but then Elizabeth felt herself pulled along towards the door. The night air was bracing, but as they sat in the cab she felt sick again. The cabbie's worried Americanized eyes glared from the rearview. His photograph and a name she couldn't pronounce, and she felt his distress—that she would puke her well-fed capitalist American guts all over his paved-with-gold-street of the back of this shitty cab. Garlic and armpits, cumin and soiled money. This cab a maelstrom; this Plexiglas a Petri dish of solidified Manhattan air. She felt her body float along 49th Street, to her apartment, her bed, her eyes closed as she let sleep finish out the day.

Elizabeth woke in a fever. Jacqueline's body against her, hot under the blankets. Slight snoring sounds, a face without makeup, puffy in the morning light. What power did she have now, this middle-aged woman, like her mother sleeping beside her? Swollen and blemished in this innocent sleep? She looked at her mouth, the way it curved downwards and pulled at her lips; and her skin, the wrinkled flesh that she had kissed. Her skin was loose—it flowed over her body like water, holding her reflection. Jacqueline Jimson-Weed had been a young, unpublished poet once, who dreamt of how it would be once her words bloomed in the world.

Saturday was sunny, and Elizabeth persuaded Jacqueline to walk around town. This way the day would pass more quickly. They had lunch in the Village, and then browsed the used bookstores, and Elizabeth watched as a young woman came up to Jacqueline by the poetry rack.

"Aren't you Jacqueline Jimson-Weed, the *poet*?"

The girl was young and pretty, with a nose-ring, and a tattoo on her left arm of a butterfly.

"Yes." Jacqueline smiled. And then the expectant pause.

"I loved *Women Without Men!*" the girl complied. "It's a complete refutation of Hemingway! It's been so inspiring to me. I'm trying to be a poet myself."

"Is that so?"

"Yes. I'm in the Creative Writing program at Hunter. I saw you when you lectured there last year."

"And your name is..." *Her eyes surreptitiously followed the curve of the young girl's breasts.*

"Amy...Amy Passary."

"Well, Amy, perhaps you'd like to send me some of your work."

That was all she needed to say. She didn't even look at Elizabeth, but she knew she had witnessed the whole scene. It was about power—what she could bestow, what she could take away.

As the girl left, Jacqueline turned to Elizabeth.

"That was a nice young girl...a poet at Hunter."

They left the bookstore and walked to a café, (Jacqueline suddenly wanted a glass of wine), and they grabbed a seat by the window. And as the people passed by outside, Elizabeth saw Michael. He moved in his typical hurried manner, body bent slightly forward in a rhumba against the wind, back-pack slung over one shoulder with his pile of books. Past the restaurant he went, without a glance in any direction but forward. Elizabeth decided to spend the afternoon in the café drinking wine, hiding in the window. By the time they got home she was drunk. She barely felt Jacqueline's hands.

Before she opened her eyes she heard the rain. Sunday morning was gray and rainy, which meant that Jacqueline would want to spend the day in bed. Elizabeth thought of Michael, hurrying by, on the way to work on his thesis. Wouldn't that have been ironic if she saw him with a woman...or better, a *man*, a secret lover, as she sat there in the window with her Lesbian dominatrix. She had told him of that first time—the night Jacqueline invited her to dinner. It was an experiment, she said. She assured him it was over.

"It's raining."

Jacqueline's voice, soft against the pillow. And then a hand on her stomach, to the hair below the navel.

"Maybe we should have breakfast in bed."

"Yes, I'll get some bagels."

"That's not the breakfast I had in mind..." Jacqueline's mouth moved into something not quite a smile as she slid beneath the covers, coming to rest between Elizabeth's legs.

A warm tongue, and soon, in spite of herself she became aroused. Grabbing handfuls of hair she pulled her in deep when she heard a noise; the door outside; someone fumbling with the lock. The door swung open and Michael appeared. (He had planned to work on his thesis. On Sundays it was always so quiet here.)

"Elizabeth?..."

Jacqueline's head shot out from beneath the covers.

"Who's *this*, Elizabeth? Is this *Michael*?"

"Michael, I can explain..."

"Is this your *publisher*, cuz I know this sure ain't Martha's Vineyard."

"Michael, I..."

He glared at them both and then stormed out.

"You told him you were in Martha's Vineyard?...With *James?*"

There was silence.

"Oh, Elizabeth, I'm sorry." She grabbed a sweater from the floor. "Kind of a mood killer, wasn't it?...*He'll* be all right. May I use your phone?"

"Sure."

Outside the rain came down, torturing the glass.

"Hello James, it's Jacqueline...Yes, it's raining here too...New York...yes, in Manhattan. I came to see Elizabeth Aphelion...yes...yes she...yes, she has *several* new poems...would you like to speak with...yes, she's right here..." She handed her the phone.

"Hello?"

"Elizabeth, so good to finally speak with you. This is James Brume, Jacqueline's publisher. I've read all of your poems and I must say, I really love your work, I truly...It's just that, well, we need five or ten more poems to fill out the book...you understand. I love your stuff, really, I...now as soon as you finish them I want you to send them out, okay? And then we can get your book published...Have you considered a title yet?"

"Yes, *When Days Are Overcast.*"

"Yes, after your...that's very nice...Good, it's been good speaking with you. We'll meet soon and celebrate. May I speak with Jacqueline again, please?"

"Yes...yes I know, James...all right, well good then, I'll...I'll see you soon...yes, well you know how it...I'm sure...yes, yes I...all right, good-bye James..."

She hung up the phone and looked at Elizabeth's face.

"It *will* happen."

They spent the day in the apartment, in and out of clothes, but Elizabeth's thoughts had become the day. The rain which washed away the sky, which gave the streets a fresh glow, which made the cars sizzle as they drove past. The sound of cars on a rainy street had always been comforting.

Soon it was dark and they ordered a pizza. They made love again before going to sleep, and when Jacqueline left the next morning, the poem Elizabeth had begun on Friday was finished:

I've been weaned of love—
sucked ev'ry drop from the
desiccated breast
until I had no taste for it.

I spit your acid milk
and I see demons rise;
I find your hair and mine
intertwined

like coiled serpents
guarding the gate—
the rotting door I opened wide,
and lost myself inside.

19

Fred Orbis spent the end of his workday staring at his desk, at the newspaper opened to page 15. He was disappointed. The second chapter of what he intuitively felt was his masterpiece was still languishing in the journalistic backwaters.

> *Woman found dead in alley. Sylvia Scarlatina, a 21 year-old model, was found dead in an alley on 8th St. Cause of death unknown.*

What did it take to get a good review? It reminded him of some of the polite, pithy responses he'd received regarding *Fortune's Fool.*

> *The Editors regret that they cannot use the material submitted. We wish you continued good luck with your work. (This is good luck?)*

or...

> *We are sorry but we cannot offer publication. We receive so many submissions that it is impossible to comment on the work.*

The "work" in question was 700 pages long. It represented 10 years of his life and was reduced to 2 generic impersonal lines from the royal *"We"*—those same lordly publishers who went into panegyrics over their latest best-selling diet book, or memoir of a serial killer. The question still remained: *Where was literature?* But then he thought of Joyce. Even Joyce's own brother thought *Finnegans Wake* incomprehensible—this book which consumed the last 18 years of his life, which he died thinking a failure. Fred Orbis looked back at the article in the paper. The world had become insufferably banal. Even something as inspired as death by a Virginia ham sandwich went unnoticed.

Sly Syl of the sylvan glancing glade in the alley 'er maker's reached. High Ho senz O'Billity-Bobbin' narveck flumers unabinnybom. Klack! Und then donum superadditum pax obitus, marzy blam and baked ham. Virginy, but no virgin she, with mouth awide and pinguis he, with smarching slonth wee-blonny bloke blonded, anna Heavy-sent messy jar pardoned. Atta boy inna minute's mirth may, gezalten, gezeiten, besetzung, begone!

Now *that* was a death notice. He gazed at the computer screen, when Roger from the Art Department appeared in the doorway.

"I'll see you tomorrow, Mr. Orbis." But he lingered for a moment, as he stared at Fred Orbis's face.

"What is it, Roger?"

"It's...well, did you get a haircut or something? I mean, you look...*different.*"

"*Different?* In what way?"

Roger strained his eyes but couldn't put his finger on it.

"I don't know...just...different."

"Yes, a haircut."

"It looks good. I'll see you tomorrow, Mr. Orbis."

A polite nod as he waited for the door to shut, before going back to his computer. Fred Orbis called up a special program he had developed. On the screen appeared a New York State driver's license blank, and he gazed at it for a moment as a name from *Finnegans Wake* came to him. *Chudley Magnall.*

Chudley Magnall...422 Zwivell Lane, Troy, New York 17751.

He clicked *'Print'*, and as he waited he took out a sheet of photos. With an *X-acto* knife he cut out a photo of himself and pasted it onto the new license, and then he put it through the laminating machine he'd purchased a few weeks back, when preparing for his first date. Tonight he would be *Chudley Magnall.*

He thought of what Roger had said, because lately he had thought this himself. Ever since the date with Belle Horizonte he was changing. Granted, he had become a murderer, (and with Sylvia Scarlatina a *double* murderer), but if one could possibly overlook this, because something *marvelous* was happening as well! With each murder he was less hungry, and he saw himself now as the butterfly inside an enormous chrysalis. His hopes of losing weight, which had always been dashed on the empty plates of yet another dinner, were starting to become realized.

Fred Orbis left his office and walked to the shipping room, where they had an industrial-strength scale for weighing huge parcels. The scale went up to 500 lbs., but whenever he had stepped on it in the past the needle and the springs had strained beyond their limit. Today, however, there were pounds to spare.

He had lost 60 pounds since his epiphanous date. For the first time in memory his clothes felt a little big.

He knew it was her from a block away. She stood out from the masses, resplendent in that celebrated glow of specious beauty. The limousine pulled up to the curb and he opened the window.

"Are you Tawny Haustorium?"

The woman's long legs led her to the car, and as she bent over her hair cascaded down in luxurious golden strands.

"Yes." A breathless smile.

"I'm Chud Magnall, please come in."

"Do you always drive your own limo?"

So far, disappointingly predictable.

"Well, it's such a nice evening."

He could almost read her thoughts. "He's fat...he's really fat!"

Fred Orbis turned to her.

"You are even more beautiful in person, than in the photograph you included in your letter."

"Oh, thank you. And *you*," her voice became softer, "it must be so exciting to be a movie producer!"

"Yes, it is. In fact we're in the middle of casting for..." He mentioned a huge Hollywood star. "For his brand new picture, and we still haven't found the 'love interest'. We've seen so many girls, but not the right one."

"Did I mention I was an *actress*? I said I was a model, but I'm also an actress. I've been taking classes."

"You don't say? Well, you *are* the right type, but..."

His mind wandered. How funny, that all his life he had obeyed the rules. He brushed after every meal, he did his homework, he respected his elders, he obeyed the Ten Commandments, he even flossed, but all his life his life had been a disaster. And now, when he had renounced goodness, embraced evil, and become a sinister murderer, things were finally looking up.

"What? What *is* it?" Tawny asked, moving closer to him in the seat.

"Well, it would involve some nudity."

"That's okay."

"Full frontal nudity..."

"That's fine. I brought some pictures, some nudes. Maybe you'd like to see them."

"Well, yes, that would be..."

"Or *maybe*..." She slid over a little closer, and undid the top button of her blouse. "Maybe you'd like to see the real thing..."

Her fingers, so beautiful and innocent. It was the way of the world, everyone ready to sell what was most dear.

"Or maybe..." She moved closer still, and those same innocent fingers found the zipper on his pants. "Maybe we can do something *else*..."

"Tell me, Tawny..." He gently pushed her away. "Don't you think I'm *fat*?"

"What?" *(Why had he pushed her away? No man had ever done that before.)*

"I mean, let's be honest. Don't you find me just the least bit repulsive?"

"What, I..."

"Repulsive, repugnant, odious."

"I don't..."

"Revolting, repellent, disgusting."

"I don't know what you mean."

"Fat, aren't I *fat*?"

"Well, *sure*...but you're a famous movie producer."

"So, if I *wasn't* a famous movie producer..."

"I don't understand."

"You wouldn't happen to know *Latin*?"

"What, you mean, like the *lambada*?"

"Ne fronti credi..."

"What?"

"Trust not to appearances."

She stared at him through bewildered but beautifully mascaraed eyes. Chudley Magnall was like no man she had ever met.

"Okay, so you're fat. But what about the movie? I don't mind nudity..."

"I'm *extremely* fat."

"What? "

"Blimplike, humongous." He kept his eye peeled for an appropriate dark alley. "One might go so far as to say that I'm..."

"What? I don't know. What?"

"Obese. Say it, I'm *obese*..."

"Okay, you're obese!"

"What did you say?"

"I said you're *obese*! Jesus, I wanna...Can you take me home, I mean, I don't feel so..." Then she saw him laugh as if the whole thing had been a joke or a test. "What?...Wh, what is it? Was that, was that some kind of...was that like some kind of *screen test* or something?"

"Yes," he smiled, "I wanted to see your emotion. And it was...*inspiring*."

"Wow...Well, I've been taking those acting classes, like I said, and...well, my teacher, he says I..."

"Yes, I can see it. You're quite expressive. In fact, I think I've seen enough."

"You mean, I got the *part*!"

"Yes, there's just one thing..."

"What, the *nudity*? I mean, I told you I don't mind, I..."

"No, it isn't that. There's a bag in the back seat. Can you reach over and get it for me?"

"*This?*...It smells like food."

"Yes, a little snack. Would you mind taking it out of the bag."

"It's a sandwich."

"Yes. Corned beef and Swiss actually, with a little Dijon. May I have it, please?"

"But I thought we were going to dinner?"

"I'm not hungry. The sandwich is for you."

The car came to a stop in the middle of a dark alley. Fred Orbis waited for the moment of realization, and then he brought the corned beef and Swiss in one sweeping motion into her beautiful mouth, holding it there until the life passed from her beautiful eyes.

"*Adieu.*" he said, pushing her body out the door. "*Omnia mors aequat.*"

A half hour later he returned the limo and stood on 7th Avenue, as he tried to hail a cab. One by one cabs drove by, until finally one pulled up.

"Whoa, I hope my tires got enough air in 'em." said the cabbie.

Fred Orbis's good feeling was rapidly deteriorating in the face of this cabbie's sophomoric wit, and he glared back and hoped he'd remain silent.

"What, were ya out for a *jog?*" The cabbie laughed to himself as he reached into a paper bag, and brought out a cheeseburger. "You wanna bite?...Nah, looks like ya already ate. Listen buddy, I was wonderin' if I could get your autograph, see, cuz my kid, he's a real fan of the Goodyear blimp..."

Fred Orbis noticed a deserted stretch of road by a warehouse.

"Pull over there."

"Whatever you say." The cabbie pulled over and Fred Orbis handed him a fifty dollar bill. "Hey, *thanks* buddy!" He was about to apologize for his wisecracks when he saw the cheeseburger, pushed by an enormous hand into his throat. The last gasps of air wrenched from his lungs as he clutched and squirmed, and then the entire bag of fries swiftly followed. The last thought the cabbie had was of being buried beneath an enormous mound of McDonald's French fries.

Fred Orbis wiped a handkerchief across the door handles as he exited the cab. He left the fifty on the seat and the cab under the pregnant gloom of a decaying warehouse, and he walked home in light. The light of the Renaissance shone upon each of his steps, the time of limitless possibilities. Was it his imagination, or was his step actually lighter, more brisk on the potholed street? He thought of his first words, *"I eat! I eat!"*, and for most of his life he did, but now he felt sated, filled to the brim with possibility.

Ganis Ganymede Satisfactus voluptas. Brot the brilly brod neely anna mumpt. Bumpity bumpity bellows bumped, ana Pellows pumped along long-grain granus. Gravus graymalken gossamer entreat? In gorged then vile, in villa virago shute the shilly-shal, lonz thema f'week. Fallow farl not a whit witless wany one, goes away hot light, finey shot, whispers wail a'wane.

Her face was flawless. Or perhaps it was completely flawed. Darby had stopped on the sidewalk as other Manhattanites moved past, and she stood like a buoy anchored amidst the ever-flowing current. There was a poster, the latest fashion model working her way into the collective consciousness, and Darby Montana stood before it. What had happened between sperm and egg to result in such a face? The eyes, the nose, the mouth, the hair molecularly aligned in a kind of misty perfection. The human face as an *incipit*, the first line of a novel, full of implication. She remembered reading an author once who imagined a novel containing only incipits; of first lines where everything else was implied, and this was what she saw here.

Darby moved closer. It seemed to her a battle between dimensions. Here she was, an undistinguished representative of the three-dimensional world, confronting an ambassador of the world of two. Darby's world, of jarring angles and buildings cutting into sky, of floating metal rivers and noisy gray air, of people, so many people, alone beneath Heaven's eye. How could they stand it, brushing elbows each day against their anonymous selves? And then, in this two-dimensional haven beyond the photograph's frame, this woman stood as an invitation. The Faustian bargain made each day, as the world of three dimensions opted for the world of two. But *why*?

Her face implies the rest, we read it in her eyes, we know her world is different from ours, where people walk by unkempt with bulbous noses and hair in disarray, and petty concerns which become their lives—where the prevailing wind blows a bland uniformity. We are anonymous in our ugliness like the lifeless buildings, and as Darby stared at the poster she saw herself not in the photograph, but in the rectangular frame. What was beauty but three-dimensions becoming two? Into the model's sea green eyes she went, as if looking through a keyhole. The barest glimpse of something more inside. A gateway, but instead of Cerberus, a 19 year-old girl, and beyond her somewhere the Elysian fields.

The people rushed past. Stopping on the sidewalk was unusual in New York. The only ones who did were the "crazies"; those whose minds had broken beyond anonymity to transcend the dimensions. No longer of three; surely not of two. Perhaps they had become part of time itself, and like time, a reminder of life as fleeting; of ideas' airy nothingness, and the collective vision which kept the sidewalks flowing like a river, alive as long as it flowed. But wasn't this everyone's secret, to escape the anonymity? The woman of the perfume ad had succeeded. She was universally desired, she was the first line of a novel which everyone wanted to read, the fulfillment of a wish. Darby felt lost as she stared at the face. Wasn't perfection just as anonymous? Surely Rembrandt would have preferred a bulbous nose, but Darby didn't even have the distinction of being ugly. She was plain—indifferently, relentlessly, hopelessly plain! What had happened between sperm and egg to result in such blandness? Couldn't they have waited just another day, another week, when a new combination might have turned out differently? She felt inside a spirit still strong that used to be indomitable, but usurped by what her face and her body had become—a nothing, when all her life she had felt inside a something.

135

"Darby?"

She heard her name through the crowd, and when she turned she saw Philep.

"Hi, how are you?"

"Hi. I'm okay. I was just out for a walk."

"Do you wanna go grab a bite?...My treat."

"Sure."

They walked to a café. The place was nearly empty, and they grabbed a table by the window and ordered drinks.

"Philep, what we talked about the other day..."

"Yes. We got carried away, didn't we?"

"I want to know what it's like...Hell, I mean."

"But Darby, you already know. What did Eliot say? *'Hell is oneself.'*"

"And Sartre, *'Hell is others'*, but I..."

"It's *literature*, Darby, all of it, don't you see? Stories, apocrypha... products of someone's imagination."

"But they come from *some*where. How many different gods are there? What do they say, if God didn't exist it would be necessary to *invent* him?"

Philep was silent. The sound of a waiter moving a vacuum over the rug filled the air, and they waited for it to pass.

"So let's say that God never existed, all right, and somehow we're all here anyway. And so, what, we get *bored*? *Afraid*?"

"Darby..."

"So we *invent* him, right? We create the Creator, therefore he exists."

"But, what if he *always* existed?"

"It doesn't matter."

"So you're saying that by *believing* in something it becomes real, like Santa Claus."

"I'm saying that...well, if you see something *before* it happens you're a prophet, right, but if you see something that has already *happened* it's just memory."

"I'm not sure I follow."

"Time. We think it flows in just one direction, but if there's a God then he would be *outside* of it, by definition, right? He's omnipresent. Ubiquitous...We see time linearly. We can't help it. But God would see it differently. To him, the future and the past would be interchangeable."

"So what you're saying is..."

"By us creating God we're seeing *beyond time*. We invent him, which means he exists *after* us, since we invented him, but just by doing this he instantly *precedes* us, millions of years before we were born, because one of the conditions of his existence is that he's outside of time, right? And by us creating him we create this space. So maybe it's possible for us to, I don't know, have an insight into it, this place beyond time, and through it we intuitively feel God. And then we put it into a linear sequence so we can understand it."

"So you're saying that we create God because he already *exists?*"

"Yes...Or that we could create him even if he *never* existed. Just by us *imagining* him, we create this space outside linear time, and by doing that he's instantly there."

"He already exists...the *causa causans*."

"But we created him."

"And his existence precedes our own."

"And *every*thing."

The waiter came by, and they ordered more drinks.

"So, Darby, what about the *Devil?*"

"It's the same...Philep, last week, when you were the Devil, and I...How did you *know* those things?"

"They were...they were just generalities, Darby..."

"No, they *weren't*. You were exactly right."

"Hmm. So what is *Hell* for you?"

"Hell hath no limits, nor is circumscribed in one self place; but where we are is hell."

"More literature?"

"I don't know, *you* tell *me*."

"Darby, what do you truly want?"

"I want...I want to be something *else*...I want to be reincarnated in a perfume ad, but remain who I am, I..."

"You want the impossible."

She was silent.

"But *why*, Darby?"

"You see what it's like. It's *always* been this way, the way people think. Look what's valued. And it'll never change."

"But..."

"I'm tired of being stuck in this..."

"But you're a..."

"I know, I'm a beautiful *person*. I'm beautiful *inside*. I want to know what Hell is like, Philep."

There was a long pause.

"You already know."

"And *Heaven*?"

"How have you imagined it?"

"I don't know, not like they say. It would have to be able to *change*. I mean, I'd go crazy if it were always the same. It would have to be able to change *completely* if I wanted it too."

"Like *this*, like those people outside, like this city?"

"Yes...like this."

"So what's your *Hell* like?"

"Like this."

"Why?"

"Because of hope. Because I hope that it will change but it never does, and... I can't let go."

"Darby, you're so *close*...This is your place. Let go of hope and you'll *have* your Heaven."

"I've tried, I...I *can't*."

"Let go your hope of being redeemed. That there's God ready to judge you. That somehow in the end it will all come out right. There's nothing *there*, Darby, not even time. This is it *here*."

They were silent for a long time, and then Philep grabbed a menu.

"I'm starving." he said. "This talk has made me hungry." He looked at Darby, but she was quiet. "We'll talk again. When you need to I'll be here."

He motioned for the waiter as Darby looked outside, at the current of moving bodies, at the ever-flowing river.

21

Devon DeGroot searched the trash until he found a certain crinkled-up piece of paper. Opening it he saw:

Cal Igula—7 PM

He grabbed the phone.

"Donalbain..."

"Hey boss."

"Page 97 of the *Voice*...What was that ad about bacchanals?"

A rustling of paper.

"Yeah boss...*Extremely fat, but also extremely wealthy and generous man seeks beautiful hedonist women for weekly bacchanals...* whadaya, *got* somethin'?"

"Find who put in the ad. Also, write this down...Cal Igula..."

"That's Caligula, boss."

"I know...look it up...cross reference it to the stretch limos. I'll be right back."

He hung up the phone and looked at Sylvia Scarlatina's apartment. Clothes were everywhere; fashion magazines and cosmetics; the whole place reeking of perfume. On one wall, a poster with the letters LOVE stacked like building blocks. On another, photos of the latest fashion models, and beneath it, a handwritten sign...*Don't dream it—be it!* Devon DeGroot took another breath of the cloying air, and then left the apartment.

Coffee spilled over the Styrofoam cup onto his hand as he strode into the office.

"These damn lids always come loose...Any luck?"

"Well, we got good news and we got bad news..." said Donalbain.

"We checked out the ad." said Macduff. "It was put in two weeks before the first murder, under the name Gustavus Silenus."

"So, what was that, the good news or the bad news?"

"Both. The address is here in Manhattan...1627 W. 48th St."

"Wait a second, that sounds...that sounds familiar."

"It's a Dunkin' Donuts, boss."

"So the name, *Gustavus Silenus...*"

"Gustavus, King of Sweden." said Macduff.

"Jeopardy?"

"The dictionary."

"And *Silenus?*"

Kozinski turned the dictionary to the page he had marked.

"A forest spirit of the ancient Greeks, and in some myths the foster father and teacher of Dionysus."

"Diane *who?*" asked Donalbain.

"Dionysus, you..."

"Another name for Bacchus. So, I don't suppose the Post Office remembers our Gustavus Silenus?"

They shook their heads.

"What about the *Voice*? He had to pay for the ad. *Credit card numbers?... Canceled checks?*"

"Nothing. They said people sometimes pay in cash. Maybe he..."

"But we did get *this*, boss. On the day of the first murder, Gustavus Silenus rented a stretch limo from this place... *'Big Deal*

Limousines' on Seventh. There's a license number, but it's phony. And the address is the same."

"Dunkin' Donuts."

"What about..."

"He paid in cash there too. They remembered him. They said he was *very fat*."

"And then there's this. We checked out your *Cal Igula*, and guess what? Cal Igula rented a stretch limo on the night of the second murder."

"The same place?"

"No, *'Larry's Limos'*, on 17th Street. But just like before, he paid in cash...and his license..."

"The address is where *Mama Leone's* used to be."

"So, what did they..."

"They just said that he was *fat*...that's all anybody seems to remember about the guy."

"So, we have a *fat* serial killer now?" said Devon DeGroot.

"Very fat." said Donalbain.

"Corpulent." said Macduff.

"Rotund." said Kozinski.

Devon DeGroot took a sip of his coffee but it was already cold. He grimaced once, and swallowed it anyway as a kind of penance.

"So what do we have...an overweight genius who somehow changes identities, who put an ad in the Voice so he could murder young women with *lunch meat*?"

"That about sizes it up, boss."

"So..."

"That's the bad news, boss. It's a dead end. All roads lead to..."

"Zip-ola."

"Well, I want the letters in that P.O. box. Get somebody to stake out the Post Office. We need more manpower. And check out the local obese geniuses. See if there's a list somewhere of people with high IQ's who are also fat. Donalbain, find that list...Kozinski, I want you at the Post Office in case he..."

Just then Detective Arnold appeared, his face distraught. "There's been another murder."

Ten minutes later they were back in an alley.

"The girl is Tawny Haustorium." said an officer at the scene. "She's 21...she's a..."

"Let me guess," said Macduff, "a *social-worker?*"

"We found part of a corned beef sandwich stuffed down her throat."

"Corned beef and Swiss...with Dijon."

DeGroot noticed another bum, standing alongside the dumpster. "Another *witness?*"

"Yeah, but I'm not sure how *much* of one."

"You'd be surprised at some of our witnesses."

The officer brought the bum over.

"This is..." He looked back at his notepad. "Sven Kappûtkoic."

"There's that *thing* again," said Macduff, peering over the officer's shoulder, "a *circumflex.*"

The bum was big and tall, and wore a worn-out overcoat and a moth-eaten Boston Red Sox cap. He had several open sores on his face, and his eyes never seemed able to agree on their focus.

"Mr. Kappûtkoic, can you tell me what happened?"

The bum looked at DeGroot's face, but it was as if he saw right past him.

"I...I dunno, it...it went right through his legs, I...I couldn't *believe* it." He stood with his legs apart, as he followed an imaginary object's path between them.

One of the officers stepped up.

"He...he seems to have this obsession with the '86 World Series...the Mets and the Red Sox...and Bill Buckner."

"The ball going through his..."

"It went right through his legs." the bum said. "I can't...I can't under...I mean, that was it, our chance, our...I mean, 68 years since the Babe, since that goddamned Harry Frazee...and then, it went right through his..."

Devon DeGroot watched as the man pantomimed the routine grounder, perpetually rolling into right field.

"Mr...Mr. Kappûtkoic, sir...Mr. Kappûtkoic..." Finally he got his attention. "Sir, I need to know what happened the night of the murder."

"Yes." the bum said. "I was there. I had just been thinking about..." He drifted back to Game Six.

"Please, Mr. Kappûtkoic, this is very important. What happened to the young woman over there?"

"Yes, I was there."

Devon closed his eyes to ward off the approaching migraine.

"I had just been thinking about...*Women*." He turned to them with a knowing smile. "As an abstraction, of course...The perpetual *querelle des femmes*...the 'woman question', which has plagued philosophers for...is it millenni*a* or millenni*ums*? I always get those confused."

"It's both." said DeGroot. "You were saying about the woman..."

"Yes, the woman *question*. I was pondering the enigma, its inscrutable nature as it were, when to my surprise this beautiful woman suddenly appeared...albeit *dead*, of course...I must have concentrated too hard."

"He thinks he somehow conjured her outta thin air." said the officer on the scene.

"I tried to speak with her. She seemed nice enough, but then again," he threw up his hands in a gesture of *C'est la vie*, "she was *dead*. I ascertained that right away. My interests include medicine as well as metaphysics. She was dead all right, the ghastly pallor, the lividity, that sandwich stuck in her mouth...*Omnia mors aequat*... Apparently it was her time."

"What's that, was that *Latin* you just said?"

"Latin, yes! A lovely language. What a pity that it..."

"Please, what does it *mean*?"

"The *Latin*?...Death levels all things."

"Apparently he was some kind of scholar," the officer explained, "who took to drink when the Red Sox lost the '86 Series. He tried to sell us *this*..."

"His college diploma?"

"For fifty cents marked down from a dollar."

DeGroot looked back at the bum.

"The Latin..."

"That's what *He* said."

"*He?*"

"God. It's His revenge for me not believing in Him. I'm not an atheist, mind you, nor an agnostic. I have always considered myself a '*nihilistic optimist*', to coin a phrase. Nihilists enjoying a long and respected history. *Bazarov* of course being the first to appear in literature, in..."

"Please, Mr. Kappûtkoic, what do you mean *He* said? Did *God* speak to you? Did he speak to you the night of the murder?"

"Yes, He did. He came in black...which was unusual, because one wouldn't expect such a mode of dress from God, but then again, this is *New York*...He deposited the young woman on the ground, right over there."

"He came in black...the black limo."

"And he said those words, *Omnia mors aequat*. But it doesn't matter. I will never forgive Him, no matter how He taunts me with fleshly temptations. I have renounced corporeal pleasures in my asceticism. This..." he pointed to the cardboard box behind the dumpster, "is my sanctum sanctorum, and this..." he motioned to the alley at large, "my unpeopled void...except for today of course."

"You will never *forgive*..."

"God and Bill Buckner." He returned to the ground ball, rolling ceaselessly through dumbstruck legs.

Devon DeGroot walked over to the body. In death the woman's face shone of an angel, of God's chosen. Her delicate mouth set forever in an expression of wonder, (albeit, due to the corned beef sandwich).

"Where's the murder weapon?"

One of the officers handed him a plastic bag with a small piece of crust, and a few bits of meat and Swiss cheese.

"*This?* There's hardly enough here to choke a sparrow."

"Our friend over there...*Sven*...He said he dreamed of a corned beef sandwich, and...well, he was..."

"I know, he was hungry. Get his statement. And get him a hot meal, for Christsakes."

When they got back to the precinct there was more bad news.

"There's been another murder." said Detective Arnold, who looked now as if he had been overcome by plague.

"Another *girl?*"

"No, this time it's a cabbie. They found him by a warehouse, with a fifty dollar bill on the seat of the cab, and a double cheeseburger with fries down his throat."

Devon DeGroot let out a prolonged sigh.

"So our boy's branching out. Did you check the cab?"

"Yeah, the cabbie's prints were on the fifty...but the door handles were clean."

"So our guy's careful."

"Christ, if the media gets a hold of this..."

"They already have." said Donalbain. In one hand he held a bag of crullers, in the other a newspaper. He held up the headline for all to see.

COLD-CUT KILLER STRIKES AGAIN—4 DEAD

22

The muted trumpet sounded far away. Notes came out in flutters, like birds from the stillness of oncoming night. A single note strained against the darkness, grasped its emptiness and faded, like a bleeding sunset becoming ink blue. Another note, this one close, inside her now as she listened, and in it a kind of dying. Elizabeth stared at the chessboard. She wasn't sure who's move it was, and she saw Mr. Monde's face, placid and calm, a black sky coming on with night's gentle peace.

"The middle game, Elizabeth..."

She couldn't get the weekend out of her mind.

"...is where the battle is won or lost."

"Michael, I need to talk." It was the fourth time she had called, and he finally didn't hang up. "Please Michael..."

"All right."

They met by the dog run in Schurz Park. For years they had wanted a pet but couldn't in their apartments, so they came here now and then to sit and watch the dogs. And for a half hour they felt the wildness kept inside, while they dozed in apartments, or gingerly walked cement sidewalks held fast to leashes.

"Hello, Michael."

"Hi."

They sat down but didn't speak, and turned to the dogs as if it were some symbolic counterpoint, the barking dogs and their ominous silence.

"Listen Michael, I'm...I'm sorry. "

"You told me it was *over*, Elizabeth. You told me, what, eight months ago that it was a one-time thing...an experiment."

"It was."

"Oh, so that was another *experiment*?"

"You know about the book..."

"That *goddamn* book. That's all you think about."

"It's my *life*, Michael! You know what it means to me. I'm a *writer*, for Christsake."

"Yeah..."

"What's *that* supposed to mean?"

"Nothing."

"What, you think I want to spend my life cleaning *toilets*? Christ, that's what I do while you're teaching your little undergraduates, and working on your thesis."

"What, you think *that's* fun? You think I like what *I* do?"

"Well, there you go."

"What?"

"We're *both* doing things we hate."

"I didn't say I hate *any*thing, Elizabeth."

"Michael...All right, but you're doing what you do so you get your doctorate, right? Your degree, your *Ph.D.*, so you can *then* do what you want."

"So what's wrong with that? I mean, so could you..."

"Not this again."

"What? I mean, why'd you quit school?"

"I didn't *quit* school! I got my goddamn master's degree, in case you forgot"

"I didn't forget, but you could be teaching now, instead of..."

"Michael, I'm a *writer*! Can't you get that through your head? I want to *write*, I don't want to teach, just so I can be in some goddamn Ivy League..."

"But you want to clean toilets..."

"Yes Michael, I want to clean toilets...that's where I draw my inspiration."

"I mean, you've been waiting for that goddamn book for what? *Two years?* That bitch is stringing you along."

"I...I spoke with the publisher the other day. He said it's..."

"What? Is that before, or after you screwed your professor?"

"We didn't *screw*..."

"I don't know *what* the hell you do. You said it was over."

"It *was*, I just...I just haven't been able to..."

"Goddamn it Elizabeth, can't you see what's happening? Can't you see what kind of person she is?"

"What, do you think I'm an *idiot*? Do you think...Do you think I *like* what I've done?"

"Then why don't you just tell her to fuck off!"

"I..."

"Because of the book, right? The goddamn book!"

" . . . . "

"Listen Elizabeth, you have to decide what it is you really want."

"What, you mean *you or the book*?"

"No, I mean the book or your life. I mean, doesn't it make you feel *bad*? How can you write your beautiful poems, and then do what you do to get them published? And I don't mean cleaning toilets. It doesn't make sense."

"It makes *complete sense*. Do you think it's *easy*? Do you think I just have to send a few poems to the *New Yorker* and that's that? You can't get *anywhere* without connections, without contacts."

"Yeah, I saw the kind of contacts you had. I mean, Christ, she looked like your mother!"

"I'm so glad you decided to have a reasonable discussion."

She turned back to the dogs. A small poodle was being set upon by some other dogs, and although the other dogs thought it was fun the poodle started yelping in terror.

"God Michael, it's all so easy for you. It's all so clear. You just get your precious Ph.D., and the rest of your life takes care of itself."

"And what's wrong with that?"

"My life's not like that, Michael. That's not who I am."

"Well who *are* you, Elizabeth, can you tell me? Can you *see* yourself?"

"I'm a writer, Michael. I'll *always* be a writer."

"Well, good luck. I hope it's worth it." Abruptly he rose from the bench. "I have some work to do. I'll see you."

She watched him disappear, and then she turned and saw the poodle, rescued by its owner. The dog had been petrified, but as it was led away it glanced back at the other dogs with what looked like longing.

Elizabeth looked at the chessboard. She reached for her knight and captured a pawn, when her eyes were suddenly drawn to Mr. Monde's bishop. By moving her knight she had cleared a path for it to capture her queen.

"How was your weekend, Elizabeth?"

"Oh, it was all right." *(I'm a writer, Michael.)*

"I was wondering if maybe you'd like to stop now, and I can tell you the next chapter in our tale of George Washington." His eyes touched the board, and it seemed as though he held her queen. "We can leave the pieces as they are, and resume next time."

"Yes, please, the story." *(I'll always be a writer.)*

"The second test, Elizabeth. One of the enigmas of the founding fathers is the issue of slavery. The seeds of the Civil War had been sown long before the American Revolution, however, that was the time when something could have been done to prevent it. Thomas Jefferson himself put a motion to abolish it before Congress, but it was defeated. And then, there was a kind of collective veil pulled over everyone's eyes. A tacit agreement to ignore it. But slavery wouldn't go away.

"Which brings us to George Washington. He was the richest man in Virginia, and he owned hundreds of slaves. But in the same breath, he and the other founding fathers believed that England was trying to 'enslave' them, through taxation. Blacks, on the other hand, were thought of as nothing more than property, by even the more enlightened. After all, it was in the Bible, in Aristotle. So there was this fatalistic acceptance, that even *God* had ordained that blacks were inferior to whites."

"And Washington thought this too?"

"Well, that was *it*, in a way. He tried not to think about it. He even wrote in a letter: *It's a subject that has never employed much of my thoughts.*"

"So, what happened?"

"Well, after his death he ended up freeing his own slaves in his will. But for him the question was still unresolved. The basic issue of course was humanity. Were all men created equal? What was a man? The answer was the Civil War."

"And Washington?"

"This is the subject of his second test…It is the 1820's. There is a plantation owner in Georgia named Thomas Jefferson Polk, who ironically owns 1776 slaves. There is a young slave named Opal. Her father, no one knows. Her mother dies in childbirth, and Opal is raised by 'Aunt Ruby', an old slave woman who many believe is a witch. Aunt Ruby knows herbs. She knows which roots to use to cure colic and fever, and which teas to restore vigor after a long day in the fields. And she has second sight. She sees things, and many say that she can cast spells.

"The years go by. Opal is now a young woman. She's spent her whole life in the fields. Brutal work, hot under the sun. But one day she's called into the main house. She's to be a laundress, and while she's there the master walks in and gives her a long look.

"That night she's called into the kitchen of the main house by one of the other slaves. She's told that the master wants to see her, and she's led outside to the barn. The master is there of course, and...well, every few nights she's called back, and each night Aunt Ruby comforts her. She tells her stories, and one night she tells her of a vision.

"There is a cow, and in the cow's black spots she reads the future. A day when there is no more slavery. And she sees the end of the Polk family line. A fruit picked from this very garden will rot over generations, and bring about their ruin.

"Ten years later the master's son frees all of his slaves, but unfortunately dies of pneumonia soon afterwards. And as for Opal... well, she's free now, but this is Georgia, and not the best place for a freed slave. Many of them wander to other plantations, many are captured...A few, like Opal, manage to get North on the Underground Railroad. And she ends up living in Philadelphia, where she works as a laundress for a white family until she dies."

"George Washington was Opal."

"And through her he learned about humanity, and equality."

"So what happened to that family? The *Polk's* that Aunt Ruby predicted would come to ruin?"

"That will be answered when I tell you of the *fourth* test, Elizabeth. Next week we'll hear of the third..."

Elizabeth looked back at the chessboard. There was a pawn blocking Mr. Monde's bishop. She hadn't noticed it before. Her queen was out of danger.

23

Fred Orbis could barely contain himself. He had made the front page.

COLD-CUT KILLER STRIKES AGAIN—4 DEAD

The media had even hung a catchy alliterative moniker on him which the public could embrace. It was his first good review, and it positively gushed. Gruesome details of the murders; the dark alleys; the hapless victims—the euphonious Belle Horizonte, (the woman who had started it all, and in one evening changed his life). Sylvia Scarlatina, Tawny Haustorium, the dim-witted cabbie, (who he found out today was named Manny Shemogian). The incongruity of the black limousines and the deli sandwiches. Already, noted criminal psychiatrists were offering their psychological profiles of the *"Cold-Cut Killer"*...

The frustrated working man, the common ham sandwich the symbol of his life, the black limousine him rising above his status, the beautiful woman the refined culture denied him, and in the act of murder the sandwich transforms him.

The wealthy man who recognizes the sham of his own existence, that his wealth and stature are but illusions, and in murdering the beautiful woman he symbolically murders himself and becomes reborn; the ham sandwich the link to the world of the simple and unadorned, where he feels the truth ultimately dwells.

Fred Orbis's eyes danced over the names of each of the murder weapons. A meatball sandwich, a baked Virginia ham, a corned beef and Swiss (with Dijon), and the extemporaneous double cheeseburger with fries, all now immortalized. It's true that within days of the story hitting newsprint, consumption of lunch meat and Italian sandwiches in the metropolitan area rose by 23%. McDonald's considered some kind of promotional tie-in; while executives at Burger King and Wendy's lamented that the "Cold-Cut Killer" evidently preferred the Golden Arches.

Fred Orbis read further as his paper trail vanished before everyone's eyes. He had several known aliases—Gustavus Silenus and Cal Igula—but the post office box, the rented limos, all trails that could lead to him had abruptly ended; to the dismay of the investigating police detective, one Devon DeGroot of Mid-Manhattan South Vice and Homicide. Reading further, it said that he spoke fluent Latin, and was an authority on James Joyce. They were calling him the *"serial killer for intellectuals"*.

He grabbed a few other papers. They all had picked up on the "Cold-Cut Killer" as if through some Hundredth Monkey Effect, and all were praising his efforts. But then he saw that the people who had rented him the limos had described him as being *"very fat"*, and he was disappointed. *Where was the poetry?* If only *Mencken* had been behind the counter at "Larry's Limos", he would've been *"elephantine"..."adipose"..."oleaginous!"* Why did the prose of newspapers always have to be so prosaic? Then he picked up the *New York Times* and the headline was altogether different. WAR BREAKS OUT IN MAURITIUS. Just like *The Times*, he thought, more concerned with an obscure war in a forgotten island in the middle of nowhere east of Madagascar than what's going on under their own roof. He turned back to the *Daily News*, when there was a knock at the door.

"Mr. Orbis?" It was Ralph, the associate editor. "The new layout is ready. I thought you might..."

This was the monthly feature at *Feast Magazine*, the lavish cover story of a massive banquet table loaded with food, which Fred Orbis would then proceed to devour from one end to the other, as he had done each month since he had founded the magazine. Oddly however, at the mention of this today Fred Orbis blanched.

"Is it time for that again?" he asked.

"Well, *yes...*" Ralph was taken aback at his boss's apathy, which he couldn't help but view as an omen heralding a new harmony between the celestial spheres.

"What is it *this* month?"

"It's that Scottish feast...the *Robert Burns Banquet.*"

The thought of haggis and cock-a-leekie was suddenly revolting. "No, you go on."

And for a moment, his associate editor stood nonplused in the doorway as it sunk in, that his boss on this day was passing up a feast.

Suddenly a thought hit Fred Orbis. He sprang from his chair with surprising agility and hurried to the shipping department, and while the employees went about their work, he stepped onto the industrial-strength scale and weighed himself. 60 more pounds had disappeared—which made 120 since the first murder. A quick calculation as to what he would need to arrive at a normal weight. 120 pounds divided by 4 murders equaled 30 pounds per murder. Six more murders should do the trick, and for the first time he saw the light at the end of the tunnel. A transformation. A metamorphosis. He was becoming Federico Orbisini! It was time to brush up on his Italian. As he walked back to his office, Roger from the Art Department hailed him.

"Mr. Orbis, I heard you're not going to the feast..." And then, "You look *different.* I mean, is that a new *suit?*"

They were starting to notice. He had lost 120 pounds but he still wore the same old suits, which had a kind of tent-like quality to them now.

"Che bella giornata!"

"What?"

"What a lovely day! *Mi dispiace, io adesso dobbiamo andare.*"

Roger stood for a moment in silence, as his boss walked merrily away.

Fred Orbis took the rest of the day off, and on his way home the revelation unfolded. The moronic cabbie, Manny Shemogian, had opened up a *world* of victims. *All* God's children were worthy to suffer the wrath of the meatball sandwich...but then, one mustn't repeat oneself. Perhaps tuna salad, or maybe olive loaf. This could be the first time in recorded history that someone died of an olive loaf sandwich.

Fred Orbis paused to look at his life. He had become a consummate villain; an arch-fiend; an overall bad hombre, and it was good. He felt his baggy clothes and envisioned a new wardrobe, but there were still six more victims to dispatch. And he would have to choose carefully; be circumspect. No more limos or personal ads. And as he pondered this, he was struck with an aftershock of the first revelation. The book, his new novel which had been foundering for months for lack of inspiration, suddenly became clear! Each page unfolded before his eyes as he rushed to his apartment and sat behind the computer.

Til the soul-departed seas wash your empty shores, and earth becomes a hollowed ball.

He stared at the sentence for a moment longer and then pressed *'Delete'*. A new beginning was required. *Ver perpetuum.* Fingers flashed over keys...

Hugh Vorax was fat. Very fat, and he wanted to be thin.

There it was, the first line, the incipit! This would be his story and the story of society itself—of beauty and ugliness, good and evil. A Rabelaisian, Joycean, Melvillean romp. A rollicking satire, and a poignant reflection on morals, literature, and the bestseller list—of society as caprice, and culture as ephemera. He thought of a passage from Calvino:

"The inferno of the living is already here, where we live every day. There are two ways to escape suffering it. The first is easy for many: accept the inferno and become such a part of it that you can no longer see it. The second is risky and demands constant vigilance and apprehension: seek and learn to recognize who and what, in the midst of the inferno, are not inferno, then make them endure, give them space."

This would be his answer to the intolerable question that society had posed. He looked back at his new first line. *Hugh Vorax... Hugh* for huge...*Vorax*, Latin for gluttony. *Hugh Vorax. Fred Orbis.* They shared the same verisimilitude. Hugh Vorax the anti-hero, the *evil* Gargantua. Instead of *"gargantuan"*, successive ages will say *"voraxian"*. And the title...it was elegant...sublime. *The Serial Killer's Diet Book*. The best of both worlds. In one fell swoop he had united the two camps of bestsellerdom. *The Serial Killer's Diet Book*. There it was, his ticket out of obscurity. Right then he knew that he would have to dedicate the book to Belle Horizonte. He typed a title page and signed it Federico Orbisini.

Fred Orbis decided to take an extended leave of absence from work. He was becoming conspicuously thin, and at the rate he was going his co-workers would soon grow intolerably nosy, if not downright suspicious. In his apartment he was safe. For 17 years he had lived there, and in all that time not one of his neighbors had ever said a word to him.

He looked at recent events and was pleased. His life had become a bounty, a cornucopia, and he owed it all to becoming a serial killer. How profoundly strange and ironic was life. And now he would stay home and work on the book, (with a murder thrown in every few days to burn off those unsightly pounds), and when it was finished he would emerge as Federico Orbisini, world renown novelist, existential philosopher, raconteur, and lover of women, and then he would pick up stakes and move to the south of France. But, he was getting ahead of himself. To avoid suspicion he would maintain the ruse of Fred Orbis. He walked to the bed and stuffed pillows beneath his jacket until he was as fat as ever. His plan—to stuff himself with pillows to maintain the obese shell—while underneath his body shrank to that of an athlete. He would work out; he would run in place and lift weights, to strengthen muscles lost for a lifetime in flab. He yanked out the pillows. Losing weight had become almost as easy as this.

Fred Orbis wrote 35 pages that day, and like Thomas Wolfe he wanted to announce it to the world. Striding to the window he threw it open and was about to shout out, when he was distracted by the building across the street. The "Refrigerator", as he called it. This retro-Bauhaus monstrosity, designed to cram as many people in it as possible, like so many eggs in a carton. For years he had used this building as negative inspiration. It was definitely *inferno*, of that there was no doubt. He went back to the computer, to the Internet, and in minutes he had located its architect and his address. Manhattan, the upper east side. Sure enough, when he arrived there Fred Orbis saw a beautiful old building of ornate brickwork, sculpted cornices, fluted columns, Corinthian flourishes, intricate wrought iron gates—in short, everything the "Refrigerator" was not. He looked for the name—Arthur Creeb. It was appalling that it contained the word "Art" in it, but he smiled at the irony as he rang the buzzer.

"Yes." a toneless voice responded.

"Is this Arthur Creeb, the famous architect?"

"Yes, this is Arthur Creeb." The voice slightly more pleasant.

"My name is Paul Apollyon. I'm a big fan of yours. I've come all the way from Reykjavik to meet you."

"Reykjavik?...Iceland?"

"Yes, you are very respected and admired there. In fact, I've just come from viewing one of your buildings on 49th street, the large white..."

"Yes, one of my favorites. Please, come in."

The buzzer sounded and Fred Orbis walked inside.

For an instant Arthur Creeb was disconcerted at the sight of the huge fat man who stood in his doorway, but then a smile came over his face. He was, after all, a fan.

"Please, come in. Your name was..."

"Paul Apollyon."

"Is that Greek?"

"Yes, it is."

"It's so nice to meet someone who appreciates architecture." He motioned to a photograph on the wall. "Here's one I did on Fifth Avenue..."

Fred Orbis saw what looked like an industrial freezer.

"Yes, very nice."

"And this one I did last year, in Baltimore..."

A tall obelisk resembling a gigantic stake, ready to impale a colossal vampire.

"Amazing," said Fred Orbis, "what you do to space..."

Arthur Creeb turned around now and saw something unusual in Fred Orbis's hand.

"Is that...Is that an *olive loaf sandwich*?"

Two days later, outside a loft in Greenwich Village, the Postmodern artist Dolus, (whose real name was Jerry Dolinski), was leaving his apartment, when he saw an enormous shadow blot out the street lamp. Looking closer he recognized a man, albeit an extremely large man.

"Can I help you?"

"Are you the famous artist, Dolus?"

The artist smiled to himself. It wasn't unusual for him to be accosted by fans, it was just that they were usually 20 year-old women.

"Yes, I am Dolus."

You mean, Jerry Dolinski.

"It's an honor to meet you, Mr. Dolus. I saw your latest exhibition...the gallery that's completely empty...and it was..." He searched for the right words. "A *revelation*."

"Yes, thank you." He was growing impatient with this fat person. *Now if it had been a young blonde with a tight-fitting shirt...* The artist's thoughts were elsewhere, when something caught his eye. A *kielbasa*. Well, actually, a string of kielbasas, that this fat man for some reason held in his hand.

"Isn't that *kielbasy*?" he asked.

But before he could say another word, they, the kielbasas, or it, the kielbasy, was rammed down his throat, the last one hanging from his mouth like a Christmas ornament, as he sunk to the ground.

Two days later, outside of his Riverside Drive townhouse, the famous fashion designer Per Golesi was approached by a very large man, carrying the latest issue of *Cosmopolitan*, featuring the designer's latest diaphanous creation, on the latest anorexic-yet-buxom model. At first the designer tried, as he did with all common people, to look past this unsightly blob as if he didn't exist, but with Fred Orbis this proved to be impossible.

"Would you *mind...*"

"Excuse me, but aren't you the famous fashion designer, Per Golesi?"

The man took an exasperated breath, that he had to suffer on occasion, the likes of this repulsive fat slob.

"Yes, what is it...the *magazine?*" His thoughts were already uptown, a party of all his beautiful friends.

"Yes, would you mind autographing it for me. My little sister is such a fan..."

The designer grabbed the magazine in one rude motion and took out a gold pen, and as he scrawled his name over the young model's implanted breasts, he glanced up in time to see a whole Genoa salami, like a wayward zeppelin about to crash. An audible gasp, as his eyes closed in a final peace.

Looking over, the doorman saw a disappearing shadow, and then the world famous fashion designer sprawled on the ground, a huge Genoa salami jutting from his mouth. It was the first time he had seen such a thing in twenty-five years as a doorman, and he smiled to himself, content.

24

Darby Montana debated whether to put candles on the table. Dining by candlelight was something she enjoyed, but just by having them there was the implication of something more. We all spoke silent languages, in secret dialects.

First Possibility:

A man is coming to dinner. The table is set with milky white candles, silverware, a gourmet meal. He arrives and senses the mood. The lighting, subdued. Music, Coleman Hawkins—smoke-filled tenor of two AM jazz, and languid slow dancing. A bottle of wine with two long-stemmed glasses. And there *she* is, her face in candlelight and shadow. Her dress, her décolletage, and in a shared glance they agree to a night of passion. And now the delicious savor of anticipation.

Second Possibility:

The apartment is brightly lit. Loud music, upbeat Motown. The woman wears a floppy sweatshirt and jeans; her hair tied in a fuzzy elastic band. The mood is casual. He expects others to drop by at any moment. She will answer every phone call. They will have dinner, and then perhaps watch a video—a comedy, or action-thriller.

Darby thought of the first scene because this was what she missed. She remembered another scene, years before.

Third Possibility:

She meets a handsome man and invites him to dinner. When he arrives everything is as in the *First Possibility*—the lighting, the music, the shared glance. A week later she discovers that he has *many* "girlfriends"; that his relationship with her is based on the fact that she's rich.

After that she is careful not to let on about her money. But then...

Fourth Possibility:

Another man, the same scene—candlelight and wine, a fine dinner she'd prepared. A glance across the table, and in his face she sees that he's bored. (A look like no other.) In a panic she engages him in conversation. *(She'll win him over with her depth and intelligence! Her vibrant mind!)* But he doesn't want words. He wants this exact scene complete to every detail, except with someone else.

Darby looked at the candles in her hands, and then put them on the table.

"What the hell," she said, "it's only dinner."

When the candles were lit there was a knock at the door.

"Hi, Darby, I brought wine. I hope you like red."

"Yes, it's fine. Let me take your coat."

As Philep walked in a smile came to his face.

"What is it?"

"Your apartment, it's so *different* now."

"You mean without the *others*? I hope you don't mind, but I invited Iona to join us."

Philep laughed.

"So, how have you been, Darby?"

"Good, how 'bout you?"

"Fine...What's wrong? Is something troubling you?"

"I've...I've been thinking a lot about what we talked about the other day...at lunch."

"Yes, that was quite a talk."

"You know how in Drama there's a term, *Deus ex machina*."

"Yes, God in the machine. Is that how you see *me*, Darby?"

"Yes."

"Is that why you called, and invited me here tonight?"

She took a long breath.

"What's it like, Philep?...*Hell*?"

"What did Homer say, *'a place of shadows, where nothing is real?'*"

"Dammit Philep, I'm *sick* of literature! I mean, *all* of it, the Bible, the Last Judgment, philosophy, religion. They're just *opinions*. Some fiction somebody made up so they wouldn't feel that life was meaningless!"

"So what does it mean to *you*, Darby? Life, death?"

"I don't know. I *want* to believe, but...I mean, no one really *knows*! That's it, that's what it all comes down to. Not the Bible, not Dante, not...*James Joyce*. No one, except..."

"Darby, do you believe in Good and Evil?"

"Yes, well...I mean, how could I not?"

"Duality. The duality that governs our lives. You spoke of transcending... What if this longing we have to transcend is simply to get beyond duality to *oneness*? Then what would dying be but an opportunity to attain this?"

"So, it's beyond Heaven and Hell..."

"Beyond *thought*...beyond comprehension."

The food was ready and they had dinner, and afterwards Darby turned to Philep.

"Last week, when you were the Devil, and I..."

"Yes, the Devil and Darby Montana."

"I'm *serious*, Philep."

"I know, I'm sorry."

"I'm ready."

"What?"

"I said I'm *ready*."

There was a long pause.

"Are you *sure?*"

"Yes, I'm sure."

"You're positive..."

"Yes."

"All right."

"But there's one thing. It must be..."

"I know. It will happen *gradually*, Darby, as you wish. Each morning for seven days you'll notice the changes. At first they'll seem subtle, but then..." He looked into her eyes. "What was it you wondered? What would have happened if the sperm and egg had waited another day, another week? This will be you a week later."

Darby stared at his face, and then her eyes were drawn to the candles.

"And what about..."

"*Hell? Heaven? Eternity?*...Darby, any questions you have now have no answers. All I can say is that you'll find it quite interesting... Like New York without the pollution."

"What, no fire and brimstone?"

"For others, Darby, not for you."

"So what do I have to do, shall I get a pen?"

"No." Philep laughed, and then he noticed the candles on the table. "These candles... Think about what we've discussed. If you change your mind, simply blow them out. If you agree, let them burn out by themselves."

"And that's *it?*"

"That's it."

"Will I see you again, Philep?"

"We'll see each other again...and we'll have lots to talk about."

"Philep, I was wondering...how you found me?"

"You found *me*, Darby. I heard your voice...Please, give my regrets to the others for not seeing them again."

He started towards the door when she embraced him. She wanted to say thank-you, but he smiled and put his finger to her lips.

"Good-bye, Darby. Take care."

She looked at the candles on the table, at their wicks consumed by flame. For a long time they held her gaze, and then she walked to the bedroom and shut the door.

Detective Arnold sat at his desk and brooded. It was happening again, the vortex that was Devon DeGroot was somehow drawing in all of the city's evil—harpies, basilisks, incubi, succubi, all swirling around his doomed ship. The last time Arnold felt this way he had been shot three times. The only hope was if the promotion had come through—the desk job upstairs he had been trying to get for the last six months. He looked at the other detectives. They seemed oblivious to the encroaching evil, and all at once it seemed to Detective Arnold that he was in a play; that they were actors in some absurd drama, authored by some cruelly indifferent dramatist.

Act IV. Scene I.
[6th Precinct, Mid-Manhattan South. Offices of Homicide and Vice] Two police detectives stand around a coffee machine.

Macduff.   A pastrami on rye.
Donalbain.   *[Writes it on a pad as Macduff hands him a five dollar bill]* Okay, you're down for a pastrami on rye.
Macduff.   What about you?
Donalbain.   Here's me. *[Points to list]*
Macduff.   Chicken salad? No way!
Donalbain.   Whadaya mean, *no way*? I got as much of a chance with chicken salad as you got with pastrami on rye.

Macduff.   *[Shakes head]* I got a feeling about this.

Donalbain.   What? Divination by *lunch meat?*

Macduff.   Right. *Delicatessenomancy.*

Enter *Kozinski*

Kozinski.   What's goin' on?

Donalbain.   It's the "Cold-Cut Killer Pool". You try to guess the next murder weapon.

Kozinski.   How much?

Donalbain.   Five bucks. Everybody's in it.

Kozinski.   *[Hands Donalbain a five]* Okay. Let's see, how 'bout...a pastrami on rye.

Macduff.   *[Smiling at Donalbain]* What did I tell ya?

Donalbain.   Macduff already picked that.

Kozinski.   Okay. How 'bout a chili dog then...with onions and relish.

Donalbain.   *[Checks list]* Nope, McMurphy in motor pool has that.

Kozinski.   Well, what about Liverwurst?

Macduff.   *Liverwurst?* Yuck! What a way to go!

Donalbain.   *[Checks list in depth]* Nope, there's no liverwurst. Is that what you *want? Liverwurst?*

Kozinski.   Yeah, what's wrong with liverwurst? It's an honored and respected lunch meat.

Macduff.   It tastes like paste mixed with chicken shit.

Donalbain.   Liverwurst for Kozinski. *[Kozinski hands him a five]*

Macduff.   Hey, Arnold? You want in on this? *[Arnold shakes his head and remains silent]*

Enter *Devon DeGroot*

DeGroot.   What's news?

Donalbain.   *[Holding up "Cold-Cut Killer Pool"]* We got a...

Macduff.   A *lead,* boss. *[Glares at Donalbain with an "icksnay on the ool-pay" look. Donalbain hides the pool]*

Donalbain.   Right. *[Shuffles through papers on his desk]* Here, boss... that list you wanted.

DeGroot.   What? What's this?

Donalbain.   The list of geniuses in New York. *[Hands him the list]*

DeGroot.   Are these the *obese* geniuses? Christ, this list is three pages long!

Donalbain.   Well, boss, we just got their IQ's. We were gonna cross-reference the names to their driver's licenses in the DMV to find out their weights, but...

Macduff.   The computers were down.

DeGroot.   What do you expect? It's the DMV! *[Examines list]* Have you looked at this list? Do you believe who's on it?

Macduff.   We were as surprised as you, boss.

DeGroot.   *[Scrutinizing list]* Here's *Reggie Jackson,* for Christsake!

Macduff.   180 IQ, boss.

DeGroot.   But *Reggie Jackson?*

Macduff.   He's on the list, boss.

DeGroot.   *[Looks further]* James Dempster?!... *[Donalbain and Macduff nod in unison]* Senator James "Jimmy" Dempster?

Macduff.   We found that one hard to believe ourselves, boss.

DeGroot.   I mean, *Jimmy Dempster?*

Macduff.   198 IQ, boss.

DeGroot.   *[Shakes head in disbelief]* I mean, if Jimmy Dempster is a genius, then I'm the King of Siam. The guy's a moron...an imbecile.

Kozinski.   He might be the next President, boss.

DeGroot.   *[Shakes head in despair]* It used to be that the Presidency *meant* something. If Jimmy Dempster were alive in 1776 he'd be the village idiot.

Macduff.   I know boss, but...

DeGroot.   Is this all we have?

Macduff.   Afraid so. *[Everyone is silent—the office under a funereal pall]*

Enter *Arthur Creeb*, the Postmodern architect's ghost.

Ghost.   *[In an unearthly wail]* Avenge me! Avenge my death! *[Devon DeGroot stares in amazement but the others go about their business as if nothing is amiss]* Avenge me! Avenge my death!

DeGroot.   Who are you? *[He speaks to the ghost directly, the others oblivious to the dialogue]*

Ghost.   I am the ghost of Arthur Creeb, the self-important architect. I have been gruesomely murdered, my life snuffed out prematurely by an olive loaf sandwich.

DeGroot.   *[His ears prick up]* An olive loaf sandwich, you say?

Ghost.   Yes. By an extremely fat man. His name...Paul Apollyon.

DeGroot.   Apollyon, the destroyer. The angel of the bottomless pit. Rev. 9:11.

Ghost.   I know that now. But at the time I was concerned only with my own fame and renown. I never read the Bible, only my press notices and good reviews. I was in *Who's Who*. I was a chair on the *International Federation of Architects and Freemasons*, and the founder of the *Creeb Institute for Postmodern Study*, in Newark, New Jersey. I had an IQ of 182. Thank *God* I was smarter than Reggie Jackson. But alas, the flame of celebrity winks out all too quickly, *tempus edax rerum*...and now I am here, in Erebus, doomed to walk in darkness until I can be avenged.

DeGroot.   When? When did this happen?

Ghost.   Last night. My apartment. 47 E. 86th St... Apartment 3-E.

DeGroot.   This man...this extremely fat man, can you...

Ghost.   A message will come to you. Decipher it, or else you will be damned like me.

DeGroot.   A message?

Ghost.   Avenge me! Avenge my death!

Exit *Ghost*.

Macduff.   Somethin' wrong with the coffee, boss?

DeGroot.   *[To Donalbain]* Is that a pool? *[Points to "Cold-Cut Killer Pool" on desk]*

Donalbain.   *[Nervously]* Um, yeah boss, we just...

DeGroot.   How much?

Donalbain.   *[Noticeably surprised]* Um, five bucks, boss.

DeGroot.   *[Hands him a five]* Olive loaf. Put me down for an olive loaf sandwich.

Donalbain.   *[Scans list]* There's no olive loaf, boss. You're down for an olive loaf sandwich. *[Donalbain, Macduff, and Kozinski trade furtive glances]*

DeGroot.   All right, Donalbain and Macduff, come with me. Kozinski and Arnold, stay by the phones.

Donalbain.   What's up, boss?

Macduff.   Yeah, where're we goin'?

DeGroot.   There's been another murder.

Act IV. Scene II.

[6th Precinct, two days later. The phone is ringing.]

Macduff.   Are you gonna *answer* that? *[Arnold stares at phone]* Hey Arnold, answer the phone for Christsake! It's drivin' me crazy.

Arnold.   *[Reluctantly picks it up]* Yes...yes...all right...all right. *[Hangs up]*

Macduff.   What is it?

Arnold.   Some artist, name of Dolus...found in the Village with a string of kielbasy stuffed down his throat.

Macduff.   *Kielbasy?* Damn!

Kozinski.   What did *you* have?

Macduff.   Anchovy pizza.

Kozinski.   Hmm, I had a BLT.

Macduff.   Did anyone get kielbasy?

Donalbain.   *[Scanning list]* Well, Mendenhall in Internal Affairs had Polish sausage.

Macduff.   Internal Affairs...Fuck 'im.

Enter *Devon DeGroot.*

Donalbain.   Looks like our boy has struck again, boss.

DeGroot.   What?

Arnold.   Some artist in the Village, named Dolus...

Macduff.   Found with a string of kielbasy down his throat. What did you have this time, boss?

DeGroot.   *[With rising anger]* Gentlemen, I hate to remind you that it's our *job* to *catch* this guy! He's making a *mockery* of us. How hard can it be to track down an obese genius serial killer, for Christsake! *[Takes deep breath to control temper]*

Kozinski.   But no one ever sees him, boss, except for those bums...

DeGroot.   *[More composed now]* What about that *one* bum, Dr. Randall Jared?

Donalbain.   Our expert on James Joyce? *[DeGroot nods]*

Macduff.   Still no luck, boss. There are quite a few alleys in New York City.

DeGroot.   Well, I want to know everything there is to know about the latest victim. Kozinski, you go to the scene...Macduff...

Macduff.   What, boss?

DeGroot.   *[Shakes head despondently]* Nothing. *[Walks to office and shuts door]*

[An hour later]

Macduff.   That artist, Dolus...Do you know his real name was *Jerry Dolinski*? He's what they call a *Postmodernist*.

Donalbain.   What's *that* mean?

DeGroot.   It means he can't draw.

Macduff.   No shit, boss. You know what his latest exhibit was? An empty gallery, can you *believe* it?

Kozinski.   *What?*

Macduff.   Yeah. The entire gallery was empty. Some *artist,* eh?

DeGroot.   And the architect, Arthur Creeb...He was a Postmodernist as well.

Macduff.   But how's that fit in with the three girls, and the cabbie?

Kozinski.   Maybe it's some kind of abstruse critique of society.

Macduff.   *Abstruse,* that's a good word...*Crossword puzzles?*

Kozinski.   *[Smiles]* He's making a statement. He's some disgruntled fat genius, holed up in his apartment all his life.

DeGroot.   And what does he do? He puts an ad in the *Voice.*

Macduff.   Because he hasn't gotten laid in thirty years...

Kozinski.   And he gets a response, but she's repulsed because he's obese, for Christsake.

DeGroot.   And he decides to get his revenge on women, who all his life have treated him as a non-entity.

Donalbain.   The other two girls.

DeGroot.   And on the way home from the third girl's murder he takes a cab.

Macduff.   And the cabbie makes some crack about what a fat slob he is.

Kozinski.   So he kills the cabbie...

DeGroot.   And it's his epiphany.

Donalbain.   His *what*-any?

Macduff.   Epiphany, numbskull. It's a revelation.

Kozinski.   Sure. By killing the cabbie he's free to get his revenge on the rest of the world!

DeGroot.   Exactly. And he has this bug up his ass about the Postmodern. Through the murders he's...I don't know, making the world more...*pure.*

Macduff.   What's this guy, stuck in the *16th century,* for Christsake?

173

DeGroot.   Yeah...and he's trying to make the world over in his own image.

Enter *Second Ghost*.

2nd Ghost.   Hey, it's real hot here, man.

DeGroot.   *[Shocked at the second apparition]* Who are *you*? *[Once again their dialogue goes unheard by the others]*

2nd Ghost.   I am Dolus...*Ow! All right, man.* I mean, I'm Jerry Dolinski.

DeGroot.   Are you all right?

2nd Ghost.   Yeah, well it's this *place*, man. These guys here are real pains in the...*Ow!* Every time I say something they don't like they hit me with this, I don't know...*thunderbolt* or something. I'm the artist who...*Okay, okay, so I could never draw! But that's what the Postmodern is all ab...Ow! Will ya cut it out! That shit hurts! Will ya let me talk to the man?...Jesus!*...Sorry...I came here to warn you. There will be another murder.

DeGroot.   Who? When?

2nd Ghost.   I wish I could say, but it's like, all foggy and dark here, man...everything's in shadows. It's like, I can only speak to you symbolically. *Fructu non foliis arborem aestima.*

DeGroot.   *What?* What's that?

2nd Ghost.   I don't know, Italian or something.

DeGroot.   It's Latin, but what does it *mean*?

2nd Ghost.   How the hell should *I* know? I'm a Postmodernist... *OW! All right, I'm a simulacrum! I'm a simulacrum!*...What the hell's a simulacrum? *Ow! Jesus, that hurts*...You better stop him.

DeGroot.   The killer? What does he look like? What's his name?

2nd Ghost.   I don't know. He's fat, man. We're talkin' *ob...Ow!* Well he *was*, did you see the *size* of him? God, I hate this place.

DeGroot.   Where are you now?

2nd Ghost.   I don't know. *Hey, where am I again?*...Hell, I'm in Hell, man.

DeGroot.   What's it like?

2nd Ghost.   Well, it's a lot like...*Ow! Ow!*...Listen, I can't talk anymore. Remember, *Fructu non foliis arborem aestima.* I gotta go, man. *What?...Oh yeah*...Avenge me. Avenge my death!

Exit Second Ghost.

Macduff.   What're you doin', boss?

DeGroot.   *[Scribbling madly on a piece of paper]* Fructu non foliis arborem aestima. *[Hands it to Macduff]* I want this translated, ASAP.

Donalbain.   *[Looking on]* What is it, Italian?

Macduff.   It's *Latin*, Nimrod. Are you okay, boss? For a few minutes there you looked pretty peculiar.

DeGroot.   It's nothing. Just find what it means.

[Three hours later]

Macduff.   That Latin is from *Phaedrus*, boss. An ancient Roman fabulist, circa 40 AD. It means *"Judge a tree by its fruit, not by its leaves"*...Why do you wanna know *that*, boss?

DeGroot.   He's going to kill again.

Macduff.   The Cold-Cut Killer?

DeGroot.   And it has to do with that phrase. What were we talking about before?

Kozinski.   The Postmodern.

DeGroot.   It's a simulacrum.

Donalbain.   A *what?* *[Looks to Macduff and Kozinski but they shrug their shoulders]*

DeGroot.   He's going after everything he thinks is phony. Fake. Sham. Image over reality.

Macduff.   Like the models.

DeGroot.   Like the models, but something else.

Macduff.   What, boss?

DeGroot.   I have no idea.

175

Act IV. Scene III.
[6th Precinct. A dour mood prevails because there has been another murder]

Kozinski.　　His name was Per Golesi...the famous fashion designer.

Macduff.　　There's your tie-in with the models, boss.

Donalbain.　　He was found with a foot-long salami rammed down his throat.

Kozinski.　　*Really?* I *got* salami! *[Beams at the others]* Look it up, Donalbain.

Donalbain.　　*[Looks through latest Pool]* You put down *hard* salami, Kozinski.

Kozinski.　　So?

Donalbain.　　It was *Genoa.*

Kozinski.　　Damn!

DeGroot.　　Gentlemen, that makes seven dead. *[Shakes head in disgust]* And this happened right outside a townhouse on Riverside Drive, for Christsake! You mean to tell me there were no *witnesses?* *[Temper flaring]*

Macduff.　　Well, no. We questioned everybody, boss. The doorman says he didn't see a thing...just the guy on the ground with the salami stuck down his throat.

DeGroot.　　*[Calming himself]* So, we have three young models...and now we have a fashion designer...two sides of the same coin. And we have an architect and an artist, both of dubious distinction.

Macduff.　　This guy's hung up on the arts.

DeGroot.　　So who's *next?* A musician? a writer?

Enter *Third Ghost.*

3rd Ghost.　　This place is appalling, really. I mean, how can you expect me to live in such a...I mean it's all *gray.* Who was the designer, *Babar?* It's like I'm inside of an...*no, no please, not the thunderbolt, I'll...yes, I'll be good, I... I promise!*

176

DeGroot.   Who *are* you? *[By now, used to these supernatural visitations]*

3rd Ghost.   I am Per Golesi, the famous...*Ow! All right!*...I used to design woman's clothes...*What?...Yes, if you insist. Where's that piece of paper...* [Receives a document from an invisible source and reads from it] I, Per Golesi, was an enslaver of women, who kept them perpetually locked in a false view of themselves. Because of me, millions of women became anorexic, and had costly and dangerous breast implants so they could look like, in my own words, a "stacked 12 year-old"...*Must I go on, I mean...Ow! Ow! All right! All right!*...My entire career was built on envy and greed, and I am heartily sorry for the shame and confusion I've caused women everywhere, by setting up such impossible standards and calling them reality...*There, are you happy?*

DeGroot.   Who are you talking to?

3rd Ghost.   Them.

DeGroot. Who's *them...God?*

3rd Ghost.   *[Cautiously, for fear of the thunderbolt]* My gracious hosts wish to remain anonymous.

DeGroot.   Where are you?

3rd Ghost.   I have been informed by my hosts that this is Hell...*all right, Erebus*...but a rose by any other name...

DeGroot.   What is it like?

3rd Ghost.   It's like New Jersey in July...*Ow!* I mean, it's actually quite lovely! Like the tropics...I have been sent to you as the last of the three...Heed our warning. Soon you will receive a message. You must decipher it at all costs, or else be doomed, like me...It's so awful, everyone here is *fat...Ow! Ow! I'm sorry your Excellency, your Greatness*...Oh yes...Avenge me! Avenge my death!

Exit Third Ghost.

Donalbain.   Do you *believe* this?

Macduff.   What?

177

Donalbain.   I just got another call. Somebody wanted to turn in their "fat" neighbor...claimed he was the "Cold-Cut Killer"... That makes 879 this week.

Macduff.   That's amazing.

Kozinski.   People don't like *fat* people.

Macduff.   New Yorkers, ya gotta love 'em! I remember this one guy, he was *so* fat...

Arnold.   *[Hands mail to DeGroot]* Mail's here, boss.

DeGroot.   *[Sorts through mail]* Look at this return address. *[Shows others]*

Donalbain.   Kennie Sangfwa...Parsippany, New Jersey.

Macduff.   *Sangfwa?* That's a word, isn't it? I heard it on *Jeopardy.*

Kozinski.   *Sangfroid.* I've used it in crossword puzzles. It's French. It means...

DeGroot.   It's an anagram.

Macduff.   What?

DeGroot.   The name's an anagram. *Look... [Gets piece of paper and writes the name, and then rearranges the letters]*

Donalbain.   Kennie Sangfwa is *Finnegans Wake?*

DeGroot.   It's our boy. *[Opens letter, then turns immediately to others]* I want that bum back in here.

Donalbain.   You mean *Sven?* The *Red Sox* fan?

DeGroot.   No, the *other* bum. Our Dr. Randall Jared, the world's foremost expert on *Finnegans Wake.* It's imperative that we decipher this message. Arnold, Donalbain, Macduff, Kozinski...I want you to scour every alley in the city if you have to, but *find that bum!*

Exit *Donalbain, Macduff, and Kozinski.*

Arnold.   *[Hesitantly]* Boss, I was wondering...

DeGroot.   What is it?

Arnold.   That promotion I talked to you about. I was wondering...well, if you heard anything?

DeGroot.   Not yet. Be patient. I've given you my recommendation.
Arnold.   I know, boss, thanks, but, it's just that the sooner...
DeGroot.   Besides, with this case we can't spare anybody anyway. *Goddamn budget cuts!* How am I supposed to run an investigation with all these goddamn cut-backs? *[Looks avuncularly at Arnold]* Be patient. I'll talk to them today.
Arnold.   Thanks, boss.
DeGroot.   Now find that bum.

Exit *Arnold.*

Devon DeGroot stared at the letter on his desk...

> Onus Mundi the airy bus takes a'midtow conducing dee, dee-dee. Brashing the bim bound Artie Face, cool bossy brings brift a lung lent lease. Den Archie tak no artin hymn, wrecked tangle O' Live O'Dyin eyes, is donus mundi make! Bar-oak composter too-dimage, wheedle de-dee juneau a Sam-I-ham or Sal am I? Big apple eon, dis Troy labile vent, the odiisques in cunabula. Sellebus sickubus salve, to wait, to whit, toulouse, to fie! O Willy, O Wony, O'Nanzave erneck? Unseamy agricolus, inda hellus swoon. Mad-essen Rusk aurum—veneris septem vie—to ovum acetorum hircinious ewe.
>> *The nasty nay may make yer day,*
>> *or else you be dammin hell'away!*

Five hours later:

"We got him, boss!" said Macduff. He led in the eminent Dr. Randall Jared, the world's foremost authority on *Finnegans Wake*—a tatterdemalion in greasy stains, and rotted food.

179

"Is he drunk or sober?" DeGroot whispered.

"It's hard to tell."

"Where did you find him?"

"An alley down by NYU, boss."

"He said the uptown alleys were too snobby." said Kozinski. "The ones in the Village were more *literary*."

"*Litter...airy!*" Dr. Jared said with a bright smile. "You see, both properties of a New York alley, hence the ideal place for me. In fact, I had just gotten settled in my new domicile when I received your invitation. I wore my good coat for the occasion." He pulled on the ragged edges of the worn, soiled cloth.

DeGroot motioned for him to sit down.

"Dr. Jared, we have a very important assignment for you... you being the world's foremost expert on James Joyce and *Finnegans Wake*."

"I met the most delightful person the other day." Dr. Jared began. "A fellow scholar, a man of letters, a most amusing fellow... although seemingly obsessed with something called the '*World Series*', and someone named *Bill Buckner*...One meets the most interesting people in the infrequently traversed by-ways."

"Dr. Jared." DeGroot was growing impatient. "We have a letter here. We were wondering if you could translate it for us?" He handed the letter to the bum, and for a moment a whiff of decomposing cabbage rose in the air.

"Where did you get this?" the bum asked.

"It's evidence in a murder investigation. It's vital that it be deciphered."

The others moved downwind.

"This is in *Finnegans Wakean*. It shouldn't be too difficult...*It went right through his legs*."

"*What?* It says *that?*"

"Oh, no. That's what my new *friend* always says, it went right through his..."

"Dr. Jared, *please*..." He motioned to the letter. "If you will. It's very important."

"Yes, of course." He turned back to the letter with the bearing of a distinguished, albeit dilapidated scholar, as he went through it line by line.

"*Onus Mundi*...the world's burden...He has a high opinion of himself, whoever wrote this...*The airy bus*...that's Erebus, the place in Hell where the newly dead dwell...*takes a̓midtow conducing*...a play on takes a bus to midtown, this police precinct, and the third part is that he will 'take you for a ride' on the 'bus', which is Erebus, or Hell...He's very confident that he'll confound you."

"It *says* that?" asked DeGroot.

"Right here..." The bum pointed to the next words. "*Conducing dee, dee-dee*...*Conducing* is confounding and making a dunce of, and this is *you*...*dee, dee-dee*, for *Detective Devon DeGroot*..."

"So he's calling me a fool."

"More like a challenge, as if he's challenging you to a duel." He read on. "*Brashing the bim bound Artie Face*...here we have brash and artifice...What were the names of the last three vicitms?"

"Creeb...Dolus..."

"Dolus is Latin for artifice. And bashing 'bimboes', if you will, who are somehow bound or choked, but also bound by their destinies, by societal pressures to fit an unreal image. But also bound for death, as in hell-bound..."

"It says all *that*?"

"*Finnegans Wakean* is the most expressively deep and rich of all languages." Dr. Jared explained. "If you wrote all that *Finnegans Wake* actually meant it would take over 5000 pages. It is the supreme triumph of the English language, liberated into its true grandeur and beauty...But I digress. Back to the letter...*cool bossy*..."

"Kielbasy!" erupted Donalbain.

"Yes! Very good. You see, even a mind mired in the quotidian can understand and appreciate it."

Donalbain smiled proudly.

*"Brings brift a lung lent lease...*this is about the brevity of existence, made even briefer when there's no more air in your lungs!" he chuckled to himself. "The choking image again...*Den Archie tak*...then the architect...also 'tack', as in a course of action, and 'tacky'...crass, vulgar...*no artin hymn*...this is good, it says there is no *art* in him..."

"The architect's first name was Arthur." said DeGroot.

"Ah! He's commenting on his name, as well as the shallowness of his work. But also 'art in him' becomes *ardent hymn*. This is religious to whoever wrote this. A kind of sanctifying rite is being performed here...a purification...*wrecked tangle*...rectangle and 'wrecked angle', or a tangle of lines, again commenting on the banality of the architect...then *O'Live*...Was he by chance choked to death by an olive loaf sandwich?"

"Yes."

Macduff winked at the others, because "Olive loaf" had won big for DeGroot in the "Cold-Cut Killer Pool".

"O'Dyin eyes is...this is 'Dionysus', another name for Bacchus..."

"The bacchanals."

"But it's also 'dying eyes'...The killer gets pleasure from gazing into the eyes of his victims. He sees an innocence there. This is what he wants to find...And then here, he admits that he's the killer...*donus mundi make*. Although he's saying that perhaps he's not their murderer, but rather their savior. *Donus mundi*...the world's gift....Might I trouble you for a drink?"

"Get him a cup of coffee." DeGroot said to Donalbain.

"This next line...*Bar-oak*, obviously baroque, and *composter* is composer, although the juxtaposition implies that this person is a sham...he shares something with a baroque composer, but he is referred to as a *'composter'*, meaning..."

"We get the idea."

Donalbain handed the bum a cup of coffee, along with a cinnamon cruller.

"Um, this is good. Thank you...This here...too-dimage is a play on 'too dim', meaning this composter...but it also implies 'too damaged', as well as 'two dimensions'...Perhaps this person is involved in something two-dimensional, like painting, or..."

"Photography." said DeGroot. "He was a fashion designer."

"Ah..." Dr. Jared nodded. "*Wheedle de-dee*...he's poking fun at the detective here. And then he asks if you know him...'d'ya know' becomes *juneau*...but it also implies that it will be a cold day in Hell when you find him. But it's also a play on Noah's ark, and Genoa salami...There's also a ham sandwich in here, and Sam the Sham and Dr. Seuss, and this...*Sal am I?* He's asking rhetorically if he isn't in fact the savior, the bringer of salvation..."

"So, he has a God complex..."

"Well, not *the* God, but a god...like the ancient Greeks and Romans. He's someone hopelessly lost in a romantic view of the past. The grandeur that was Greece, the glory that was Rome, *etcetera, etcetera*...I wouldn't be surprised if he also fancied himself in the Middle Ages, like some courtly knight, rudely awakened to the 20th century...Here's another classical reference...*Big apple eon, dis Troy*...Big apple of course needs no translation, but it leads into..."

"Apollyon...the destroyer."

"Yes...I applaud you on your Classical education, sir." He executed an approving bow. "Here again his delusions of grandeur... *eon* implies the magnitude of his own deeds, along with Troy, but here *'dis Troy'*, as in 'dis', meaning to dissemble, to disregard or disrespect, so in a sense he's putting himself beyond the ancients, telling us that he *is* Apollyon...*Labile vent*...Labile is changing, and also a play on 'bile'. And vent, he's venting his spleen, but in many guises...he's protean."

"The different identities."

"*The odiisques in cunabula*...odalisques are female slaves or concubines...meaning they are a slave to something...fashion perhaps, and through this become concubines...*Incunabula*...the earliest traces of anything, like a demon dormant for eons suddenly rising...It also means any books printed before 1501, so here again the medieval mind. And also he's probably a writer...but not popular by any means, although he *wants* to be...*Sellebus sickubus*...he's saying that he was sick of his celibacy, but by trying to break it he released a succubus..."

"A demon."

"And also a further reference to the demoniac female form... and then *salve* is 'slave', but also salve as in a palliative...*to wait*... meaning the pain of his waiting. This man has spent his whole life waiting, but he's also advising *you* to wait."

"For the next victim?"

"It appears so...Also, wait is a play on 'weight'...apparently he's quite fat...but then *to whit*...he's both praising his own wit, and challenging you to a battle of wits...*toulouse*...from the French painter, who was a dwarf and an outcast...how he sees himself, as an outcast. However, through this ritual he's somehow transforming into someone else."

"What's this, *to fie?*"

"It's a curse, an imprecation. He's cursing you. *To fire!...Go to Hell,* so to speak. And then this...*O Willy, O Wony*...will he or won't he, meaning will you catch him? *O'Nan* is you...or rather, what he *thinks* of you."

"How's that?"

"*Onan* is the Greek god of masturbation."

DeGroot shot the gimlet eye at his detectives to keep them silent.

"He goes on to say that you must save your own neck by saving the next victim's...*unseamy*...of course, the unseemly nature of the whole affair. He feels that he has been drawn into it somehow against his will. But also unseamy is 'you see me'...and then he goes on to tell you where to look..."

At this Devon DeGroot's eyes opened wide.

"*Agricolus*...Latin for farmer...and then, *inda hellus* is a play on 'in the dell' and 'in hell', and also inda for *indago*...Latin for 'track down or hunt'. But it *really* means in the delicatessen...He's telling us which delicatessen...*Mad-essen*...italicized for poetic purposes... 'Mad-eating', the madness of gluttony, one of the Seven Deadly Sins. But also Madison Avenue, the advertising capital, and the birthplace of bulimia...And then, here...*Rusk aurum*...*aurum* is gold, and *Rusk* is 'Ruskie' or Russian, or in this case 'rush'. But it also implies *risk*...So, 'gold rush', the 49'ers..."

"Madison and 49th." said Macduff.

"Precisely."

"When?"

"*Veneris* is Friday. *Septem* is seven o'clock, and *ovum acetorum* is egg salad sandwich."

Macduff and Donalbain winced, because they had a stromboli and a knish in the next Pool.

"He's telling you that this is your only chance to catch him... and then..."

"What is it, doctor?"

"See this here...*hircinious ewe*...he says you smell like a goat!... He concludes with a song, a kind of jig he made up, especially for you...this of course implying that the 'jig is up' if you catch him, but it's also a taunt that you won't, in which case the jig will be up for you...*The nasty nay may make your day, or else you be dammin hell'away!* He's saying that if you don't stop him you will be damned, and you will also damn yourself."

The doctor looked up now, exhilarated.

"That was great! I feel splendid!"

185

"Thank you doctor," said DeGroot, "we couldn't have done it without you."

"*Finnegans Wakean* is a most beautiful language. I'm surprised that more authors haven't taken to employing it…The man who wrote this is a true scholar. I would be pleased to dine with him sometime, and discuss philosophy. If you see him give him my card…"

The doctor handed Devon DeGroot a soiled, dog-eared, handwritten business card:

Dr. Randall Jared, Ph.D.

The Alley off Seventh and Bleecker.

"Thank you, doctor. I'll give him your best." He turned to Kozinski. "Please escort the doctor out, and get him a good meal… and then take him to Goodwill and get him some decent clothes, for Christsake!"

"So what now, boss?" asked Macduff. "I mean, do you think all that stuff is really *in* there? "

"Yeah," said Donalbain, "I mean, how much faith are we gonna put in the Doc?"

"You and Mucduff stake out the delicatessen."

"But boss, it's only *Wednesday*."

"That's all right. We'll go in six hour shifts. You and Donalbain take the first watch. Then Arnold and I will relieve you. If he shows we don't want to miss him."

"*Damn!*" said Donalbain. He held the latest "Cold-Cut Killer Pool" in his hand.

"What is it?" asked DeGroot.

"It's McMurphy from Motorpool…He has '*Egg Salad Sandwich*'."

Donalbain and Macduff shook their heads in frustration, while Detective Arnold buried his head in his hands.

Her eyes were a brown that was almost black. There was a darkness there that compelled her, and she thought about this thing called a mirror—glass backed with silver, a quarter-inch thick—but as she gazed at it she saw depth in the flat surface. What must early man have thought, in coming upon his image in a puddle on the ground—that another man lived in the water? And what happened when he realized that it was himself? How did the world change because of this? Elizabeth Aphelion saw her own face looking out, but one mirror implied many. Her reflection, and then her face reflected back, on and on, and which was real?

She remembered the phone call. The cringe throughout her body when she heard Jacqueline Jimson-Weed's voice.

"Hi, Elizabeth. I'm going to be in Manhattan this weekend. I thought I might..."

Her own voice, like an actor mouthing lines.

"Yes, that'll be great."

"Then I'll see you on Friday."

She vaguely remembered something about her book, *(her goddamn book)*. It was time to go to work. But then, it was Wednesday, Mr. Monde's. An hour of house cleaning, and then a game of chess, or a story. This one day a week kept her sane.

The poems sat on the dresser, the new ones she had written. And she'd give them to Jacqueline, and Jacqueline would say that they were fine but that the publisher wanted five more, or ten more, or a *million* more—when would it end? (Michael was right.) But then, what if this was her only chance? She looked out from the mirror as if trapped inside herself, and she thought of the dogs in the park—their one furious moment before going back to sleep. And this was what she dreaded. The sleep.

From Mr. Monde's apartment the city was quiet. The world's inertia came to rest here, and she felt restored. She didn't even mind the housework, like a daydream, dusting the old books. An old volume noticed for the first time, Marlowe's *The Tragedy of Doctor Faustus.* On the first page: *Faustus—Latin for lucky.* At this Cleo hopped from the couch and trotted to the door. Mr. Monde was home.

"Hello Cleo...Hello Elizabeth."

"Hello Mr. Monde."

"I was wondering, Elizabeth, if you like baseball?"

"Baseball?" The question seemed incongruous coming from Mr. Monde, and she almost laughed. "I guess so. I mean, I've seen a few games."

"Well good, because baseball sets the scene for Washington's third test. Would you like to hear the story?"

"Yes, I would."

"Good." He walked over to the painting on the wall. "Look at our old friend George...Do you believe that someone can discern a person's inner life, simply by looking at their face?"

Suddenly she was uncomfortable.

"They said of Washington that his face showed a constant conflict and mastery over passion. We've already discussed his passion. Now let's speak of his temper. There was a battle...August, 1776...

four months before Trenton. A place called Kip's Bay, not too far from here, in fact. British ships cannonaded the shore for two hours, and the din was so loud and frightening that the Colonial troops fled the beach as the British landed without a musket being fired. Washington had just ridden five miles from headquarters, and when he saw his troops running away, their guns and ammunition strewn across the ground, he went into a fury. Thomas Jefferson had said that *'if Washington's temper broke its bonds, he was most tremendous in his wrath.'* And this day, astride his horse, he drew his sword and rode towards the enemy as if to take them on by himself, only to realize the futility, and return in a rage. His officers thought him so vexed that they believed he sought death over life, and they watched him throw his hat to the ground and shout, *'Good God, have I got such troops as these!'* Washington's temper almost cost him his life that day, and that would have cost the country a great deal more. His temper was something that plagued him his entire life, and this is the subject of the third test..."

Mr. Monde walked to the kitchen and brought back two bottles of beer.

"To get us in the spirit of the game." he said. "I've always loved baseball. I used to like the *Yankees*, but that was a long time ago. Nowadays professional sports has gotten so...well, it's not like it used to be."

"When I went to Smith I saw a *Red Sox* game once." said Elizabeth.

"I've always *disliked* the Red Sox. But to the story...The year is 1911, a golden age for baseball. There are clubs everywhere. Every town and every factory has a team. And in a little town in Vermont called Indian Head, there is a club called the *'Warriors'*. They are led by a fiery, white-haired manager by the name of Josiah Moses Kreel, although everyone calls him 'Hickory'..."

"Hickory?"

"Years before when he was a player, he was called out on strikes by the umpire and he didn't appreciate the call...so he went after the ump with his bat, which was this thick club of hickory wood."

Mr. Monde paused to take a sip of beer.

"So, after his playing days are over, Hickory Kreel becomes a manager. And he leads the old *Cincinnati Red Stockings* to two straight pennants at the turn of the century. But then, there's another *incident*...a disputed call on a close play, and Hickory Kreel runs from the dugout with his bat, and...well, the umpire goes to the hospital for six months, and Hickory goes to jail.

"When he gets out he tries to get another managing job, but no one will hire him. So he rides the rails, does odd jobs. But then a year or two later he wanders into a small town in Vermont. They have a ball club called the *'Warriors'*, and are *'between managers'*... some scandal involving a teenage girl...And so, Hickory Kreel lands the job.

"The first year the team spends in the cellar, because they aren't very good. They're always complaining about not getting paid on time, and that their uniforms are old and ratty. And Hickory, well, he scours the soup kitchens and railroad yards for prospects... players who want to win more than they want to complain, and before you know it, the *Warriors* start winning. You see, in spite of his temper, Hickory Kreel is a great manager. He could have been one of the best, but...Anyway, by the summer of 1911 the *Indian Head Warriors* are one of the best teams in the league, in a neck-and-neck pennant race with the *Littleton Lions*, the perennial champs of the White Mountain League.

"Well, the summer winds down, and on the last day of the season the two teams are tied, the final game to decide the pennant... It's hot, a real scorcher, and on the day of the game the temperature soars into the high 90's. And let me tell you, there's no love lost between these two teams.

"But before I tell you about the game, I should tell you about the players, the *Indian Head* starting nine...Hickory Kreel had assembled quite a cast of misfits and ne'er-do-wells. 'Lefty' Vandevoort, their starting pitcher, had been a hobo and a drunk. In fact, Hickory met him in a boxcar."

"When he was riding the rails?"

"No, in a poker game."

"So, he was a left-hander?"

"No, he was a *right*-hander. He took the nickname '*Lefty*' so he could confuse the opposing batters.

Elizabeth smiled.

"Then there was 'Cork-Screw' Collins. *He* was the left-hander. They said his curve ball was so good that the opposing hitters ended up curled around like a cork-screw when they swung and missed...The catcher was this big Russian named Vladimir Gromykin. They called him 'Tolstoi', because he was always reading *War and Peace* in the dugout. He had been a Hussar in the Russian Army, so the story goes, and had fought a duel with sabres. And in fact, he had this big scar that ran all the way down his face...The infield saw 'Havana' Hufstetler at first..."

"*Havana Hufstetler?*"

"He claimed that his father went up San Juan Hill with Teddy Roosevelt, but it was really because he liked to smoke Havana cigars... Then there was the second baseman, Norton James Walkonstop..."

Elizabeth laughed.

"Norton James Walkonstop doesn't sound like a baseball player's name."

"I know. That's why they called him 'Pig Iron Pete', because he used to work in a foundry...Let's see, the short-stop was a kid they called 'Farmboy.'"

"Because he lived on a farm?"

"No, he came from New York City, but his last name was *Farmer*...The third baseman was this big German fellow named Otto Schmelling, who wore this thick handlebar mustache."

"What did they call him?"

"*Bismarck*. In the outfield they had 'Flea Circus' Flannagan in center, 'Two-times' Roudebaugh in right, and 'Cannonball' Mertz in left."

"Because he threw like a cannonball?"

"No, because his grandfather lost an arm at Gettysburg to one. It was handed down as a family heirloom...the cannonball, not the arm...and his grandson, Mordechai Mertz, kept it in the dugout."

"The *cannonball?*"

"For good luck...Which brings us to the game. Would you like another beer?"

"Not yet, thanks."

"By the third inning there is still no score, but 'Cork-Screw' Collins is running out of gas. He stayed out a bit late the night before, you see. And this rookie pitcher at the end of the *Warrior* bench keeps asking if *he* can go in the game. The kid's pretty good, but Hickory hardly ever lets him play. You see, his name is Chester Alan Arthur Polk..."

"You mean..."

"One of the great grandsons of Thomas Jefferson Polk, the slave owner. And for reasons that not even Hickory is aware of, he *hates* this young pitcher. So he leaves 'Cork-Screw' in the game, and by the end of the inning the *Lions* lead 2 to 0.

"A few innings later, the Warriors score two runs to tie it, and it's like this until the bottom of the ninth...'Knot-hole' Simms is the first batter, and 'Lefty' Vandevoort strikes him out."

"Lefty the *righty?*"

"Yes. But the next batter is 'Freight Train' Benedict, the *Lions'* best and meanest player, and the crowd goes wild. You see, Benedict played for the *Warriors* the season before, but he skipped to the *Lions* for more money. Anyway, 'Lefty' ends up walking him, and meanwhile there's this constant heckling between the two dugouts, in four or five different languages. The next batter is 'Dago' Randazzo, and he bunts 'Freight Train' over to second."

"*Dago?...*"

"These were less enlightened times, Elizabeth...This of course brings all kinds of commotion from the crowd, the winning run on second...two outs. And of course, Chester Alan Arthur Polk says *'Put me in Coach, put me in!'* and Hickory yells, *'Sit down!'*...The batter is 'Slide Rule' Rubosky."

"What, was he a *mathematician?*"

"Hardly. He had this rule about always sliding with his spikes held high."

"Charming."

"It was a different game then, Elizabeth, like a *war*, as Ty Cobb would say...So, we have a situation here ripe with possibility. It's now 98 degrees. Tempers are high...The on-deck batter is 'One Eye' Watson, who's in a slump, so Hickory tells 'Lefty' to walk 'Slide Rule' to pitch to 'One Eye'."

"Why do they call him *'One Eye'*?

"He always keeps his eye closest to the pitcher opened, and the other one closed, so it won't distract him."

"Does it work?"

"Not lately. However, 'Lefty' is too careful, and he walks 'One Eye' to load the bases, putting the hated 'Freight Train' Benedict on third. This brings up one of the team's better hitters, the *Lions'* first baseman, a kid they call 'Joe Irish'...The first pitch is a strike. The next, strike two, and the fans are suddenly hushed. But the next pitch is a liner to left, and as 'Freight Train' Benedict roars home, 'Cannonball' Mertz fires a strike to home plate. There is a horrible sound, like two trains colliding. A cloud of dust, and then the umpire shouts, *'Safe!'*, and all hell breaks loose! Hickory Kreel grabs his bat, and is about to rush the field when he feels a hand holding him back. It's the young pitcher, Chester Alan Arthur Polk. *'No, Coach.'* he says, and Hickory raises his bat to bash the kid's head in when their eyes meet, and in that instant something happens, something indescribable. Hickory sits down, he puts his bat aside."

"I'm not sure I understand." said Elizabeth.

"You see, if he hadn't intervened...well, let's look at the same scene played out a different way. The umpire shouts *'Safe!'*, and Hickory grabs his bat. Both benches rush the field, a *donnybrook*, as they used to say, and Hickory is like a man possessed. He spots the first baseman, the kid who got the winning hit, and he sees red. He hits him with a full swing of the bat, and he kills him.

"The first baseman, the kid they called 'Joe Irish', was Joe Kennedy, who six years later would have had a son named John Fitzgerald."

"JFK..."

"Yes. But Hickory holds his temper. He even congratulates the opposing manager. And after the season he retires to a farm, somewhere in Virginia, while Joe Kennedy, for better or worse, becomes a millionaire."

"That's some story, Mr. Monde."

"It was Washington's hardest test so far. There was a moment there when he..." He looked at Elizabeth. "But, there's still one more test. And this will be the hardest of all."

"You mean it hasn't happened yet?"

"It's happening right now, as we speak."

"And how is he doing?"

"Very well. But like in chess, Elizabeth, even the best opponents can falter, they can make a mistake."

Mr. Monde stroked Cleo behind the ears, and she made a sound like a sigh.

"Or something happens, something unexpected."

The cat opened her eyes, and for a moment seemed almost to smile.

Fred Orbis looked in the mirror and was happy. He was a shadow of his former self, but then again, he had cast a very large shadow. His math had been flawless. Seven murders, times 30 pounds per murder, meant that he had lost 210 pounds, and this was nothing short of miraculous. True, at nearly 300 pounds he was still obese, but this was one of those cup half-full or half-empty kinds of things, and as he stared at his new body, visions of the life that awaited danced nimbly in his head. But then, one mustn't count one's chickens...There'd be plenty of time for celebration after three more murders. And he had to make sure that he stopped at three. Heaven help him if he was forced to kill beyond this limit, and he got too thin.

He reflected on the past few weeks. *Fortunae vicissitudines.* To think it all started with a personal ad, and then the chance meeting with Belle Horizonte. How unfathomable was the world! A few months before his conscience was clear, his soul unblemished, and he was utterly miserable. Now, seven murders later...Thoughts of St. Augustine, *felix culpa.* The Fall of Man necessitated the Redeemer, and he, Fred Orbis, was the world, (or at least as *fat* as the world); Belle Horizonte the Christ, and through her he'd been redeemed. He looked now on that first date as something holy—a Sacrament. True, at the time he had felt bitterness, when his romantic view of things had been rudely shattered, but can you blame him? Had he ever known a woman, or a woman's tenderness? Not even his mother, who left to join a convent when he was a month old. So consequently, they were something mythical. The maiden, pure and chaste—he, the noble knight. And since he had never known anything else, the myth sufficed.

From another viewpoint, what were those first three dates but the drama of Adam and Eve; the expulsion from the Garden? *Reality*, that's what he had found, and he liked it. The world was a disgusting, venal, corrupt place, but so what? He was finally *happy*—the feeling, so new and unprecedented. And what was it like, this happiness? It filled him as the tons of food had filled him, but with food he was never full, whereas this happiness filled him completely. It seemed that he had stumbled upon a corollary: *The overall lack of happiness in the world filled everyone with a need to consume, and this appetite was never satisfied. And behold the result. But where there is happiness there is satisfaction, contentment, and instead of homo consummatus we have homo animus contentus.* The world according to Fred Orbis seemed to be nothing more than a wrong turn on the road towards happiness.

He stared at himself in the mirror and saw who he would become, and then he gazed beyond at his ideal world. First of all, if people gave up the blind rage to consume there would be no more ugly buildings, because ugly buildings only went up because of money. This would eliminate over half the buildings in Manhattan. Imagine the space, the light, the sky...things that many New Yorkers had never seen before. Then of course, no spurious art movements would flourish, since they would be recognized immediately for what they were, *inferno*. Professional sports would be abolished as a mindless misdirection of energy, and hence there would be all these empty stadiums sitting around, and what better place to put all of this so-called art and so-called literature that crowded the galleries and bestseller lists? And then, once every stadium was filled, a magnificent bonfire, as the collective consciousness was purged. Purified, through this burnt offering to the Gods of Aesthetics. And throughout the land these mountains of flames would be lamps lighting the way to a new Golden Age, the glory that was Greece, the grandeur that was Rome, reborn! Corporations would be dismantled, since corporations were the embodiment of this misdirected pursuit of happiness, and all CEO's would be forced to run Food Banks and soup kitchens, or else be exiled to someplace remote like Greenland, or Antarctica. And the media. He couldn't help but notice the parallels between *"media"* and *"Medea"*, both devouring their children. Commercials would be gone, since they were about money and money was *inferno*—and since TV was fueled by the dollar it would cease to exist as we knew it. No longer would there be formulaic shows, with trite plots and stereotyped characters inspiring envy and lust in the populace. No, in Fred Orbis's ideal world all shows would be in *Latin*—so if someone wanted to watch TV they would have to get a Classical education. And in one fell swoop literacy would skyrocket, aesthetics blossom, sensibilities expand. Cabbies would discuss Plato, housewives contemplate Descartes, and philosophers would be the new Superstars! They would be signed to million dollar contracts, their faces on every maga...*Hold on there,* Fred Orbis thought. There wouldn't be any *money*, so this wouldn't work. See how pernicious it was, that even *he* could suffer a momentary relapse! It was insidious and pervasive and the sooner it was abolished the better. But then, for the sake of argument one might ask, "If we were to eliminate money then how will we get our food and clothing?" And he would respond, "When one is philosophical one doesn't worry about such things. Consider the lily..." "But then, what would we do for diversion? Surely even the happiest of men might need an occasional distraction." And he would point to his bookshelf. "There is Homer, Virgil, Cicero...

Dante, Shakespeare, Cervantes...Melville, Joyce, Orbisini..." And they would skulk away to their dimly lit rooms, and from beneath hidden floorboards bring out one of the forbidden texts. Tom Clancy or God forbid, Stephen King, and they would devour the words in secret by candlelight. Throughout the land secret societies would form, clandestine book groups meeting in places like the *Chestnut Tree Cafe*, where spy thrillers and romance novels, and New Age self-help books would proliferate. Soon there would be a subterranean sub-culture, whose aim was nothing less than the overthrow of the order which Fred Orbis's will had imposed for the good of humanity. But, ignoramuses as they were, they saw nothing of his vision, of how he had brought them a new age of enlightenment. Consequently, secret police would be necessary to flush out the vermin. Two private armies—one in brown shirts, mostly hooligans, who would uncover these factions, and impose summary and appropriate punishment— the other in rakish black, the elite who would eventually replace and surpass in terror the thuggish brownshirts. There would have to be some kind of propaganda machine set in motion, because obviously people couldn't be left on their own to decide such things as proper reading material and appropriate philosophies. Ergo, everything would be sanctioned by the state. And if anyone diverged from this doctrine—concentration camps. The aforementioned sports stadiums and arenas, albeit charred from the book-burnings, would be used as gulags for the growing number of dissidents, and if the dissidents became too many...well, some kind of systematized control would have to be imposed. First *sterilization*...but then, if it persisted, extermination. Meanwhile, the underground groups of rebels would have banded together, and grown so large and powerful that there would be rumors of revolt. Hence, purges, pogroms, and assassinations become the norm, as the blackshirts are loosed upon these traitors, while the state propagandists continue their brainwashing of the loyal population, filling them with a frenzied hatred for all things *not them*, meaning *inferno*. The war industry is in full swing and fortunes are made, as money has been reinstated in order to pay for armaments. A war is declared behind closed doors—"Eliminate all Philistines, Illiterates, and Postmodernists"— what is called the *"Solutionis Ultimus"*...The day comes when the battle is joined between Good and Evil, the survival of the human race depending upon the outcome.

Fred Orbis was depressed. He had begun as Adam and had ended up as Hitler. It was the *world*! There was some kind of centripetal force towards Evil. No matter what you did you were doomed, and any hope of change was...*hopeless*. But then, why after all did he worry so much about it? The world was big, it was all grown-up, it could take care of itself. And the more you looked at it, the more it seemed not quite right in the head—a bit off, disturbed; as if there had been one too many nuclear detonations beneath the Nevada desert. The world, for lack of a better word, was *crazy* that was a given. So, where did you go from here? He thought of two other words, the Latin *solus* and *ipse*—alone and self, the roots of the word *"Solipsism"*—the philosophy that there is no reality other than the self. There was something to be said for this. The first commandment of the existentialists was "The world is absurd.", and Fred Orbis was nothing if not an existentialist. Camus said that the only serious question was whether or not to commit suicide, and Camus chose life. But this begged another question. What do you do *then*? How does one make peace with the absurdity? Give up *hope*? Surely not...he had given up hope all his life, as far as meeting a woman was concerned, and had been miserable—and then, the moment he finally met one his whole life changed for the better. But it wasn't a happiness through good deeds, or making the world a better place. It was through glorification of the self, the self as the only reality, and the measure of all things. It was Solipsism, and what was wrong with that? He was an *'Existential Solipsist'*, to coin a phrase, and it was good.

He left the mirror in the bathroom and sat down behind the newspapers and magazines, spread across the table. He was big news. *The Cold-Cut Killer* was everywhere. Since the murder of that fashion designer the world took notice. He had made both the cover of *Time* and *Newsweek, (but weren't they the same?).* Talk show hosts and late-night comedians made endless cold-cut jokes. Stock in Oscar Meyer soared, and he could almost feel the yearning from those he had slighted. Tuna companies prayed for him to use a Tuna Salad sandwich; fast-food chicken places pined for him to get a bucket to go; and corporate pizza execs wondered why he had yet to use a deep-dish with the works. Whole industries had become dependent upon him. He had even seen kids with "Cold-Cut Killer" T-shirts, but the thing that meant the most sat before him now on the table. *The New York Times* had given him its imprimatur. He had made the headlines at last.

Fred Orbis sorted through the newspapers and uncovered a magazine—a glossy Postmodern art rag called *Afflatus.* Inside there was a certain critic, a shameless proponent of the Postmodern whom Fred Orbis had taken a disliking to. This critic had praised the work of that hack Jerry Dolinski, and had even called him a genius. *(He'd show him the true meaning of genius.)* He turned to the article. Livingston Good was his name, and he lived here in Manhattan. Through the miracle of the Internet he found his address. How had serial killers managed in the old days, Fred Orbis wondered? A glance at his watch, the band noticeably loose on his wrist. He had to be at the deli at Madison and 49th at seven sharp, but he sincerely doubted that that detective, Devon DeGroot, would ever decipher the little message he had sent. But nonetheless, he had to keep his part of the bargain. And this would crown his victory even further, since he would have given them the chance, and they would have blown it.

He sat down behind his computer. 200 pages of the novel were already written, and at this rate it would be finished in no time. Of course, that still left the pesky matter of how to get it published, but he shook his head. There would be no negativity. In this brave new world negativity was not allowed. Somehow, just like everything else of late, fortune would smile upon him. *Fortunas favet obesus...* fortune favors the fat. Within minutes his still plump fingers hovered in a blur over the keyboard, like a flock of overweight literary hummingbirds. One chapter, then another, until it was time.

He went to the closet and grabbed his suit. Actually, he owned seven or eight suits, but they were all the same shade of gray, and he laughed that for some reason all these years he had unconsciously dressed himself as an elephant. New suits were in order—custom-fit Armani—he had seen the shop uptown; his reflection in its window. But he was getting ahead of himself—there were still quite a few pounds to shed, and one didn't stop three quarters of the way up the mountain. Grabbing the pillows from the bed, he stuffed them in his clothes until he looked like his old self, and then all was in readiness. He rubbed his hands together in anticipation, and then exited the apartment.

Meanwhile, across the street from the deli on 49th and Madison, two police detectives sat in an innocuous gray sedan.

"Do you think he'll show?" asked Detective Arnold. He grew more nervous by the minute, and he kept touching his bullet-proof vest to make sure it was there.

Devon DeGroot's eyes never left the store.

"I feel it." he said. "I know it."

Arnold sighed to himself. He had found out about the promotion, he didn't get it, and now there was no way out. With a pained expression he watched the hands on his watch as DeGroot watched the delicatessen, and as he sighed again there was a call from headquarters.

"DeGroot..."

"There's been an accident, boss...your wife."

"My *wife*?"

"A car accident. She's at Mt. Sinai."

"*What*? What *happened*? Is she *all right*?" And like that he forgot about the Cold-Cut Killer. Devon DeGroot loved his wife passionately, and never more than when she was in danger.

"It happened about a half hour ago, boss. A car swerved into her lane...a drunk."

"How...how *is* she?"

"Not too good. You'd better get over there."

"Mt. Sinai?"

"Yeah."

"Kozinski...thanks." He hung up and turned to Arnold. "Keep your eyes peeled. I know he'll show. I gotta go to the hospital...my wife..." A pause to get himself under control, and then he looked back at Arnold before dashing away.

Arnold looked at his watch. Quarter to seven. With each minute his heart beat faster. *Twelve* of...*ten* of...*seven* of...He looked at his watch. *Five* of...but then, wasn't his watch *fast*? Didn't he always keep it five minutes *ahead*? A glance at the deli. Nothing. It was a wild goose chase as he'd known all along; that letter a red herring. Imagine, basing an investigation on the ravings of that drunken bum from the alley! What kind of police work was *that*? *Goddamn it!* Why didn't he get the promotion? It was always the same, you work your ass off, you put your life on the line, and for *what*? He looked at his watch. Three minutes to seven. Surely his watch was fast. It was already *past* seven o'clock, the Cold-Cut Killer hadn't shown up. A last look at the deli, and he was gone.

Fred Orbis arrived precisely at seven, for he was nothing if not punctual. He looked at the man behind the counter—an honest, hard-working man to be sure, but probably a man ignorant of the finer things, through fate and circumstance. But in a way, Fred Orbis was doing what he did for him, for this man and all those like him, for Fred Orbis was the patron saint of possibility.

"I'd like an egg salad sandwich, please...and a large dill pickle, just in case."

"Just in case?" the man asked.

"In case I'm still hungry."

"What kind of bread do you want it on?"

"Something coarse and abrasive."

"Coarse and abrasive, huh? We got *Jewish rye*, that's pretty coarse. And then there's *pumpernickel*." The man held out the loaf for Fred Orbis's inspection.

"Yes, that looks very coarse, very hard."

"But it's *fresh*..." the man insisted, his pride momentarily wounded.

"I'm sure it's *very* fresh...*Pumpernickel* will be fine."

The man wrapped the sandwich in waxed paper along with the pickle, and handed them across the counter.

"I'm the *Cold-Cut Killer*." Fred Orbis announced as he paid for the sandwich. He pointed to the headlines in the newspapers and tabloids, in a rack by the cash register.

The man regarded him incredulously, as he did most of his customers.

"Have a nice day."

Fred Orbis fumbled through his pocket for the address of Livingston Good as he walked towards an awaiting cab, and from the other direction came Jacqueline Jimson-Weed, converging on the same cab. She had just returned from a wild afternoon with that young poet from Hunter College, (who had proven to be quite the find). And after a shower and change of clothes she was on her way to Elizabeth Aphelion's, when she collided with an enormous man the size of a pachyderm.

"I'm sorry." he said. And he watched as the look of disgust took shape on her face.

"What a *revolting man*!" And as Fred Orbis digested her words, she snatched the cab.

His gaze lingered on her black hair in the rear window as the cab sped off, and in a flash he was at the curb, and through sheer force of will summoned another taxi. And although he knew it was hopelessly hackneyed, he said, *"Follow that cab."*

As Jacqueline Jimson-Weed rode towards Elizabeth's apartment, she wondered what she'd say when the topic of Elizabeth's book inevitably came up. She of course couldn't tell her that her editor had decided to put the book on the back-burner. It was a poetry book after all, and wasn't exactly a priority. What could she say to keep it alive, that he wants more poems? That had worked in the past, but perhaps she had overused this. Maybe she could say that the editor had switched gears...that he liked her love poetry so much that he wanted her to do an entire book of love poems! Yes, that was it, and she paid the cabbie and walked towards Elizabeth's apartment, just as a wall rose inexplicably from the sidewalk to block her path. Standing back to gather it in, she saw that it was that immense fat man who had almost knocked her down in front of the taxi—the one she thought resembled a dirigible. He must have gotten upset that she stole his cab—New Yorkers could be so touchy—so she decided to cut the Gordian knot.

"Get out of my way, you disgusting, obese *slob*!" As her words hung in the air she tried to maneuver around the behemoth, but it was like trying to run around the horizon. "Will you get out of my way, you..." And then she saw the egg salad sandwich and it dawned on her, (for news of the Cold-Cut Killer was everywhere). "You're the..." the rest of her words garbled by egg salad, and the dill pickle.

Fred Orbis watched with fascination as she struggled vainly in his grip, and when the light went out in her black eyes he felt an overwhelming peace. He carried her body to the alley, and then mentally subtracted thirty more pounds. His only regret was that Livingston Good, the champion of the Postmodern, had escaped his wrath. There were two murders left, and these were to be special. Suddenly the world beckoned. It was a glorious evening. Manhattan had never looked so splendid, and he decided to walk home and drink in the cool night air, and feast on the smell of spring flowers.

28

Darby Montana opened her eyes and it was morning. She brought her hand to her face to feel if there was any difference, but she couldn't tell. In the kitchen she saw the melted candles, and then she went to the bathroom and confronted the mirror. Her face looked the same, she was disappointed. But when she looked deeper, her eyes seemed brighter, her cheekbones more pronounced, her face more oval than square. Her hair was shinier, its color more rich, and as she opened her bathrobe her body was a bit curvier where it had always been straight. Philep said that it would happen slowly, that at first the changes would be subtle. She looked at her eyes, the window to the soul. Was there any reproach there for the bargain she had made? Was there any hint of remorse or apprehension? But her eyes looked beautiful. It had happened. She was changing.

So what then was the soul? Until today a theory, a word tossed around in metaphysics. But now something real. Could she feel it? She thought of what Descartes had said—*the soul as the pilot, the body the machine*—like a car to its driver. And then she remembered what Liv Good had said about a Ferrari: *"It's still a damn fine car."* Perhaps this Cartesian view of the soul was too simplistic, because according to recent events she was now a driverless car, but yet she felt that soon she would pilot this brand new Ferrari off the showroom floor and into the world. She still had her will. Her will, after all, had sold off her soul as if it were an old lamp at a garage sale. So if the soul wasn't the will, what was it? Not conscience, because she still knew right from wrong, (and she had no desire to become a serial killer). And it wasn't conscious*ness*, because she still felt deeply. So what the hell *was* it? She went to the window and threw aside the drapes. Outside, trucks and cars and people moved past as always, but the light was somehow different. Even in the dirty pavement, in the hazy air, in the soot-stained buildings there was a kind of radiance. So what was this thing, the soul, a kind of useless organ like the appendix? She returned to the mirror. In the time it took for her to look out the window and walk to the bathroom, her lips had become fuller, her hips more round, her eyes more inviting. It had happened. She was changing.

"Hello Darby." It was Iona Bentley, shortly after two o'clock. Ever since Philep the meetings had begun two hours earlier. "Is he...Darby, you look...are you wearing *makeup?*"

"No, I don't *wear* makeup."

Iona scrutinized her face.

"You look...*different.*"

"I've been taking vitamins."

"Really? What kind?"

The bell rang. Liv Good and Anna Coluthon.

"Hi Darby. Are you wearing *makeup?*"

"I asked her the same thing. It's vitamins, dear. Darby's taking vitamins."

"Really? What kind?"

"You look...is Philep here?"

"No, he's..."

"Seriously Darby, I've been feeling run down lately. What kind of vitamins are you taking?"

"Echinacea."

"*Echinacea?* I've *heard* of that. Isn't that some kind of *root*, or something?"

"Where's Philep?"

The bell rang again. Barton and Melanie Snide. As Barton walked in he paused and looked at Darby's face.

"I confess at being nonplused by your nascent pulchritude."

"He means you look different." said Melanie.

Courtney Imbroglio arrived.

"Where's Phil...Darby, did you get a new *hairstyle?*"

"It's vitamins." said Iona.

"Echinacea." said Liv Good.

"Isn't that some kind of *bark?*" asked Courtney.

"Where's Philep?"

"Yes Darby..." said the others. "Where's Philep?"

"He asked me to tell you that he was called away."

"What?"

"Called *away?*"

"On business..."

"But..."

"He left the country. He went back to...Luxembourg."

"Oh..."

And there was a silence akin to mourning, followed by a pilgrimage to the wet bar.

"Well, what are we going to *talk* about then?"

"Are we smoking again, dear?"

"Yes, Courtney," said Liv, "what about your latest romance?"

"I've decided I like smoking better than I like men. So what are we going to *talk* about?" her words managing to escape between puffs of her cigarette and gulps of her drink.

"I had a weird thing happen to *me* the other day." said Iona. "My house cleaner..."

"Your *house cleaner*?"

"Yes, I found *this* under a book on the coffee table."

"A *penny*?"

"Yes, isn't that strange. There was a penny beneath the book I keep on the coffee table in my living room."

"And you think your *house cleaner* put it there?"

"Yes, I mean, how *else* would it get there? I'm not in the habit of putting pennies beneath the objects in my house." she laughed. "I mean, why would she *do* such a thing?"

"Have you asked her?"

"Well, no, I mean...what if it's some kind of, you know, some... bizarre Satanic cult, like she's a *witch* or something...You've seen *Rosemary's Baby*."

"But a *penny*?"

"Who knows how crazy people behave? I mean, this is *New York*. Look at the *Cold-Cut Killer*..."

"Iona's right." said Liv Good. "That city out there's a mess! I mean, do you know that I get *death threats* because of my reviews."

"Well, at least that means somebody *reads* them."

"Very funny! I'm *serious*. Sometimes I don't even want to leave the house. That city is *Hell*. I mean, look at the people it attracts. This *Cold-Cut Killer*, for instance..."

"But they say he speaks six languages."

"And was a Noble Prize-winning physicist."

"And that he...something *snapped*."

"But that's my point. Even a *genius* in this city can snap like that, and become the Cold-Cut Killer. This city is *death*."

"Then why don't you move to the country?" asked Courtney Imbroglio.

"What, with all the *bugs*?...And all the farmers talking about combines, and *feed*..."

"Did you hear about his latest victim? Some Lesbian poet, with an egg salad sandwich and a dill pickle shoved down her throat."

"Was she Postmodern?" asked Liv.

"No, *Lyrical*, I think."

"Good, I was starting to worry...after what happened to Dolus."

"Did you know his real name was *Jimmy Dolinski*?"

"It was *Jerry*, dear."

"So, what about your house cleaner?" asked Darby.

"You mean about the *penny*?...I let her go."

"You *fired* her?"

"Of course. Do you expect me to keep some *psycho* under my roof?"

"I can't believe you fired her."

"Well, what would *you* have done?"

"I clean my own house."

"How commendable."

"And you're not afraid of serial killers?" asked Liv Good.

"I don't know. This one sounds kind of interesting. I mean, they say he's a man of ideas. That's a hard thing to be."

"*I'll* say."

There was a pause as everyone looked at Darby Montana. Like a painting she felt their eyes, and for a moment she was self-conscious, but then she brushed her hair from her face and her radiant smile lit up the room. Outside there was a horn honking, followed by shouting back and forth, and as she listened to the noise on this filthy Manhattan street, she thought of Heaven.

Devon DeGroot had a strange dream. He was in the middle of Times Square, at a table behind a chessboard, and his opponent was the *Michelin* tire man. Cars and trucks and taxi cabs whizzed by, but the two of them were intent on their game. DeGroot was winning, but then there was the blare of a horn and he looked away and saw Detective Arnold, driving by in a police cruiser with a passenger who looked like Alexander Hamilton. And when he turned back to the board his opponent had captured his queen. The air suddenly became unbreathable. Pollution from every car exhaust and smokestack, decay from every garbage can and dumpster seemed to have gathered here into a collective effluvium, which went right up his nose as he gasped for breath.

He awoke and found Lafayette, his big golden retriever, asleep next to him on the bed, breathing his noxious dog-breath into his face.

"Get off!" said DeGroot. "You *know* you're not supposed to be on the bed." But then he saw the sad look on his face. They were both sad because Mrs. DeGroot wasn't there. Still in the hospital, although the doctors said that she was out of danger. He gave the dog a pat on the head, and then got ready for work.

Devon DeGroot cut across 56th onto Madison to avoid a traffic jam, and as he passed the corner of Madison and 49th something caught his eye. The deli they had staked out the past few days. In its window was a sign:

The Cold-Cut Killer Shops Here!
Egg Salad Sand. Special!

DeGroot pulled to the curb and rushed across the street.

"I noticed your sign."

The man behind the counter smiled proudly.

"Yes! Last night he was here. He bought an egg salad sandwich, and a dill pickle!"

He held up the *Daily News*:

EGG SALAD SANDWICH CLAIMS 8th VICTIM.

"That was *my sandwich*! I sold it to him! Would you like one? We have a special today."

"No. Last night, do you remember what time he came in?"

"It was seven...*Seven o'clock Wheel of Fortune*...eight o'clock *Beach Lookout*."

"What?"

"My shows." He pointed to the TV set. "Seven o'clock *Wheel of Fortune*...eight o'clock *Beach Lookout*."

"And he came in when *Wheel of Fortune* came on?"

"Right. Seven o'clock."

At this, Devon DeGroot felt fury, rage. He was thankful that Arnold wasn't there because he surely would have wrung his neck. A glance around the store.

"Don't you have any cameras? For surveillance, or security?"

The man reached behind the counter and brought out a 30-.06 double-barreled shotgun.

"Who needs cameras when you got a *30-.06*?"

212

Devon DeGroot started to reach into his pocket for his identification, but found the shotgun pointing at his chest.

"I'm a *police officer*." he explained. "I'm just trying to get my identification."

"Alright...but *slowly*." The man's finger noticeably itchy on the trigger.

Devon slid his hand inside his coat, and carefully brought out his ID.

"You are Devon DeGroot...police detective?"

"Yes."

"What do you want?" he asked coldly. The shotgun remained fixed. Apparently a sign wasn't forthcoming that *Devon DeGroot Shops Here!*

"Can you describe the man for me?"

"The Cold-Cut Killer?...Sure!" All smiles now, he spread his hands in the air, all the while holding the shotgun. "He was fat." the man gesticulated. *"Enormous."*

Devon DeGroot found it hard to concentrate—what with his boiling rage, and the shotgun being waved about.

"Would you mind coming down to the Precinct, to give a description?"

"I just did."

"But sir, this is important."

At this the bell rang and someone came in.

"I'd like three egg salad sandwiches, please."

"Dill pickle?...The Cold-Cut Killer always has a dill pickle with his egg salad."

"Sure, why not. Three dill pickles...Does he really shop here?"

"All the time. We're old friends." When the woman left he turned to DeGroot. "I got 200 egg salad sandwiches back there. I can't leave the store."

"All right. But how 'bout if I sent a police artist down *here?*"

"An artist? To draw my picture?...*Sure!* Can I give it to my wife?"

"You don't seem to under...the police artist will be drawing... Of course." DeGroot nodded. "After you describe the Cold-Cut Killer, he'll do your portrait."

At this the man seemed quite pleased, and he stowed the shotgun behind the counter.

Two more people came in.

"An egg salad sandwich, please..."

"I'd like *four* egg salad sandwiches to go, please...and don't forget the pickles."

Dispirited, Detective DeGroot walked back to his car.

"Egg salad! Damn." said Macduff. "That crackpot doctor was right!"

"What do you want for the *9th* victim?" Donalbain asked.

"Stuffed cabbage...no, meatloaf...no, *yes*...meatloaf."

"Where's the *fiver*? Kozinski, you want in on the next Pool?"

"Yeah, deviled ham."

"One *'deviled ham'* for Kozinski..."

At this Devon DeGroot came in, his eyes like flaming torches.

"Where's *Arnold*?"

"Um, he hasn't come in yet, boss."

At this DeGroot went into a rampage. Picking up a chair he smashed it to pieces, and then he went over and demolished the coffee machine.

"No more cold coffee!" he shouted. When he went into his office he slammed the door so hard the glass window shattered.

"I guess we won't ask him if he wants in on the next Pool."

They were all silent as Arnold walked in.

"Hey guys." He was in a good mood because of last night. He hadn't seen the paper yet, and then he noticed the broken chair and the coffee machine. "What's goin' on?"

"*Arnold!*" It was DeGroot, grinding his shoes on the broken glass. "Get in here!"

Moments later...

"Have you seen this?" Devon DeGroot shoved the *Daily News* beneath his nose. "I was just over at that deli. The guy has signs up. *The Cold-Cut Killer Shops Here!*, for Christsake."

"But boss, I waited till past seven..."

"Save it. At seven *Wheel of Fortune.*"

"What?"

"You betrayed me."

"But *boss...*"

"Forget it, you're through. I want your badge and your gun. Until further notice pending a hearing, you're suspended."

"But..."

"Now get out of my sight!"

As Arnold slithered away Macduff appeared.

"Boss, the mail's here."

DeGroot sorted through the mail to take his mind off Arnold's betrayal, when he came upon a letter.

"Look at the return address."

"Anna Graham...*So?*"

"Look...Parsippany, New Jersey."

"Like our friend, Kennie Sangfwa."

DeGroot tore open the envelope and saw an index card with bold block letters.

I MUST STOP EVEN FIST

"I Must Stop Even Fist...What the hell's *that* mean?"

"It's an anagram." said DeGroot. "See...*Anna Graham*...anagram."

"It's him, boss."

"Kozinski, Donalbain...Get in here!" DeGroot handed them each a pad and a pencil. "Write this down. It's an anagram. We have to find out what it means."

Everyone went to work.

After a few minutes of scribbling, Donalbain announced, "I got it...

SUMO PENIS TIT VEST

"*Sumo Penis Tit Vest?* What the hell's *that?*" asked Macduff.

"It's what it says."

"But that doesn't mean *anything*."

"Well, what do *you* got, Einstein?"

IS IT SEVEN TUT MOPS

"*Is It Seven Tut Mops?*...And *that's* supposed to mean something?"

"Sure." said Macduff. "It's a question...the question is being posed..."

"Is it seven tut mops?" said Kozinski.

"Right!"

"What did *you* get, Kozinski?"

VENUS MIST SETTI FOP

"What the hell's *"SETTI"?*"

"I don't know, isn't that like the abominable snow man?"

"That's *Yetti.*"

"Oh..."

"What did *you* get, boss?"

POST FESTUM VENISTI

"Ah, *boss?*..."

"It's Latin. We need to get it translated. Macduff, where did you go last time, with that other Latin phrase?"

"The Library, boss. They have all these Latin books there. It's amazing!"

"There's no time for that. *Here...*" DeGroot handed him the soiled, dog-eared, hand-written business card.

Dr. Randall Jared, Ph.D.

The Alley off Seventh and Bleecker.

"Him again?"

"Go."

"*Sumo Penis Tit Vest.*" Macduff said to Donalbain on his way out the door.

"Is It Seven Tut Mops!" Donalbain called after him.

"Kozinski..." said DeGroot. "I want you to take a police artist to that deli and get a description of our man. He was in there last night...at seven o'clock."

Both Donalbain and Kozinski saw the Krakatau that was Devon DeGroot, and they quickly made their exit.

Macduff walked into the alley and came upon a philosophical discussion.

First bum.   [*Sitting on the edge of a garbage can*] It's the brain. What could be smarter than the brain?

Second bum.   [*Takes swig from bottle in paper bag, then passes to first bum*] It's the stomach.

First bum.   The *stomach*?

Second bum.   Right. Because it's smart enough not to digest itself. See how long the *brain* would last down there.

First bum.   So then, if the stomach is the smartest part of the body, then the fatter you are...

Second bum.   Precisely. Wittgenstein said '*The human body is the best picture of the human soul*'...

First bum.   But Wittgenstein wore women's clothing...

Second bum.   So did Schopenhauer.

First bum.   *Schopenhauer?*

Second bum.   Or maybe it was Kant...Aeschylus says...

First bum.   Tell me again about the game...

Second bum.   *[Smiling proudly]* It was Game Six, and if the *Red Sox* won they would have broken the curse of the Bambino.
First bum.   Bambino being...
Second bum.   Babe Ruth...The Babe.
First bum.   Whom that scoundrel Harry Frazee...
Second bum.   The bastard.

"Gentlemen..." Macduff said as he approached them.

"I *know* you." said the first bum, who in fact was the eminent Dr. Randall Jared, the world's foremost authority on James Joyce.

"I know him too!" said the second bum, who was actually Sven Kappûtkoic, the former scholar and *Red Sox* fan, who took to drink after the disastrous Game Six of the '86 World Series.

"Would either of you be able to help me out?" asked Macduff. "I have some Latin that needs to be translated."

"Latin..." said the first bum. "Piece o' cake!"

"*Veni, vedi, vici...*" said the second bum.

Macduff handed them the piece of paper.

"*Post festum venisti.*" said the first bum to the second. "Would you like to do the honors?"

"By all means, the honor is *yours*." The second bum bowed graciously to the first.

"*Post festum venisti*...You have come after the feast."

"You...have come...after...the feast." Macduff said as he jotted it down. "But what does it mean?"

"It means you missed dinner! So anyway, it's the Sixth Game of the Series. The *Red Sox* are up three games to two..."

"In the best of seven..."

"Right. And they're ahead 5—3 in the bottom of the tenth, when..."

"Thank you gentlemen."

"You're most welcome. Our door is always opened."

"It means *You have come after the feast*, boss." He handed him the piece of paper.

"You have come after the feast..." Devon DeGroot mulled over the words as Kozinski came in with the police artist's sketch of the Cold-Cut Killer.

"He looks like the *Michelin* tire man, boss. Do you want me to put it on the wire?"

"Yeah." DeGroot reluctantly agreed. "The media's gonna *love* that."

And after the late edition of *The Post* hit the streets, fat people throughout the city stayed in doors. And when the Dow closed for the day, stock in Michelin had risen 6 points.

When Elizabeth Aphelion heard about the Cold-Cut Killer's latest victim her heart skipped a beat. But then almost instantly she became downcast. Without Jacqueline Jimson-Weed, what was to become of her *book*?

Frantically she searched for the number—the phone bill the day Jacqueline sat on the bed and called her publisher.

"Hello, may I speak with James Brume, please."

"This is he."

"Hi, this is Elizabeth Aphelion...Jacqueline Jimson-Weed's..."

"Yes, Elizabeth, what an awful tragedy. Just awful. You must be..."

"Yes, I don't know what to say, I'm...I mean, it was *awful*, but...I was wondering, about the book. My book of *poetry*...I was wondering if..."

"I'm sorry, Elizabeth, didn't Jacqueline tell you? We've decided to put it on the shelf for awhile."

"The *shelf*? What do you..."

"Some other projects are more pressing. We've decided to hold off on your book for the time being."

"For how long?"

"Well, I don't know. I can't say right now, but...how 'bout this. Call me in six months, okay, and we'll see how things are? Fair enough?"

Elizabeth was silent.

"Elizabeth?"

"Yes, six months then."

"Good-bye Elizabeth."

She stared at the phone, and then dialed Michael's number.

"This is Michael...leave a message..."

She hung up, wondering how she could have ever been with someone with such an unpoetic answering machine. *Two years* she had waited for her book to be published. *Two years* wiped away like that, and what was left but to start again? Life was such an incredible pain in the ass, and it just got worse. She thought of Sylvia Plath, and Hemingway. Was suicide about great weakness or great strength? Maybe she had to live more. Maybe with more years under her belt she'd understand what they understood—but what to do in the *meantime*? She had even been fired from one of her house-cleaning jobs, and now she had to get another client *fast*, in order to pay the bills. But what if she just gave this up— New York—this city? Hadn't she thought about moving before? But she always pictured herself in a new place as a published poet, not a nobody house cleaner. What would she do for work? What everyone else did, survive. But didn't anyone ever *question* this? And wasn't the answer anything but hope?

Elizabeth Aphelion stared at the headline in the newspaper, and then turned to the classifieds. There were hundreds of jobs all the same, offering little money and no future. She called a few, but they were already filled.

31

New York City was gripped by *"Cold-Cut Killermania"*. As grisly as the murders were, there was something about them which inspired the populace. The idea of having food rammed down a throat, it seemed so logical; the *reductio ad absurdum* of a capitalist, consumer-driven society; that one engorged themselves even at the point of death. It was poetic, and this poetry wasn't lost on the masses. Cartoons portrayed the Cold-Cut Killer as a kind of rotund Robin Hood, emerging from Mama's kitchen to right a symbolic wrong. Restaurants throughout the city put up signs: *The Cold-Cut Killer Eats Here*, and mothers across the country felt a warm, matronly affection towards him. To them he was the faithful son who was always on time for dinner, who happily cleaned his plate, and always asked for seconds. Editorials appeared in newspapers and magazines, focusing on the symbolism of the Cold-Cut Killer. And one noted writer even offered to write his biography, and was instantly besieged by publishing houses brandishing million dollar advances, even though nobody had any idea who the Cold-Cut Killer was. But soon that would change, Fred Orbis thought. His book was almost finished.

The only people who saw the Cold-Cut Killer differently were the Postmodernists, who took to traveling in groups, and stayed clear of delicatessens. But Fred Orbis, as much as he would have liked to continue his swath across the New York art scene, was through with the Postmodern.

He looked past the headlines to an article on page seven:

Senator Dempster to Address Manhattan Mensa Group

Senator James "Jimmy" Dempster, Rhodes scholar, Yale graduate, and noted genius with a 198 IQ, will address the Manhattan chapter of Mensa, Tuesday evening at 7 o'clock. A reception to follow.

"Fool's faces stick to walls." Fred Orbis said to himself, as he stuffed the pillows beneath his clothes.

As geniuses from all over Manhattan began to filter outside, a large shadowy figure sat in an innocuous gray sedan parked across the street. Fred Orbis watched as strains of Palestrina's *Missa pro defunctis* played on the rental car's tape deck, and then he saw Jimmy Dempster step into his limo and pull away. They drove uptown, where the esteemed Senator had drinks in a restaurant with several important-looking men, and then a few hours later, Fred Orbis followed him to a dark, quiet street in the upper East 80's. He watched as a scantily-clad young woman opened the door to her apartment, and greeted the Senator with a big kiss. Some genius, he thought. It had only been a few hours, and *already* he'd discovered him with his mistress. Fred Orbis shook his head. Shouldn't all that made up the Senator's life by rights have been *his*? He remembered that fateful day in fourth grade, when Jimmy Dempster read the story which rechristened him *"Obese Orbis"*. And then the battery of tests, and somehow he scored in the bottom percentile, while Jimmy Dempster was hailed as a genius. And from that moment on the world shamelessly dumped its bounty upon this simpleton's head, when it should have given him a dunce cap. Fred Orbis looked at the sandwich on the seat of the car. It was headcheese on Wonderbread, and he laughed at the symbolism.

Hours went by as he waited, headcheese sandwich at the ready. A glance at the limo. It was the middle of the night, the chauffeur asleep. Finally, at two in the morning the door opened from the apartment, and a noticeably disheveled Senator Dempster emerged. Fixing his tie he turned towards the limo, when suddenly all light was sucked away by an enormous shadow. When his eyes finally focused he saw a man, an enormous man, and he gazed into his face.

"Do I *know* you?" he asked.

And then the moment of recognition (followed by headcheese and Wonderbread). Jimmy Dempster watched as his life passed before him, and he had no regrets. From fourth grade on it was a good life. He was a respected Senator and a genius, and was never wanting for a mistress. In death his face wore an insipid grin.

The next evening an innocuous gray rental car pulled up to a quiet neighborhood in Brooklyn, and an enormous fat man with a liverwurst in his hand walked to a house and rang the bell. Several minutes later, an elderly woman with bluish hair opened the door, with a bluish poodle dog yapping at her feet. At first, she thought it was the delivery boy from the butcher shop, as she squinted behind her glasses. But then... *"Obese Orbis?..."* And then, "Obese Orbis!"

"Sic semper tyrannis!"

The shadow moved forward like an eclipse, and then came the liverwurst. Mrs. Pressman had always hated liverwurst.

After dropping off the car, Fred Orbis walked home humming highlights from Handel's *Messiah*, when an unmarked police car drove by.

"Look over there..." said Donalbain.

224

"It is bal*loon!*" said Macduff. They glanced at the police artist's sketch of the Cold-Cut Killer, and then back at the fat man walking down the street.

"It's *him.*"

Within seconds they were out with guns drawn, and moments later, after squeezing the enormous fat man into the squad car, they were back at the station house at Mid-Manhattan South.

"Looks like we got ourselves the Cold-Cut Killer!" said Macduff.

"*I* spotted him." said Donalbain.

"Where's DeGroot?"

"At the hospital." said Kozinski. "Wow, so you guys got the *Cold-Cut Killer*...I guess that's the end of the Pool."

Meanwhile at the desk, Fred Orbis was fingerprinted.

"Empty your pockets, please." said the desk sergeant.

And Fred Orbis proceeded to empty everything, including the pillows which lined his clothes, and after seven or eight pillows were stacked on the desk, the desk sergeant went over to Macduff.

"Um, maybe you should come over here for a second." He pointed to the pile of pillows, and then at the slim man in the incredibly baggy suit.

"*Damn!* Another Cold-Cut Killer copycat. That's the *tenth* one this week!" Macduff glared at the man in the ridiculous suit and at the stack of pillows on the desk, and saw his promotion vanish. "Get him outta here!"

"Shall I take the pillows?" the slim man asked.

"Just get outta here."

Fred Orbis grabbed everything and exited the police station, and as he walked home he distributed the pillows among the bums he passed sleeping on the sidewalk. He was exhilarated. Never had he felt this good. There was a night breeze, and he opened his enormous suit to the wind, and like a sailboat floated effortlessly, silently homeward.

Each morning for a week Darby Montana woke up and faced the mirror. The transformation was astounding, and by the seventh day the face that looked back was that of an exotic Mediterranean beauty. Her hair was full, deep black, like the night sky of a Sicilian countryside. Her eyes, dark and glistening, like the Tyrrhenian of a new moon. And her body, instead of a packing crate was an hourglass.

With a new hairstyle, and new clothes to show off her figure, she walked down the sidewalks of Manhattan, spending half the time stealing glances at herself in the windows.

And *men*...Suddenly she was an object of desire. Men's eyes covered her now as once they had ignored her, and sometimes she smiled, and sometimes she walked on as if she didn't notice, but either way she was thrilled. What a topsy-turvy world it was, where a few seconds of an appreciative glance made up for almost anything. She drank in the looks as she imagined herself in their eyes. They *wanted* her. They had no idea who she was or what she was like, but they wanted her. And in a way, it was remarkably refreshing—the uncomplicated candor of lust. She had spent her life being invisible, but now she was the Mediterranean sun, in a tight dress and high heels.

Darby stopped in front of her favorite bookstore. She remembered catching a glimpse of herself in this window, months before, staring at a body so square and lifeless. But now she followed every curve, until she noticed a man in the reflection doing the same. She started to turn around, but then she smiled and walked away.

"You are *beautiful!*" he called out. "You look like *Sophia Loren!*"

And she turned in her steps.

"In Italiano..."

"What?"

"Say it in *Italian.*"

"I'm sorry, I don't speak it."

"Too bad."

She walked on as if she were a model, the sidewalks of Manhattan her runway. But then, she remembered the meeting. It was Wednesday, she had forgotten to call everyone to cancel the Wednesday Afternoon Discussion Group. She hailed a cab and instantly one appeared, and somehow they arrived safely at her apartment, even though the cabbie's eyes never seemed to leave the rearview mirror.

Moments later the bell rang.

"Hi Darb...oh, excuse me. Is *Darby* here?" It was Iona Bentley.

"No, she's not. She was called out of town quite suddenly. I'm her cousin Sophia. I'm going to be house-sitting for awhile."

"She was called out of town? Not bad news I hope?"

"On the contrary, quite good news."

Liv Good and Anna Coluthon appeared.

"This is Darby's beautiful cousin, Sophia." Iona announced. "Darby was called away quite suddenly."

"Yes. She was sorry that she didn't have time to call you, to explain that the meetings will be on hiatus for awhile."

"When do you expect her back?"

"Not for some time."

"So she'll be gone for...where did she *go?*"

"Sicily...To visit our family."

"Darby's family is from Sicily, dear."

Barton and Melanie Snide arrived.

"This is Sophia..."

"Sophia Montana."

"She's Darby's cousin from Sicily."

"Ah! *Sei molto bella.*" said Barton Snide.

"*Grazie.*"

Courtney Imbroglio arrived, and was taken aback at the beautiful woman in Darby's doorway.

"This is Sophia Montana...Darby's cousin."

"Darby never mentioned you."

"She's from Sicily, dear."

"Are you a *model?*" She searched Darby's face for a family resemblance.

"No. I'm a *philosopher.*"

"So there are no more...what do we do on *Wednesdays* now?"

"There's this new show that just opened." said Liv Good. "This *Post*-Postmodernist name of..."

"*Post*-Postmodernist?" said Courtney.

"It's the next thing. They're picking up where the Postmodern left off."

"And that would be..."

"They've eliminated the '*art gallery*' from the equation."

"So where's the show?"

"Today it's on the corner of 57th and Lexington."

"What, like a sidewalk art display?"

"Well, actually they've eliminated the '*art*' as well..."

"I don't get it."

"Many don't because it's so radically new. You see, this artist designates a time and a place for people to go and *look...*"

"Go and *look*...At *what?*"

"That's just it! Everyone sees something different. It's like a light is shined on an ordinary moment, and for a few minutes it becomes *art.*"

"So let me get this straight," said Courtney, "people go to this street corner and just *look*...and that's the guy's exhibit...that's his art?"

"The man's a genius."

"I think I'll go shopping."

And this became the exit cue, as one by one, the members of the Wednesday Afternoon Discussion Group bid Sophia Montana *arrivederci*, and floated back to the secure immutability of their lives. Lives unlike Heaven, but certainly not like Hell—more like a well-appointed Purgatory with room service.

Darby shut the door and felt her breasts swell against her dress. In the doorway she had been reborn and christened Sophia Montana, and the world's eye gave her its blessing. She wondered if Philep could see her, and she mouthed the words "thank you" and *"grazie"*, and then went to the closet to decide which dress to wear for dinner. Reservations for one—although she didn't expect this to be the case for much longer.

"I still can't get over it." said Donalbain.

"What?" asked Macduff.

"A headcheese sandwich and Jimmy Dempster."

"And it was Wonderbread." said Kozinski.

"A kind of poetry to it, huh?"

"Sometimes the universe just works. What did *you* have?"

"Bagel with sundried tomatoes. *You?*"

"Philly steak with peppers."

"Anybody get headcheese?"

"You kidding?"

Devon DeGroot came in, sans his customary cup of coffee, looking downcast and disgruntled.

"No coffee today, boss?"

And then they remembered, he had renounced coffee until the Cold-Cut Killer was apprehended. Since the ill-fated night of Arnold's betrayal Devon DeGroot had become obsessed, as if somehow his life depended upon the outcome of this case.

"I just got back from Brooklyn." he said. *"Look..."* He handed his detectives some police photos of a little old lady and her dog, both with liverwurst rammed down their throats.

"And the dog, *too?*" said Donalbain.

"It's a *poodle...*" said Macduff, as if that explained it.

"And what's that...*liverwurst?*"

DeGroot nodded, as Kozinski mentally berated himself for not sticking with liverwurst in the Pool.

"Jeez! I've seen some grisly murders in my day, but *this* one..."

"It's appalling." said Macduff.

"Heinous." said Kozinski.

"It's victim number *ten*." said DeGroot.

"*Eleven*, if you count the dog." said Donalbain.

DeGroot silenced him with a glare and turned to the others.

"So what the hell's going on? First we have three young models... then a cabbie and three Postmodernists...then this Lesbian poet... then the noted '*genius*', Senator Jimmy Dempster...and now this 87 year-old lady..."

"And her..." Donalbain was about to say "*dog*", but wisely shut up instead.

"That poet, what was her name?"

"Jacqueline Jimson-Weed, boss. She taught at Smith College, in..."

"I know where it is."

"It's where Sylvia Plath went."

"Sylvia *who*?"

"Plath. An American poet..."

"For *four hundred*." said Kozinski.

"It was for *two* hundred." said Macduff.

"Gentlemen..." said DeGroot. "What happened to our pattern? What's this lame-brain Senator and this old lady have to do with the other victims?"

"Maybe they were closet *Postmodernists*, boss."

"That poet, she was Lyrical. She had nothing to do with the Postmodern... And Jimmy Dempster, I don't think he could even *spell* Postmodern."

"He could've been the next president, boss."

"So this saved him from being impeached. What about the old lady, Mrs. Pressman? She was a retired school teacher, for Christsake."

"Maybe she was the Cold-Cut Killer's old teacher." offered Donalbain. "I remember *my* third grade teacher, *Mrs. Andretti*... boy was she mean. She used to..."

"Find out where she taught, and then get a list of every class roster she ever had."

"But boss, that was before computers."

"I don't care, it must be in a file cabinet somewhere. I want that list!"

"So, where do we go from here, boss?"

DeGroot shook his head.

"How 'bout *this*, boss?" Macduff held out a soiled napkin with a coffee stain on it. "*Anything?*"

"It looks like a soiled napkin." He walked to his office and shut the door.

Macduff turned to the others.

"We're in deep shit!"

The newspapers had a field day with the latest victims. Full-page photos were everywhere of the old lady and her poodle, laying side by side dead with liverwurst in their mouths. The *ASPCA* and *PETA* staged protests and symbolic candlelight vigils, but they were virtually ignored, because apparently the Cold-Cut Killer had struck another nerve. It appeared that there was a deep-seated collective hatred for poodles ingrained in society. They were symbolic of all that was annoying, and through this ritual death, the Cold-Cut Killer had attained the status of cult hero. People began sending liverwurst sandwiches to their bosses; to their wives or husbands; to their mother-in-laws; to ungrateful teenagers; to the rude teller at the bank; to basically anyone who pissed them off, and within days the supply of liverwurst in the tri-state metropolitan area had been exhausted. Supermarkets and butcher shops and corner delis frantically clamored for shipments from Omaha and Des Moines—both now claiming to be the *"Liverwurst capital of the world"*. Liverwurst millionaires were made, fortunes accumulated, and by the end of the week a liverwurst sandwich was on the cover of *Time* magazine. Not to be outdone, *Newsweek* ran a cover story on the horrors of factory farming, specifically in regards to liverwurst. Liverwurst's gray, pasty visage began to appear everywhere—billboards, magazines, T-shirts, TV commercials. The "Cooking Section" of *The New York Times* ran a recipe for liverwurst soufflé, and by the end of the week liverwurst was declared to be the "official lunch meat of the *New York Yankees*". The Cold-Cut Killer had spawned *"Liverwurstmania"*.

That night Devon DeGroot had another dream. He was in Times Square, in the middle of the street but there was no traffic, no cars, and not a person in sight. He looked up at the signs. They were all turned off. Manhattan was a wasteland, and as he walked down the street he heard the wind whistling between abandoned skyscrapers, and he had the eerie feeling that the rest of the world was all dead. Litter and newspapers blew past his feet, and he saw a headline:

FBI Net Ten in Phony Liverwurst Ring.

Walking along he listened to his footsteps, echoing off the pavement in this concrete canyon, and never had he felt so alone. At that moment a sign lit up overhead—one of those moving billboards where words appear, and then float across like a current of water.

"Greetings, Detective DeGroot." it said.

"What's happened?"

"It's the end."

"The *end*? The end of *what*?"

The sign shut off, the words disappeared.

Devon DeGroot called out, his voice echoed across the empty city, until all was silence and the wind.

34

Miles Davis' *Blue in Green* played on the stereo as the rain came down. The song was the melancholy that seemed to fill this Manhattan Sunday. Each chord on the piano was the rain, the brushes on the drums the traffic outside, the muted trumpet the longing he felt. It was everywhere, there was so little happiness.

Mr. Monde sipped his wine as the piano took its solo, and he looked at the newspapers on the table, the headlines about the Cold-Cut Killer. It had been like this for weeks now, and it was almost over. He thought of the endgame in chess—most of the pieces were gone, and you were face to face with your opponent. And there was the moment of realization, when one would win and the other lose and immediately after this, for those who have spent their lives playing the game, a kind of sadness. Mystery was the only thing that kept the sadness at bay. The world needed more of it, but man had this insuperable need to explain.

He listened to the notes of the saxophone, the melody born to the afternoon, the rain holding a whisper, like a lone car passing in a hiss on the wet street. Soon it would be time for him to go. He took out a sheet of paper and wrote, "Dear Elizabeth," as the trumpet returned—the brittle, metallic notes; fragile, on the verge of breaking.

35

Consummatum est. Fred Orbis put his manuscript in a cardboard box, and walked out into the city. After making several copies, he took a cab uptown to the Armani shop, where he had seen the beautiful suits. He had already gotten rid of his old clothes—the elephantine suits, the cavernous shoes, the billowy boxer shorts—and had ordered a casual outfit from a mail-order catalogue, in anticipation of this day. And as he left the cab and walked towards the store, for the first time in his life he felt normal. He saw his reflection in the window—it wasn't much different from anyone else's. When a salesman approached, he smiled and said that he wanted to be fitted for seven or eight suits, and the salesman nodded approvingly. He was brought to a fitting room, where a stooped-over man with a ribbon of measuring tape around his neck began taking his measurements. Fred Orbis explained the kinds of suits he wanted, and the little man made small talk as he measured away.

"So, what do you do?" the tailor asked.

He handed Fred a pair of pants to try on, his hands flashing through the air, making cryptic marks in chalk.

"I'm a novelist, existential philosopher, raconteur, and lover of women."

The little man looked up for a moment, and then made a few more chalk marks.

"What are your novels *about*?" It was the man being fitted next to him.

Fred Orbis turned and saw someone who radiated success; who effused possibility. He told him the story of *The Serial Killer's Diet Book*, (no one had ever asked him about his writing before), and when he was through the man handed him his card.

Sydney Charon Literary Agency

"I'd like to read your book." he said.

So Fred Orbis reached into his satchel and handed him a copy.

"And you are *Federico Orbisini*?"

"Yes, I am."

Three days later Fred Orbis received a phone call.

"Mr. Orbisini?"

"Yes."

"This is Sydney Charon...We met at Armani's the other day..."

"The literary agent."

"Yes. I read your novel, and I *loved* it...In fact, I had dinner with a publisher the other night and I told him about it, and... well, to make a long story short, he made an offer. So I shopped it around the next day, and...well, I have four publishers interested."

"Four *publishers*?" He was momentarily stunned. "In my *book*?"

"Yes."

"*The Serial Killer's Diet Book?*"

"Yes. They're all *very* interested, considering the book's timely nature, what with the '*Cold-Cut Killer*', and '*Liverwurstmania*'. Tell me, how did you get him to tell you his story? No one even knows who he is."

"*He* approached *me*. He said he always respected my work."

"So, you've written other things, then?"

"Yes, in Italy...in Italian."

236

"So it's true that the Cold-Cut Killer speaks five languages?"

"Six."

"*Amazing*! I know several writers who would have *killed* for this story."

"Me too."

"I'm sorry, I haven't even asked you if you'd like me to represent you. Mr. Orbisini, I would be honored to be your agent."

"Well, *sure*, why not."

That evening there was a knock at the door. A messenger had brought an ice bucket with a bottle of *Dom Perignon*, with a note attached saying that the book had sold, and there was a two million dollar advance.

The next morning Manhattan was resplendent, and Fred Orbis decided to walk downtown to meet his new publisher. Elegant in his new suit, as he walked down the street he noticed women noticing him. True, he had always been noticed before—small children had pointed at him as if he were a Brontosaurus plodding down Fifth Avenue, and adults had gazed uncomprehendingly at his endless layers of fat—but now it was something altogether different. In the eyes of these women was unequivocal lust—the *Seven Deadly Sin* he had longed for the most. They *wanted* him. They saw him walking down the street, suave and handsome in his Armani suit; they knew nothing more about him, yet they wanted him. It was as simple as that.

The building was on the left. *Tartarus Publishing*, one of the largest corporate publishing conglomerates in the world. And as he walked along the sidewalk he looked to the right at the street corner. Masses of people huddled there, waiting to cross—all with care-worn expressions, exhausted, beaten-down; filled with an inexpressible sadness, and a hope that would never be fulfilled. The light changed, and he saw several bums in tattered coats, with cardboard signs saying: *Will Work for Food.*

At the building's entrance was a man holding three Dobermans on a leash, but as he approached they let him pass. Fred Orbis paused to reflect. Could happiness simply be going left instead of right? He glanced back at the street corner, as anonymous people drifted off into silent desperation, and then to the left at Elysium, and he walked inside and was welcomed.

"Mr. Orbisini..." A well-dressed important-looking man, in a suit the equal if not the better of his own, held out his hand in greeting. "We are so pleased that you've decided to sign with *Tartarus*. A book like yours, a book so complex and diverse I'm sure will enjoy lasting renown. However, considering the recent spirit of the times if you will, we want to get the book out there as soon as possible. In fact, it's being printed as we speak."

"You can *do* that? So *fast*?"

"We're one of the biggest corporations in the world, Mr. Orbisini... we do what we like." He handed him a drawing on poster board. "This is how the cover will look." Kielbasy and assorted lunch meat playfully intertwined with the letters of the title. "It should be on the shelves by the end of the week. Congratulations, it's already a bestseller."

"What? What do you mean?"

"The advance sales have been phenomenal."

Fred Orbis looked at the mock-up of the back cover, where several world-famous literary figures sang his praises.

"These people have read my *book*?"

"Reading books is not the issue, Mr. Orbisini. It's about *selling*... and people *buying*. In a way, what's between the covers is irrelevant. That's what *this* is..." He pointed to the glowing reviews the book had already garnered. "It's about *illusion*. We create the illusion that there's something inside that people want, that they need, and this is what we sell. I can't remember the last time I *read* a book." he laughed. "Again, we're so pleased that you've signed with us. If there's anything we can do, please feel free to call, day or night."

"Thank you." They shook hands, and then he and his agent departed.

"We've already sold the paperback rights, and...May I call you Federico?"

"Why not?"

"And I've had several offers from Hollywood. But I think that once the book comes out we'll be able to write our own ticket, as far as movie deals go. Meanwhile, there's the book tour...and didn't you say you've written *other* things?"

"Yes, two other novels. One is called *Fortune's*..."

"When The *SKDB* is a mega-bestseller we'll have publishers selling their souls to get your next book!"

"The *SKDB*?"

"The Serial Killer's Diet Book."

"Of course."

"Next week there's a signing at Barnes and Noble, and then... I'm glad I picked that day to get a new suit!"

By the end of the week *The Serial Killer's Diet Book* debuted at number one on the bestseller list. And within days it had become part of the collective consciousness, as people everywhere, from talk-show hosts to world leaders, were grasping for a piece of Federico Orbisini. He was asked to pose for the covers of several magazines, (including *GQ*); and was invited to the White House by the President himself, who personally praised the book for its portrayal of a man struggling with issues of morality. A week later Federico Orbisini stood before the window of his favorite bookstore and looked at The *SKDB*, stacked by the hundreds. But when he looked for Fred Orbis, Fred Orbis was gone. He had somehow vanished into the thin air of this absurd world.

36

Darby Montana was not much for bestsellers, but something about this one drew her in. *The Serial Killer's Diet Book* was not your average bestseller. True, on one hand it could be read as a straight confessional memoir of a serial killer, as told to Federico Orbisini, the brilliant new writer everyone was talking about, but Darby saw it as much more. It was about the human need for transcendence, and the question of hope. The idea of beauty—image vs. reality; the question of what was authentic, and the themes of society and the simulacrum; the place of art, literature and aesthetics in such a society; the question of fate and the body, personal freedom and destiny. The existential idea of the world as absurd; the question of good and evil, and the place of the individual in such a world; and the struggle for self-realization, which led back to this longing to transcend.

It was a satire which paid homage to Rabelais and Voltaire, and it was hilarious, but its humor was rooted in serious universal concerns, its hilarity played off the seriousness of its underlying themes, and this made the book more than the sum of its parts. Darby saw in Federico Orbisini a kindred spirit, and in a way the story of the Cold-Cut Killer was her own story—a person locked inside a body against their will, longing for release. The book, in spite of its grisly subject matter, was uplifting and optimistic, and when she finished the last page she felt enlivened. She wanted to meet Federico Orbisini. She knew that of all men, he alone would understand her.

Federico Orbisini sat behind a table at Barnes and Noble, busily signing copies of his book, and he seemed genuinely happy. Darby had seen so few people like this, but here was a man who seemed at peace. She looked at his face, fresh and new; his eyes, vibrant and full of life. And when she got closer she saw a depth of passion so great that she felt both overwhelmed and helplessly drawn. In those eyes she would see herself, she thought, and for a brief glorious moment their souls would dance.

Suddenly, for some unknown reason, the crowd parted as Darby approached; her way lit by a beam of sun from the skylight overhead. The man at the desk raised his head, and in his eyes she saw the reflection of her smile, the moment for which they both had waited.

Federico Orbisini was overcome. Never had he seen a woman so lovely, so desirable, and he stood up from his chair, oblivious to the crowd.

"Sophia..."

"Sophia Montana." she said.

Their fingers touched, their eyes met, and in that gaze a kind of marriage. The meeting of lips, through the same forces that moved the planets and gave birth to stars, and after the kiss, those who had gathered round broke into spontaneous applause. And to this sound they walked hand in hand, to the waiting limousine outside.

37

A few weeks after the murder of Mrs. Pressman (and her dog), Devon DeGroot received an unexpected letter.

"Look at *this*. That old lady's nephew found this in her personal effects."

"A *letter?*" said Macduff.

"Read it."

> To whom it may concern... Your reading this means that I have departed this world for the next, and in order to rest in peace I must unburden my soul. Senator James "Jimmy" Dempster was a student of mine, in my fourth grade class at the Gottfried Wilhelm von Liebnitz Elementary School. One of his classmates was a boy named Fred Orbis. Fred Orbis was very smart, but also very fat, and out of malice towards him I switched his standardized test results with Jimmy Dempster's. From that day on Jimmy Dempster was regarded as a genius instead of an idiot, and Fred Orbis an idiot instead of a genius. I am sorry that I did this, but he was so very fat.
> Sincerely,
> Mrs. Ida Pressman.

Macduff's face drained of blood.

"What is it?"

"Um, boss...we, uh..."

"What?"

"We, uh..." He looked at Donalbain. "Donalbain spotted this guy, Orbis."

"What?"

"We *both* did, boss. A few weeks ago we brought him in."

"What?"

"You were at the hospital, boss, we..."

"We, uh...He fit the description and we brought him in."

"I don't understand."

"He had these pillows, see, and..."

"Yeah. He wasn't really *fat*. He had these pillows, stuffed under his clothes."

"Right. We thought he was another Cold-Cut Killer copycat."

"So we let him go."

Both Donalbain and Macduff inched their way towards the door.

"Leave me, both of you."

The detectives beat a hasty retreat, expecting at any moment a nuclear detonation, but Devon DeGroot just sat there, staring at the wall.

A few minutes later...

"Kozinski...Macduff...Donalbain...Get in here."

"Uh-oh..."

"Here it comes."

"I want everything there is to know about this Fred Orbis."

The three detectives glanced at each other, and then raced to their computers.

"Look, boss," said Donalbain, "here's a class roster. Mrs. Pressman's fourth grade class with Jimmy Dempster...and here's Fred Orbis."

"Fred Orbis lives a few blocks away from that deli, boss." said Kozinski. "The one we, ah..."

"There's *this*, boss..." said Macduff. "Fred Orbis is the editor of *Feast Magazine*, the magazine devoted to over-eating."

"You have come after the feast." said DeGroot. "He was telling me who he was...And he was *here?*"

The detectives braced for an explosion, but DeGroot stood up and headed for the door.

"Let's go."

They broke into the apartment with weapons drawn, but the place was empty. On the table were newspaper headlines and magazines about the Cold-Cut Killer, with Devon DeGroot's name circled in red.

"Look..." Macduff found several driver's licenses. *"Gustavus Silenus...Calvin Igula...*and somebody named *Chudley Magnall."*

"Hey, check *this* out," said Kozinski, "an article he circled about Jimmy Dempster."

"Look at this," Donalbain held up a manuscript, "it's that book about the *Cold-Cut Killer.*"

DeGroot rushed over and gazed at the title page.

"The Serial Killer's Diet Book, by Federico Orbisini...*Federico Orbisini..."*

"Fred Orbis."

DeGroot had read parts of the book because he had heard that he was in it, but he had dismissed it as a shamelessly opportunistic pandering to the marketplace.

"So this guy Orbis is the *Cold-Cut Killer*, and he's also Orbisini, and he writes about himself and gets a goddamn *bestseller?*" Devon DeGroot shook his head at the world's unbridled treachery.

"I read something about this guy Orbisini, boss. In today's *Times.*"

"What?"

"I don't know, something about a book-signing."

DeGroot grabbed the phone.

"Yeah, this is DeGroot, do you have today's *Times* there?... *The New York Times*, for Christsake!...Yeah, is there an article about some book-signing by Federico Orbisini?"

"You mean *The Serial Killer's Diet Book*?"

"That's the one."

"Yeah, here it is. Today from ten to two at Barnes and Noble, this guy Orbisini is..."

DeGroot hung up and rushed outside. A few minutes later they were at the book store.

"Where's Orbisini?"

"You just missed him." said a young woman. "The signing ended about two hours ago."

DeGroot looked at his watch.

"But it's only one-thirty, I thought the signing was until two?"

"It was, but...you know famous authors. He just got up and left...he and this beautiful woman."

"Where did they go?"

"I don't know. They drove off in a limo. It was very romantic. Would you like to buy his *book*?" She held up a copy of The *SKDB*.

"It's too late." he said to the others. "He left two hours ago."

"We'll put out an *APB*, boss..."

"We'll check the airports..."

"Just...just *leave* me. Leave me alone."

Macduff nodded, and led Donalbain and Kozinski away.

"We'll see you back at the station then, boss..."

But Devon DeGroot was far away. His face held an absent stare as he gazed at the mountain of *Serial Killer's Diet Books,* and Federico Orbisini's face.

"Can I help you find something?" the young woman asked.

"No, thank you." He walked outside, and didn't notice the truck as he crossed the street—a liverwurst truck rushing to make a delivery—and the driver didn't see the brooding police detective stepping out into traffic. There was a squeal of brakes, a hideous thud.

Devon DeGroot was in a meadow overlooking a river. Early morning, the air obscured by mist. A figure on horseback appeared, and as it approached he recognized Alexander Hamilton.

"Hello General, it's been a long time."

Devon DeGroot was speechless as the events of the past two hundred years sunk in.

"You almost did it, sir."

DeGroot looked at the rider and remembered that Christmas Eve, so long ago.

"What happens now?"

"This is the last morning of your life, General."

"And the fog?"

"The abyss."

"And how long will I..."

"'Til the soul-departed seas wash your empty shores, and earth becomes a hollowed ball...'Til the end of time. 'Til time is no more."

The rider gazed at him for a moment longer and then rode off, and Devon DeGroot watched as the fog enveloped him, as the first chill of eternity gripped his bones.

Mr. Monde stood outside a building in the old section of Prague. A rundown apartment, and from the second floor window he heard a violin. A young composer lived there—a composer he would soon visit.

Elizabeth opened the door and expected to be greeted by Cleo, but the apartment was empty. There was nothing left except for a package in the middle of the floor, and a letter.

"Dear Elizabeth..." It was from Mr. Monde. It explained about the endgame in chess, and about Washington's fourth and final test. "I'm sorry I couldn't say good-bye in person, but I was called away. The package is for you. Good luck."

Elizabeth opened the package, and saw the handwritten book of *Hamlet*.

39

The sun shone from a sky of brilliant blue as it drenched the beach with light. Ataraxia was a small island off the coast of France, and it was Federico Orbisini and Sophia Montana's new home. There was a rush of waves as Sophia emerged from the water. She was Venus born from ocean and sun, and Federico watched as her shoulders glistened, as the sun caressed her body like eyes, as the waves moved over it like lips, and he stared in silence as he remembered her taste and smell. And Sophia saw him watching her, and she smiled. Her dark eyes were dancing spirits opening a door on a room of mirrors, and as he looked he saw every pleasure multiplied a thousandfold, every desire reflected back. In those mirrored eyes he saw himself, and he heard his name on her lips.

"Federico." she said softly.

"Sophia."

Check out these other fine titles by
Durban House at your local book store.

EXCEPTIONAL BOOKS
BY
EXCEPTIONAL WRITERS

MR. IRRELEVANT
by Jerry Marshall.

Sports writer Paul Tenkiller and pro-football player Chesty Hake have been roommates for eight career seasons. Paul's Choctaw background of poverty and his gambling on sports, and Hake's dark memories of his mother being killed are the forces which will make their friendship go horribly wrong.

Chesty Hake, the last man chosen in the draft, has been dubbed Mr. Irrelevant. By every yardstick, he should not be playing pro football. But, because of his heart and high threshold for pain, he perseveres.

Paul Tenkiller has been on a gravy train because of Hake's generosity. Gleaning information vital to gambling on football, his relationship with Hake is at once loyal and deceitful.

Then during his eighth and final season, Hake slides into paranoia and Tenkiller is caught up in the dilemma. But Paul is behind the curve, and events spiral out of his control, until the bloody end comes in murder and betrayal.

OPAL EYE DEVIL
    by John Lewis.

From the teeming wharves of Shanghai to the stately offices of New York and London, schemes are hammered out to bankrupt opponents, wreck inventory, and dynamite oil wells. It is the age of the Robber Baron—a time when powerful men lie, steal, cheat, and even kill in their quest for power.

Sweeping us back to the turn of the twentieth century, John Lewis weaves an extraordinary tale about the brave men and women who risk everything as the discovery of oil rocks the world.

Follow Eric Gradek's rise from Northern Star's dark cargo hold to the pinnacle of high stakes gambling for unrivaled riches.

Aided by his beautiful wife, Katheryn, and the devoted Tong-Po, Eric fights for his dream and for revenge against the man who left him for dead aboard Northern Star.

ROADHOUSE BLUES
by Baron Birtcher.

From the sun-drenched sand of Santa Catalina Island to the smoky night clubs and back alleys of West Hollywood, Roadhouse Blues is a taut noir thriller that evokes images both surreal and disturbing.

Newly retired Homicide detective Mike Travis is torn from the comfort of his chartered yacht business into the dark, bizarre underbelly of LA's music scene by a grisly string of murders.

A handsome, drug-addled psychopath has reemerged from an ancient Dionysian cult, leaving a bloody trail of seemingly unrelated victims in his wake. Despite departmental rivalries that threaten to tear the investigation apart, Travis and his former partner reunite in an all-out effort to prevent more innocent blood from spilling into the unforgiving streets of the City of Angels.

TUNNEL RUNNER
by Richard Sand.

Tunnel Runner is a fast, deadly espionage thriller peopled with quirky and most times vicious characters. It tells of a dark world where murder is committed and no one is brought to account; where loyalties exist side by side with lies and extreme violence.

Ashman "the hunter, the hero, the killer" is a denizen of that world who awakens to find himself paralyzed in a mental hospital. He escapes and seeks vengeance, confronting his old friends, the Pentagon, the Mafia, and a mysterious general who is covering up the attack on TWA Flight 800.

People begin to die. There are shoot-outs and assassinations. A woman is blown up in her bathtub.

Ashman is cunning and ruthless as he moves through the labyrinth of deceit, violence, and suspicion. He is a tunnel runner, a ferret in the hole, who needs the danger to survive, and hates those who have made him so.

It is this peculiar combination of ruthlessness and vulnerability that redeems Ashman as he goes for those who want him dead. Join him.